CW01648415

Alien Disclosure

Amnesty

Alien Disclosure

Amnesty

Allan Kules

Book One of the Alien Disclosure Trilogy

Off-World Books

Surprise, Arizona

Cover Photo courtesy of NASA

Flying Saucer Spaceship downloaded from: widescreen full hd, fantasy images, saucerx, ufo

Small Earth image downloaded from Clipart Panda: Earth Clip Art

ISBN: ISBN-13: 978-1-7324552-2-1
ISBN-10: 1-7324552-2-8

Professionally edited by:
Jennifer Hope
www.MesaVerdeMediaServices.com

Off-World Books

Printed in the U.S.A.

Introduction

The net of secrecy suppressing the alien presence on our world is not completely secure. Openings woven into the fabric of the net allow surprising truths to escape.

However, unequivocal proof can only be met by an artifact or the unfettered presentation of the aliens themselves. In a sea of nebulous, contradictory waves of information, only this form of proof will calm the waters of disinformation and sunken historical events.

In this story, the proof is provided by an artifact (a motion picture film) that captures a presentation of intelligent life from another world. This precious celluloid record documents the meeting of President Dwight D. Eisenhower with a humanoid, not of planet earth. The basis of the story within these pages is built upon this remarkable event in our nation's and the world's history. To expose the presence of aliens on earth, the recipients of this artifact repeatedly escape capture from the legitimate and hidden forces of the US government.

The impact to humanity of disclosure is of paramount importance to society. This novel addresses these issues, fears, hopes, and desires from the perspective of the champions of disclosure as well as from the factions that are struggling to deny the existence of these visitors from afar. The story is therefore more than a simple, one-sided battle cry for instant disclosure.

The key agenda that must be implemented as part of the disclosure of alien intervention on our planet is amnesty. Amnesty must be granted to all who struggled—albeit futilely—to protect us from the truth. Absolution must be guaranteed and legally documented. This prohibition against litigation is fundamental to the health of our society if we are to resolutely proceed forward as a nation and as a peaceful world. Litigation must be set aside for all individuals responsible for any and all actions that thwarted the bona fide release of the alien presence. If this is not enacted, individuals, companies, agencies, and governments will be sued ad nauseum for the illegal actions of these governmental and industrial groups. We would endlessly drag each other into court for reparations for these deceptions, these crimes inflicted on our fellow citizens in a twisted paternalism sanctioned out of fear that the adult "children" would either remain frightened by the truth or fail to comprehend it.

These are important issues. However, this is a novel not a lecture. It is filled with adventure, sacrifice for love, acquiescence to duty, spiritual awakening, celebration, and humor. The novel is more than a journey across America with the biggest secret of the last thousand years. It is a roadmap of the issues facing humanity when—not if—an intrepid citizen presents definitive proof that alien visitors are among us.

TOP SECRET

To: SAPS 4-11
SCI – For Your Eyes Only
Breach of Artifact 54-0006-33

Regular inventory protocol was performed at 0800 this morning. The above artifact was discovered missing from its shelf in storage Locker B, at this facility. Analyst IV Fred Willow did not report for duty today nor was he documented as sick by security.

Team 3 left at 0900 to search his rental in person. Analysis of security footage of Mr. Willow's work station and his residence is underway. Security Team 1 is preparing to pursue the individual when preliminary intel is collected. We interrogated members of Fred's analyst group. We are just now hearing of his increased disaffection from secrecy mandates and his desire to make contact with a person or persons willing to daylight this artifact.

Our location as well as the nature of our artifacts may be compromised. We are considering all options—including reassignment and complete shutdown. We will have a tentative classified report by 1300.

Please advise further.

SCI Alert Protocol 27 - nmh

Memo 3:

From: Don Petrulio, CIA Station Chief

Current Assignment: Artifact Retrieval

Research and observation began in San Antonio at the UFO Conference. I identified James Broadhurst and Frank Connors. We are pursuing the likely recipient of the artifact as instructed. However, there are other teams here. I thought that we were alone on this assignment? The other teams are not DIA, CIA, or FBI.

Broadhurst and Connors left after their presentation. No sign of any artifact. Will pick up the case as instructed in St. Louis. I am not sure that Broadhurst is the recipient. Anecdotal info says that said artifact was taken by FW after a chase through River Walk. Willow appears to have drowned in canal but no body or artifact recovered.

This case is pretty sketchy. Sorry for the vernacular, but there's not much to go on here, sir. Please advise further.

Chapter 1

Saturday, September 9

"Turn left at the next corner," said James, leaning forward from his rear seat position. James Broadhurst was a prominent UFO researcher attending another confab of writers, journalists, researchers, and fans and the debut of a few new films at the St. Louis Extraterrestrial Conference. His normal conference attire was a bit old fashioned: a grey tweed jacket with pads at the elbows and an open collared white shirt. Tonight, he was convincingly disguised as a waiter dressed in a white uniform jacket and black pants.

In his middle forties, his brown hair was cut close with grey invading at the temples. His disarmingly blue eyes were proportionately set in his clean shaven round face. His easy smile, slightly rotund physique, and breezy demeanor disarmed the most ardent challengers to his serious lecture topics.

James had achieved some modest success. He had written four books in his long career. His big break came when a well-known UFO luminary took ill at a conference and James graciously offered to step in and fill the opening in the schedule. His talk on disclosure and "the Amnesty Option," as he called it then, piqued the interest of seminar organizers. After that, he became a regular on the circuit.

"Are we there yet, boys and girls?" quipped Frank from the front passenger seat. James hired his longtime friend Frank Connors, a former fighter pilot in the US Air Force, to help him with Freedom of Information Act (FOIA) filings with the Federal Government, arrange his conference schedule, and provide additional assistance—the kind of "assistance" that turned into everything from security to answering fan mail. Frank was a bit older, a bit shorter, a bit more rumpled, but was always there to bring about a successful presentation, and this was help for which James was extremely grateful.

"James, you don't need to lean forward and talk into my ear. I can hear you just fine if you sit back in *your* seat," said Maya, shaking her head.

Frank had received a call from his army buddy, Maya Jablonski, after the San Antonio conference. She said that she was interested in the research of UFOs and said that she wanted to "help." He had heard the rumor that she took a position with the CIA after her stint with the army, but nothing was confirmed and nothing came from Maya to verify it. Frank felt that she had invited herself into their fledgling operation.

He knew her well, back then. Now, he wasn't so sure. However, Frank continued to give her the benefit of the doubt, ignoring the methodology she employed to become an active member of their mission.

James was not so generous. They got off to a rocky start and proceeded to go downhill from there. Maya's forthright support and ability to quickly develop a cohesive plan for tonight's adventure confirmed Frank's confidence in her. James, however, could only voice "guarded approval" for her participation. That was as high as he could rate the athletic looking thirty-year-old's eagerness to be a part of their secret project. He was not about to let the most astounding revelation of alien visitation on earth disappear again. He had not chosen this task; it was thrust upon him. He was committed to the goal outlined to him by the giver—a scientific researcher who escaped with a fifties era artifact from a secret corporate/government facility. The artifact was supposedly the film of Eisenhower meeting with aliens from another planet. If only it was real and not some fleeting fancy by some delusional character.

The task charted for him by the thief who liberated the film consisted of a cross country race from San Antonio to the United Nations General Assembly. A staff projectionist at the UN agreed to sacrifice his career to run the film at the General Assembly meeting in September.

It was a daunting mission made absolutely compulsory by the apparent mortal sacrifice of the man who offered this artifact to James.

Sitting alone in the backseat of Maya's rental car, his mind replayed the series of events in San Antonio: the offering of the film in the alley behind the River Walk Hilton, Frank's quick action to hide the film, the chase by government agents after the man carrying the now empty film case through the crowded streets and over the bridges of the River Walk. The plunge to his apparent death into the murky waters of the San Antonio River, the clandestine shuffle of the old film reel among sympathetic conference attendees, and the disappearance of the artifact practically under the noses of government watchdogs astounded James.

They had not tested the veracity of the film's supposed content before sending it out, but something was on the film. Shadowy government agents do not usually give chase in public places for a reel of cartoons. Frank lobbied a plan to rapidly get it off their hands and to a trusted film archivist in St. Louis. There it sat, waiting to be viewed during their next scheduled UFO conference.

James thrust his shoulders back into the seat. "This would have been a lot easier if I had sat in the front," said James with a distinctive harrumph.

"It would have been worse with your nose pressed up against the windshield pointing in all directions," said Maya, shaking her head slowly from left to right. "You guys got lucky in San Antonio, at the River Walk. Judy Davenport should have never made it out of there with those guys on your case. I still don't get what happened."

"You told Maya about San Antonio?" asked James.

"Well, she seemed to already know some of it. I filled in the gaps. She's going to see it all now," said Frank. He looked out the window, averting his eyes from his longtime partner and friend.

James was clearly irritated at his business partner. A cross look on his face evolved into a surprising affirmation of how successful the San Antonio mission was. "It progressed exceedingly well. Our team there handled every facet of the operation. It went very well. I don't believe that anyone in the government thinks we have the artifact. We were very good. Didn't need a young woman pushing her way into our team here," continued James, folding his arms.

"Enough of this bickering!" said Frank, whipping his head around to face James. "What I want to know is how you know your way around this town? You haven't lived here before, have you?"

"I did what you told me to do. I memorized the directions to our destination, the address, and, anyway, we're here. Maya, could you pull over there behind that Mercedes?"

"Okay," said Maya. "What is our destination?"

"It's a theater around the corner. We're going in the back door. It's a small art house that makes a modest living with specialty films."

"So, it's a film you have?" said Maya. James and Frank were still unsure of their self-invited security and logistics guru. Too much was at stake, they thought, to divulge the details of what they had. *What if she's not the same person that I knew years ago?* Frank had thought. They were unsure about almost everything.

"Yes, but we don't really know if it's a batch of cartoons or something important. It's billed as something more. We're hopeful or fearful depending upon your orientation," said Frank.

"Okay, some ground rules. Are you prepared to see filmed images of aliens—the real thing, not just some Hollywood movie?" asked James. He was unconsciously leaning forward again, his head at Maya's ear.

Maya slowly turned around, placed her fingertips on his forehead, and gently pushed his head back in the car to a comfortable distance. "Yes, I am, Mr. James Broadhurst. I dare say I've seen many more things than you have."

"Okay, you two. This car's too small for a pissing contest," said Frank. They both looked at him and sneered. "Anyway, we're not going to spend all night in this car. Are we getting out?"

James opened his door and whispered across the roof to Maya. "We do this as we planned."

"And that includes not pissing your pants or screaming like a little girl while you watch this flick," hissed Maya, gently closing her door.

"We'll see," said James. He led the others down the block and around the corner. A short walk across the deserted street took them to an almost unseen door along a windowless wall. "I think this is it. This is the door."

In a darkened basement command center in Fredericksburg, Maryland, lit by the glare of data and images splashed on over-sized monitors, two men and one woman scanned the structured collage in front of them.

"So, how's the CIA doing now?" asked Kathleen Johnson, choosing to stand behind her chair. Kathleen, a tall, sinewy woman dressed in a blue business suit was a junior director of an unnamed agency of the hidden government. Flecks of grey peppered her short, dark brown hair. Her thin face and pointed features were assets in her arsenal to maintain order in this most secret facility. The plain features of this woman belied an inner strength and confidence that she projected to defend the company.

There was no name on the door. Members of this autonomous and top-secret facility collected and cataloged artifacts retrieved from other agencies, conducted public disinformation campaigns about alien sightings and close encounters, and thwarted any public knowledge that world governments were in contact with extraterrestrial beings. Her purpose and mission were clear and unwavering. The "government" had hired her twenty years ago, and Kathleen steadfastly defended her duty to protect Americans—to protect them from the truth.

"Same as before, Don Petrulio and his team are still falling behind," answered one of the men. "They're no closer to finding our man, nor do they have anything on Broadhurst and company."

"And where are we with the retrieval of our escapee?" demanded

Kathleen.

"I don't think he's dead. He's getting protection," answered the other man.

"I know that! Have we confirmed who's giving him the protection—some private UFO group or one of us?"

"No private saucer org has the resources. It's one of our usual suspects," said the other man.

"Okay," said Kathleen. The resignation in her voice was difficult to hide. Time and again her efforts to tamp down each leak of alien visitation was reversed by a cloaked operation within the same hidden government, under some senior director deeper in the organization set on ultimate disclosure. She mentally set aside action toward the perpetrator and who was assisting him for now. "Recovery of the artifact is vitally important. Let's put our resources where the action is. Being allied with one of our 'usual suspects' explains his relative success in handling the artifact—if he indeed has it," said Kathleen.

"True, he hasn't made any mistakes, and that's extremely unusual for a novice. Our operatives on the scene are convinced he is going to collect the film soon if he doesn't already have it. We're not sure of his intentions yet, but we believe he does have help," said one of the men.

"And you have had no luck identifying the operative giving him assistance?"

"We're checking. We're convinced it's ex-CIA or ex-DIA. Military might be an option," answered the other man.

"Doesn't Connors have military background?" asked Kathleen.

"Yes, but we don't see a connection," said the first man.

"You don't see a connection or you haven't looked for a connection?" pressed Kathleen, getting impatient with the discussion. "That film is one of the holiest of holies for the MUFON lackeys. Can you imagine if it were broadcast on CNN? At least we would hope our man at CNN would head it off, but, nevertheless, that kind of exposure cannot be tolerated. Do I make myself clear?"

The two men nodded their heads affirming that they indeed understood. "We'll start forming a list of all his military contacts and team members throughout his career," agreed the first man.

"You'll do that. And, you'll have the list of likely suspects on my desk in the morning. Broadhurst is in St. Louis for three days. Let's make sure the net is so tight that whoever is helping him is going to be squeezed to the surface. Update your operatives in St. Louis, and tell them not to get gun happy. We need recovery and detainment. We don't need a murdered UFO freak. Our policy is not to give up the assailant. It just makes things difficult with the local law enforcement who are left with a body with a hole in his head and mysteriously no one with a motive or opportunity to prosecute for the deed," said Kathleen.

"Yes, I understand," answered the second man as he picked up the receiver of the telephone in front of him.

"There's no doorknob to these theater exit doors," said Frank.

"And I left my C-4 back in my room," said Maya, not really expecting a response.

"It's supposed to be unlocked, and a small shim is up here to help us open it," said James, feeling around at the top of the door. He gently pulled on it, and the door slowly opened. Maya stuck her fingers in the widening crevice to help pry the door open. A dark hallway with only two hanging red bulbs appeared in front of them. James started to go in first, but Frank held him back.

"Let Maya go in first," said Frank. "She's security on this detail."

"What are you expecting—crack commandos bursting forth in a hail of bullets?" whispered James, unable to contain his emotions.

"No, just weirdos on crack," said Maya. "If we could pry our way inside here street people are very resourceful too. They like warm places to shoot up and crash." She pulled a small gun from her purse and held it up in front of her with both hands as she entered the building.

"Is this really necessary?" asked James, staring at Frank on the threshold.

"James, let her go. We're going into a darkened building that we don't know, and we have god knows who on our tail." Frank stared at James for a moment. "Really, Jim," he said as if to finalize this issue.

They followed Maya into the hallway and took the route and protocol that was discussed last night. The lighting improved a little once they reached the bottom of the stairs. Maya led the way, constantly sweeping the space in front of her. They reached the landing of the first flight of stairs meeting no one. Climbing the second flight and walking down another dimly lit hall, they found two doors facing each other across the narrow vestibule.

"Is this it?" whispered Maya, pointing the gun at the door.

"Yes, now put that thing away! We don't want to scare Henry out of his wits. He's probably extremely nervous about meeting us anyway," whispered James.

Frank nodded in agreement, and Maya put the gun back in her purse but continued to hold it in her hand. She knocked twice, as agreed in the instructions. The door opened slowly, and a thin, bearded man in wire rim glasses peered out.

"Is one of you James Broadhurst?" asked Henry.

"That would be me, Henry," said James.

"I hate to ask this, but can I see some ID?"

"No apology necessary. Here you go," said James, passing his wallet opened to his driver's license. Maya handed the wallet to Henry with her free hand. She expected him to look at it while she held it. He tugged at it without speaking. Maya continued to resist.

"I'm sorry. I need to take it inside. There's not enough light out here."

"Let it go, Maya," said James. Maya reluctantly unclenched her fist on the leather wallet, and it and Henry disappeared behind the door. A few moments later the door swung wide. Maya clutched her purse with her other hand in anticipation of drawing her gun. Even Frank stepped back a bit.

Henry stepped forward and thrust his hand with the wallet in the direction of James. "It's an honor to meet you, sir," said Henry, as James stepped forward to claim his property. "Please come in. I've been waiting patiently for your arrival for days now." Henry held the door open as James, then Frank, and finally Maya entered the small projection room. Maya carefully checked the surroundings, looking for exits or windows.

"You seem very cautious," he said directly to Maya.

"Oh, don't mind her. She's the self-appointed security freak for this adventure," answered James.

"Is that a gun in your purse?" asked Henry. Maya looked seriously at Henry, smiled, and then withdrew her hand from the purse leaving the pistol inside. She made no response to his question.

James thoroughly dismissed Maya by employing a combined gesture of demeaning eye roll, a rapid toss of his head shrugging off this crazy woman, and a question for Henry to refocus his attention. "I take it you received the package?"

"Yes, I did. Why are you all wearing white outfits? Do you all work in a restaurant?"

Frank responded for the group. "We needed to escape scrutiny as we left the hotel."

"Is there someone following you?" His apparent level of fear was clearly evident to the team. "I don't want any trouble. Why don't you take the package and go? Christopher said it would be safe."

"Henry, it is safe. I can attest to that. No one followed us in our car. No one detected that we left the hotel. You have nothing to worry about," said Maya. The statement of facts and the cadence of the elocution softened Henry's sense of alarm.

"We really need your help on this, Henry," said Frank.

"Okay, I know who you are," said Henry, pointing to James. "I haven't been introduced to your friends."

"This is Frank, my good friend and business associate. This is Maya, who volunteered to help us tonight."

"Pleased to meet you, Henry," said Frank, shaking Henry's hand.

"It is nice to finally meet you, Henry. Rest assured. You have a lot of friends pulling for you. Thank you for doing this," said Maya, shaking his hand. Frank mouthed the words *lots of friends?* to James behind Maya's back.

"Oh . . . okay," said Henry tentatively. "I had the equipment set up in here for a long time, but it wouldn't allow us much room to work, so I moved our operation across the hall. Shall we get started?" Henry led the way out into the hallway.

"Stop!" yelled Maya, as Henry was about to open the door.

James spoke up. "Now what?"

"She's right. Let her go first," said Frank.

Maya edged forward past the three men. "Where is the light switch for this room?" asked Maya.

"On the right, about so high," said Henry, motioning with his left hand in the air.

Maya opened the door enough to slide her arm in to feel for the switch. She flicked on the light and pushed the door open wide panning her purse from side to side in the open room.

“Surprise, surprise! The bogeyman isn’t here,” said James.

“I’ve had about enough of you,” said Maya, getting in James’s face. “This is serious business. I’m trying to protect you—all of you,” she said, scanning the faces in the room. “All you have is snide remarks; it’s always a joke to you.”

“It’s not a joke, but it sure as hell doesn’t require brandishing guns and searching through this room. What were the authorities going to do, shoot us as soon as we entered the room?” said James.

“If we’re going to get out of here before dawn, we need to get started,” said Frank.

Henry looked at the tense faces on James and Maya. They were still staring at each other. “Okay, here’s the film.” He picked it up and laid it on an open table. “I think I can get it all done in one pass. We’ll be able to watch it on the little monitor over there. But the real action is going into this computer and these units here.”

“Sounds good if you say so,” said James, a little surprised at what had to happen technologically.

“We need to collect it on the computer, and once it’s collected, we send it out to these DVD drives here,” he said, waving his hands over the electronic equipment. “I tested the equipment with another 16-mm film and it works. I’m going to create three DVDs of the raw footage. That’s what you asked for, wasn’t it?”

“Yes, that’s correct,” said Frank.

“I followed the instructions inside the box. I didn’t view the film, as you requested. I don’t have blue ray or 4K or fancy stuff like that. Besides, this old film will look just fine on DVD. What are we going to see anyway? I'd like to prepare myself," asked Henry.

"It's apparently Eisenhower visiting some military base out west in the fifties and greeting aliens," answered James.

"Muroc or Holloman?" asked Henry without any hesitation.

James stood motionless staring at Henry. He could not believe someone so young knew the stories of how Eisenhower secretly went to two Air Force bases within a year of each other, drove onto the base, and, in a prearranged event, watched flying saucers land and occupants come out and talk with the humans. There were reports that at the second meeting a treaty of some kind was signed. Here was a young man stating with certainty that he knew of the events and could readily identify the military bases. "You know about these events?"

"James, it's all over the internet. I've had a strong interest for years. Something's going on here, that's for sure," said Henry assuredly. "It doesn't take much to find these stories."

"We really need to get going here," said Maya.

"Okay, I'll load it up." Henry quickly got to work, took the film out of the box, and carefully threaded it through the projector. "It looks in good shape—not too brittle. Some of these older films you have to have special equipment to run it. Loops like these through the gate behind the lens couldn't be done. Just need to attach it to the take-up reel. The computer is already on, and the program is ready to take it. Frank, there are some folding chairs over there against the wall. I'm going to stand most of the time and monitor this machine," he said, patting the projector. "The rest of you might as well get somewhat comfortable."

Frank brought four chairs over to position in front of the monitor. James and Frank sat down first. Finally, Maya hesitantly sat on the other side of Frank.

"Is everybody ready? Let's make history!" Henry bellowed as he flicked on the projector light and pressed the advance lever on the large brown projector. At first it was white leader that ran through for less than one minute, but it seemed like hours waiting for the unveiling. The first image was a makeshift reader board claiming a date and place. "Well, that answers that question. It's Muroc, now known as Edwards Air Force Base."

"It's black and white," said Maya, stating the obvious.

"Does this film have sound?" asked James.

The image dramatically changed. A desert scene, in full color, appeared at dusk. Thin bands of grey clouds framed a burnt orange setting sun hovering atop an auburn hued mountain. The image shuddered a little, and voices were heard from behind the camera. The scene was a long shot of three silvery saucer-shaped spaceships hovering about one hundred feet off of the ground. One ship was positioned in the foreground. The other two filled up the background. The image was mesmerizing. Henry looked at his guests' faces. Their eyes, transfixed by the projected image in front of them, looked as saucer-shaped as the craft on the small screen. All faces were in a state of shock, except James who had an ear-to-ear grin. James caught Henry's gaze. He quickly formed a thumbs-up and returned his focus to the screen.

Within a few minutes, a new camera angle displayed the three ships in a new configuration, indicating that multiple cameras were used. This image was zoomed in on the lead saucer. A slight wavering in the saucer could be seen, and a soft hum that wasn't apparent before came across the speakers. "It's true then, they do waver a bit when they're close to the ground," said Henry in a soft voice.

The film continued showing different angles of the extraterrestrial craft in the aerial display. The scene ended, and white leader began feeding through the projector.

"Shit, is that it?" said Frank. The tantalizing snippet left him wanting more from this presentation.

"Hold on there. We have a lot of film left here. I think we're going to see the meeting with . . ." Henry's voice trailed off as the next scene unfolded. The sunset sky had dissolved into pitch black night. The images on the screen were lit with powerful floodlights from multiple directions. In the foreground was a single saucer-shaped craft supported on a finely configured tripod. No doorway or opening could be seen on the pewter colored skin that appeared to glisten under the glaring spotlights. The other spaceships were either gone or out of view. The camera was positioned on this one extraterrestrial craft.

The film jerked again into a second camera angle that captured the scene in landscape. At last the importance of this scene became obvious. On the right was the interplanetary vehicle resting lightly on the runway, and on the left was a group of men. Standing at the forefront was President Dwight Eisenhower. The camera closed in on the group and began scanning their faces.

"This must be the entourage of important people from the private sector. God, this is great! It's just like Michael Salla described," shouted Henry. The camera returned to Ike and zoomed back to capture the ship and the welcoming committee. An opening slowly appeared on the undersurface of the ship. A ramp promptly deployed and lightly rested on the asphalt surface of the runway with no hint of a sound. Ike stepped forward a little and waited. From inside the ship, a tall form disembarked.

Was this a man? The bipedal motion of the legs and hips didn't add up. *The gait is all wrong*, thought Frank. *But still, it looks human with two arms, two legs, and a human-looking head*. The camera position changed, and the lens focused on this seven-foot representative of a race not of this earth. Floating at head height approximately two feet to the side of the humanoid's head was a gold colored spherical drone. The one-foot diameter drone had a number of one- to two-inch asymmetrical protrusions that rotated or wavered as the humanoid walked. It seemed to be talking to the alien, rotating from time to time. It followed every move of the humanoid carefully, not interfering in any way.

The head appeared to be human. *No, that face, that face, it isn't human*, thought James. "He's real—a real alien, not from here," he said, not expecting a response.

The alien's uniform, a slight hue of grey accented with maroon red, was form fitting without appearing taut or clinging to the skin. He strode forward and stopped about five feet away from Ike. Ike stepped forward, expecting to engage in the human gesture of shaking hands. The drone withdrew its appendages and inched forward to be parallel with the alien's head. Ike looked at the floating small metal sphere. The alien held up his hand palm forward to Ike alerting the President to approach no further—or maybe it was a greeting. He spoke something to the President, and Ike appeared to relax.

Ike extended his arm as if to gesture to an open hangar. They walked side by side, with the President keeping his distance from this strange visitor. The entourage dutifully followed at a discrete distance, controlled by two military policemen. The camera followed from behind these men until the film ran out again and dissolved into the familiar white leader.

"This is incredible! I've heard about this film for a dozen years and now, now . . ." stuttered James.

"Now it's here," added Maya. "Can we stop the film for a moment?"

Without waiting for a response from the others, Henry flipped one switch on the projector and pushed a button on the recording unit.

"Why are we stopping?" demanded James.

"How much have we seen of this?" Maya asked Henry.

"It's about half done. We have about twenty minutes left on this reel," he said, waving his hand over the film reel. Maya looked at her watch.

"Okay, I just wanted to check our time."

James leaned forward to speak to Maya. "We're watching the most importantly revealing presentation of the last thousand years, and you're checking your watch!" he said incredulously.

Frank held his arm, attempting to rein him in. "Hey, she's security. We're on the clock here. It's a valid question." Frank turned to Maya and asked politely, "Do we have the time?"

"Yes, I was just having difficulty estimating the time . . . for the rest of the film. We'll be fine."

"Shall we resume?" asked Henry. Without waiting for an affirmative answer, he flipped the switch and pushed the button, and the equipment whirred into action again.

The next image was from a new camera position inside the large hangar. The scene was of the President and the extraterrestrial entering the well-lit structure. The room contained two comfortable leather arm chairs positioned facing each other at a distance of four or five feet. Behind one of the chairs was a row of seats. Ike stepped forward and extended his arm toward the leather arm chair.

The full features of this humanoid came into view. His shoulder length white hair framed a ghostly white face that appeared to glow with an iridescent sheen replicated even through the medium of fifties era film. The invited guest directly faced the camera lens for a brief moment. *Nice. An intentional act to permit us to fully catalog you*, thought Maya.

A high forehead and prominent cheekbones that framed an incredibly thin nose extending to almost non-existent nostrils. The visitor's almost colorless lips circled a human looking mouth with white teeth. The eyes were light blue with distinctly nonhuman large irises and small black pupils. Everyone stood motionless waiting for this stranger from another world to make his next move.

"May we sit and talk with you?" said the President.

"Thank you," said the guest from another world, in plain Americanized English. The startled guests murmured. "Yes, I know your language. We have had many years to study it."

The President nodded to the men, and they quietly sat in the open seats behind him. Once they were seated, the President and the visitor sat down in unison. The drone rotated one hundred eighty degrees, the glistening tools retracted on the gold sphere, the weightless device scooted back to the two-foot attentive position to the right and back, and it rotated to the "front" again. Frank smiled and thought, *So this is the front side*. As Frank stared at the round drone, he perceived that his brain received a massive download of the specs of the device floating near the alien's head. Pictures, specifications, all translated into English—but at a fantastic rate of delivery that gave him a headache.

"Welcome to earth, or should I say welcome back?" said Ike.

"Thank you. We have been in your solar system for a long time. I remember the land when vast herds of buffalo grazed on your Great Plains. It was not so long ago."

"How old are you?" asked Ike.

"I'm approximately four hundred of your years old. As a young—as you would say—pilot, I flew over these hills and deserts around this site many times. We have been watching the development of this planet with great interest. You hardly know what you have under your feet."

"Do you mean the planet's mineral wealth?" The alien's facial muscles appeared to project a smile.

The President smiled in return.

"By 'under your feet' I mean that you take this beautiful world for granted. So many inhabited worlds are out there that are so inhospitable to life, but life persists, sentient life develops. Here your world is so rich with the ingredients for life that you and all other creatures flourish. Even calamities such as the intersection with asteroids is not enough to quell the drive for life. It comes back again and again. Your species has proliferated to the point that you are a hazard to this planet's survival, and still you do not see. You assume it is all there for the taking, that it is your right to exploit."

"But it is *our* planet," protested the President. The visitor manufactured a smile again.

"This is what I mean. You somehow think that anything you do, any defilement, is acceptable on this world because 'it is *your* planet.'"

"Why are you here?" asked the President directly.

The visitor sat up in the chair, looked at the entourage of men assembled behind them, and spoke so that all could hear. "As I have said, we have been here for a long time. However, there are new arrivals in the neighborhood. There is a distinct energy signature with every nuclear explosion that your countries explode on the surface. It is, at the moment, your most telling calling card. The species that are advanced enough for interstellar travel and concurrently have the means to detect your clarion call, have arrived." The men watching and listening murmured again. "One of the species that you have detected circling the equator in a high orbit that you will probably call the 'grays' are not the most honorable of species. We can protect you from them."

"Why do we need to be protected? Will we not be able to defend ourselves? Are they a danger to us?" asked Ike.

"In a way, the answer is yes." A murmur of voices circulated quickly behind the President.

The President held up his hand. "What do you mean?"

"In all likelihood, these aliens will be willing to negotiate with you. They will offer technology to you but at a price. The question will be: is the price to your liking? There is no limit to human greed. You will strike a bargain with these visitors, but it may not be a bargain for you."

"And what are you offering us?"

"Your species is still so violent. You are now at a crossroads where you can literally blow yourselves up. You must renounce the development of nuclear weapons on a global basis. You must foster the development of your spirituality.

"We cannot put into your hands technologies that you could manifest into even more powerful weapons, because you are not ready for it. In time, when you fully understand your true selves, we can work with you as equals and share our technologies with you."

The President put his hand to his forehead and gently wiped his balding head. "What you are asking us to do is extremely difficult, especially now with our standoff with the Russians. They are a very dangerous people, and we believe that our nuclear weapons function as a deterrent to their aggressions." The President paused and then turned to the men behind him for a moment. He turned back and spoke to the visitor. "Knowing your understanding of things, this may sound illogical to you, but we are suspicious of the intentions of our fellow men. Countries have agendas; they often communicate them ineffectively, and sometimes they are misconstrued. We are trying to build trust with our United Nations, but it is not always effective. You are asking us, one by one to drop our guard, and that's how it would be: 'one-by-one.' Any country that would do what you ask would be leaving themselves open to unsavory agendas on the part of another." The President forced a small smile. "You must have guessed that rejection of your proposal was a distinct possibility."

"Yes," answered the visitor with almost no expression in his voice.

"Then why did you come here?"

"The opportunity to place this seed of understanding and truth could not wait any longer. We have ongoing projects and missions within this galaxy with thousand-year timelines. This mission was spurred on by the arrival to your planet of the others. We would have been happy to keep working behind the scenes, but a face-to-face was given a higher vote so that you would have an alternative."

"What do you mean by 'behind the scenes'?" asked the President, leaning forward again.

The visitor seemed to pick his words even more carefully. "We are talking directly to some on your planet. They want to know the truth. They understand."

The President leaned back and softly pleaded for a break. "Will you give me a moment please?"

"Yes, of course," said the visitor. The President rose smoothly from his chair and waved his group of invited guests to join him a distance away from the seated visitor. A second cameraman joined the group of men huddled with the President.

"Should this be filmed, Mr. President?" said an old man with a priest's collar looking directly into the camera lens.

The President looked directly at the camera and then back at the questioner. "Yes, it should. Someday someone may look at this recording. I want them to know what some of the world's leaders and thinkers said here today of this monumental interaction.

"I want you only to respond to a go or no-go with further negotiations," said the President. "We will debrief with all of you after our guest leaves. Can we—or maybe the question is 'should we'—negotiate under these terms to abrogate our nuclear arsenal?"

"As a man who speaks for many in the church, I find this approach simply wonderful," said Bishop Macintyre. "The promise of peace and enlightenment as a basis of our society and theirs is what God would expect of us. However, we are only men, sinners to be true. We live in a dangerous world now, and I cannot see us relinquishing our stand against godlessness and evil of the Soviet Union. Maybe someday, when we as a people are more evolved, then and maybe only then can we negotiate with this species."

"What do you think, Franklin?" asked the President.

"I can't believe I'm in concurrence with Bishop Macintyre, but I gotta say no to this. If he's been watching us for such a long period of time, he's bound to know that this is an intractable position to bargain from, knowing our present condition."

"I concur," offered another man in the circle.

"What is your take on this, Eddie?" asked the President.

"Well, it's the right thing to do. Unfortunately, it's the wrong time. I'm not talking about military issues or global annihilation. I'm sure that if full scale knowledge of their presence here comes out it will cause panic, monetary destabilization, a full-scale assault on the Judeo-Christian tradition in this country, and quite possibly a crisis of confidence in the political makeup of Western governments. Does anyone remember a little on-air radio play by Orson Welles back in 1938?"

"What do you think?" the President asked a grim-faced man.

"I've been listening to this unanimous declaration of rejection of sanity with absolute horror," responded Gerald Light. "What are we to do? Is it our fate to negotiate, apparently badly, with this other group of powerful aliens for a few trinkets and give away everything? This man speaks the truth, and we're going to send him packing? Mr. President, I urge you not to do this. Let's talk to our friends in Europe and talk to our enemies, too, and come to an agreement. We can do this, sir."

"Thank you, Mr. Light."

"Are there any other opinions, one way or another?" the President asked the assembled group of men. "Well, this is a democracy still, and the votes of this caucus have been tallied. I'm sorry, Gerald."

"The country is sorry too, Mr. President," added Gerald.

"Let's get back to our guest," said Eisenhower, and he turned and walked quickly back to his chair. The other men followed. "Thank you for waiting, sir," said Ike, as he sat down in the chair with both hands on the arms. The visitor looked up and appeared to smile.

"As I said, we are in a difficult situation on this planet. We cannot at this time renounce these terrible weapons, not just yet. Maybe there will be a time in our future when we can limit or even remove this burden from our shoulders, but not now. I am honored to speak to you, sir. A direct contact with peoples from another planet has been dreamt about by millions of this planet's citizens. I hope we can still have further discussions with you. Is that possible?"

The visitor ignored the President's question and looked over his head at the men sitting behind Ike. "Did all of you agree to this?" he asked. He slightly moved his head, as if to grill each one for a response. They said nothing.

"We had one dissenter," offered the President. "We have a democracy and—"

"And this was important to exercise your democracy. I understand," he said, still keeping his eyes aloft looking at the men's faces.

The camera angle was fixed in one position perpendicular to the two seated men facing each other. Any nonverbal reactions of the men behind the President were lost to history. The visitor and the President had up to now ignored the camera. A heavy silence hung over the meeting, with the President having nothing to say. The visitor slowly dropped his eyes. "I appreciate the single dissenter. I know who you are," he said with a slight smile.

Inexplicably the visitor slowly turned his head and focused his gaze right into the camera lens and spoke. "Is this what you want?" President Eisenhower followed the visitor's gaze into the lens of the camera.

"Whoa!" said Henry. "Who's he talking to?"

"He's talking to *us*, Henry, here, right now," answered Maya.

There was nothing left to discuss. "Thank you for welcoming me," said the visitor as he effortlessly rose to a standing position in front of his chair.

The President slowly stood to reach parity of a sort with this tall stranger. "I speak for my fellow Americans and proudly say this has been an honor to sit and discuss these issues. I would like to know if you will come back and speak with us again. We have so many questions."

"It is up to you, sir. I hope it will not be . . . very long." The visitor appeared to pause looking at the surrounding faces that were absolutely hanging on every word he spoke. His eyes recorded the weight of importance the President and his entourage ascribed to this historic meeting. Like a tourist with a camera, he seemed to be savoring it all through whatever number of senses he had, collecting tidbits of human endeavors—of what it means to be from here, an inhabitant of earth.

"This is my last mission to earth. My son is very interested in working with you. He has taken the earth name Bastian. Maybe when he is ready to meet with people from this planet, you will be ready for him.

"I hope that the presence of my friend did not scare you," said the visitor looking directly at the ever-present metal sphere suspended near his head. "He bristled at the thought that you would touch me. He looks harmless, but had the physical interaction gone forward, my friend would have neutralized you. That would not have been good for détente. I am old, and my friend has been with me for as long as I can remember. Establishing good friends is hard to do, no matter the planet in the cosmos." The alien smiled again. The President genuinely returned a deep, tearful smile. "Goodbye, Mr. President. Goodbye, gentlemen." Without another word, he turned to the wide opening in the hangar and walked resolutely back to his ship. The visitor did not turn around, but walked up the lighted ramp of his ship. A voice in the background could be heard urging the control tower to turn off the radar. The three ships rose silently, hovered for what seemed minutes but was probably less than thirty seconds, and then rose uniformly into the night sky. The three discs reached a point above the base and inexplicably just vanished. The scene abruptly closed with the white leader coursing through the sprockets and rapidly whipping around on the take-up reel as the film completely ended. Henry dutifully turned off the whirring projector and stopped the DVD machines.

Chapter 2

Saturday, September 9 – Late Evening

The first four human beings outside of the government-controlled secrecy net to see unequivocal proof of alien visitation to earth sat silently in the small room. James had come to witness an historic event, one that he believed would free him from the doubt of family and friends convinced that he was deluded and confused about the truth. Here, in less than an hour, the facts were exposed. The truth was revealed.

James stared at the fifties era film, still fixated on the projector. *A simple device*, he thought, *plain and ordinary, but having the power of hundreds of megatons on society. It sits there calmly saying nothing, waiting for someone to lay bare it's combustible truth . . . with a flick of the switch.*

The implications for humankind were astounding. *This is sheer madness*, thought Frank. *We can't show this! It's too much. We should destroy it now.* Frank cautiously turned his eyes toward his longtime friend. *He'd never forgive me, never. The ultimate betrayal.*

The rapturous smile on Maya's face dissipated ever so slightly. Her soft lips closed, and she listened to the voice transmitted into her head. *Awesome, Maya, simply awesome*, said Adam, speaking directly to Maya through the equipment in her head. *I know that you can't talk to me right now. So . . . I'll answer your question. I saw it when I first started here. I didn't have the resources to steal it then. Anyway, I'm at home. Barbara sent on this alert to me. She didn't want to disturb you. The sensors you installed on your rental are going on and off. They're lighting up our board here. Be careful getting out of there.*

I know that you have to stop in and see him in Pittsburgh. He needs to come out of the proverbial closet. You know him. He will listen to you. He controls so much. I can hear your thoughts—well, I can't, but if I could, you probably want me to shut up because we've been over this too many times. Maya groaned.

Okay, just two things more. If you can speed up here a bit and get to New Jersey one day early, our team can put together the video for the UN. No pressure now. Oh, isn't that a wonderful cosmic link? The alien visitor in the film is the father of your Bastian. I'm just saying. Bye, honey, and keep it safe.

Maya was used to the interruptions. The "lot of friends pulling for the mission" could view the scene in front of her eyes through the surgical implant of devices behind her optic nerve and listening units in her ears. The mission was too important for the world. She put aside her reservations about the invasive methods that she had to undergo. Maya herself was now the cyborg hero of the Saturday morning cartoons that she loved to watch as a child.

The feeling in the room was a porridge of euphoria tinged with sadness. Their faces reflected the exhilaration of seeing a flat-out, hands-down validation of the truth, the hard-core reality of extended alien visitation to earth. Chewing at the extremities of that marvelous high-spirited elation was an encroaching despair that an emissary from the stars was spurned and sent away. Power, greed, and fear won the day, and war—cold or hot—was cherished. Peace was sacrificed in the front lines.

"I thought I knew this story. Reading about it from one researcher or another it seemed plausible. Now that I really know, I can't express the pain that I feel. It's as though I didn't know anything at all," said James, unconsciously rocking forward and back in his chair.

"All these years, all these years, and it's all true. Everything that you have lectured about is right and true. I supported you, Jim, but I must admit I had doubts," said Frank, rubbing his head.

James looked directly at Frank and reached to clasp his friend's arm. "I know, Frank. I've had doubts too. Things like the Twining memo could have, in all honesty, been construed in another way. The MJ-12 papers, though enticing, could have been a hoax."

"Don't give it all up, James. You dishonor your colleagues with this aura of apprehension and disbelief," said Maya, turning in her chair to face him. "Some people involved in the Hudson River sightings could amazingly jog under the slow moving and silent running craft and actually keep pace with it for a while. Richard Dolan's painstakingly documented military and law enforcement accounts scream truth to the reader. And besides, your brothers Friedman, Stringfield, Maccabee, Vallee, and Pope would be downright disappointed in you. All of us harbor doubts about life beyond the periphery of the limited vision of our narrowly focused lives."

"You surprise me, Maya. Stringfield, really?" asked James, beaming a smile in her direction.

"Yeah, I would go to Linda Moulton Howe's website and download all of his reports of downed craft. I would reread them over and over."

"James, thank you for the kick ass look at this film. I am honored to watch it with you. Just to bring us back up to reality for a moment or two, I know that you want to take these DVDs with you, but what do we do about this old film?" asked Henry, switching the reels to rewind the film.

"I believe the plan is to ship it out," answered Maya.

"That's true," said Frank.

"Listen, this has been the pinnacle of my life up to now, but I would like to get rid of this as fast as I can. I enjoy my freedom. I know this is your life and this could be a real coup for you, James, but I suspect that there are people following you and watching you since you picked this up." Henry pulled up a wooden stool and sat next to the projector peripherally watching the film rewind off the take-up reel.

"We can't walk out of here with that," cautioned Frank.

Henry abruptly turned his back to Frank and fiddled unconsciously with the projector. "Well, you can't leave it here either."

"You can't help us out by mailing it tomorrow, Henry?" asked Maya in her most feminine voice. She looked up at him from her chair with hopeful expectation in her eyes.

"Very sweet and cajoling, very persuasive . . . but no," said Henry. The take-up reel emptied, and the white leader of the film flopped around on the projector until Henry flipped the switch off. "Besides, what are you going to do with these DVDs?"

"Get it out," answered Maya curtly.

Henry furrowed his brow. A look of astonishment coursed across his face. "Out? Out where?"

"We would rather not say what the venue is, but out to the public," said James.

"Do you think much has changed since the days of Ike and the Bishop Macintyre? You're going to cause mass panic. The world is not ready for this." Henry nervously placed the film back into its case fumbling with the lid.

"You're not running down those stairs and screaming in the street at the sight of this. You were ready," said James.

Maya stepped back toward Frank and whispered in his ear.

"I also knew each man who sat behind the President. I knew the circumstances under which the President attended this meeting. I know of the species of alien that he met, the so-called Nordics. I know that parts of the shadow government have regretted the rejection of this 'Nordic' ever since. I know that other parts are greedily thankful that we hooked up with the 'grays' instead, despite all of the problems. It was like watching a movie of a book that you've read a hundred times."

In slow, measured words James answered. "I believe that the time is right."

"Yeah, you believe. Well, how many days do I have before the world knows?" asked Henry.

"About one week," answered Frank, stepping forward while failing to hide a worried look on his face.

"I have one week to cash out my investments and convert to silver and gold and move to my place in the country," said Henry.

"It's not going to be that bad. There are a lot more people like you out there. Radio talk shows, magazines, and hundreds of websites have been talking this up for decades to the point that a majority of Americans accept UFOs as a fact. The fear factor is much lower than you are painting this out to be," said James, taking the film box as Henry handed it to him.

Henry shook his head and shuddered. "Do you remember that Steven Greer book a while back where he's in a small group of people and he's 'vectoring in' an alien craft and one of his team members who he trusted, who he thought was 'prepared,' goes bananas when this thing comes in for a landing approach. Her fear was so palpable that the ship departed immediately to the consternation of Mr. Greer. Put that on a global scale and crank it up one thousand percent for those that we know are not ready."

"This is getting us nowhere!" exclaimed Maya. She got up and snatched the film box from James's hand. "Thank you, Henry, for your work and your hospitality. Do you have a couple of CD cases for those DVDs?"

"Yes, I do . . . I'll get them for you," said Henry, trying to hide his astonishment at Maya's abruptness. He exited the room and closed the door behind him.

"You are a piece of work," said James.

"We don't have time for this," answered Maya curtly.

"We need about twenty, maybe thirty minutes to get back to the hotel and 'our morning shift.'"

"By my watch we have about three hours to do that. What the hell's the rush?" demanded James.

"If you haven't noticed, we haven't slept much. That forced nap we made ourselves take last night after dinner won't keep us at our optimum all day tomorrow. And there's no contingency in your thinking for the 'what-ifs.'"

"Why do I get the impression that there's a whole heck of a lot you're not telling us? What were you two whispering about?" James asked.

Henry returned to the room with three brightly colored CD cases. "You couldn't find something flashier?" asked Maya sarcastically.

"They'll be just fine," said Frank, taking the cases. He proceeded to open the drives on the DVD recorders and placed the discs in the cases. "One for you and one for me and one for Maya," he said, handing them out.

"Let's go," announced Maya.

"Thank you so very much, Henry, for helping us out. We parked a block away so I believe that no one will link us to you. I'm sure you'll be alright. It will be okay about the disclosure, you'll see." James shook Henry's hand and patted him on the back. James padded out of the room and into the hall. Maya passed by Henry and gently squeezed his arm.

"Great job on these, Henry," said Frank, waving the DVD in front of him. "You're sure you can't send the film for us?"

"I don't want to get that involved in this. I hope it will be an obscure story that I can tell my children someday."

"I'm sure it will be a story you can tell your children someday, but I assure you it won't be obscure." Frank patted Henry on the back and joined the others descending the stairs.

"So, what were you two whispering about? Frank here looked like he saw a ghost." James pressed the exit door shut feeling with his fingers to verify that the edge of the metal door was flush with the metal frame.

"Just security stuff," said Frank, picking up the pace to walk across the deserted street mid-block with Maya.

"Is someone following us?" said James in a raised voice.

"Pipe down there, ace," whispered Maya, turning to reproach him.

"Jaywalking is probably a crime in this city too," said James.

"If that's our only crime tonight, I'll be most thankful," whispered Maya, reaching the other side of the street. She walked a little faster to get to the corner of the intersection. A single-story retail structure positioned at the corner offered her a view of the cross street. She stopped momentarily, looking through the corner windows.

"Looks okay," she said, stepping around the corner. The three figures cautiously followed the sidewalk to their car. The darkened thoroughfare was quiet. The only sound came from their footfalls on the concrete pavement as they pushed on to their vehicle at the end of the block. Maya scanned both sides of the street. Some parked cars lined the street. *Residents of the second-floor apartments nearby*, thought Maya. She could see her vehicle still parked near the corner. *Maybe we weren't followed*, she thought. "This could work out," she said out loud.

"It will," said James.

"It won't," whispered Maya. A virtual silhouette of a figure stepped into view at the unlit end of the block. A stocky man wearing a sport coat cocked his head in the direction of Maya. He stood motionless for a moment and squared his torso to the three walking toward him.

"Walk away! Walk away!" said Maya in a heavy whisper.

The stout, blunted profile of a man disappointed Maya. He approached with purposeful footfalls on the concrete sidewalk. "I don't think he got the message," whispered Frank.

The spectral shape seemed to disappear as it progressed into the dark interior of the street. "James, get to the other side of Frank." He complied without hesitation or question. Maya grasped the film case a little tighter as the figure loomed larger with every step.

Maya stopped walking forward. She analyzed each movement of shoulders, arms, and legs, looking for the slightest infirmity, an injury that was instigating favoritism of another muscle group, anything to give her an edge. Frank whispered something to James. This was Maya's show. Frank knew he was there to protect James.

The stocky man slowed his gait ever so slightly as he passed Maya. He smiled at her. Maya did not reciprocate. Frank pressed his back into James and pinned him against the wall. He positioned his body directly between the arriving threat and James.

Two paces more and the stranger deftly turned around, pulled a revolver affixed with a silencer from his coat, and pointed it at Maya. "I'll take that now," he said unequivocally.

Maya slowly rotated on her heels to face the aggressor. "No, I'd prefer to hold on to it," said Maya.

"I know you. You're Maya, Maya Jablonski," he said with a hint of awestruck recognition. "I would prefer that you hand it over. I just need that film now. It doesn't belong to you."

"It doesn't belong to you," answered Maya, slowly moving the film back and forth from one hand to the other across her hips.

"I must insist. It goes back to where it came from—where it belongs. Now it's time to hand it over. Set it down on the ground and push it over to me."

"And risk damage to the contents?" said Maya, twisting the box in front of him. "Why don't you come over here and I'll hand it to you?"

Frank edged closer to the stranger with the gun. "Come on, little lady. Do as I say or else I'll be forced to shoot you to pry it from your mitts."

Maya slowly started to comply with his request. As if it was choreographed in advance, James slumped to the sidewalk, still maintaining his hidden position behind Frank. Frank moved sharply, not toward the man but a short quick movement of his body and hands to distract the man from Maya. "Hey!" shouted the stocky aggressor. He swerved his revolver towards Frank, who had already stepped back throwing his body in front of James.

Frank's momentary distraction was enough for Maya. She shifted her weight on one foot, held the box in her left hand, and in a discus throwing motion catapulted the film in the direction of the man's groin. Just before the projectile hit him, he had discovered the ruse, repositioned the revolver in the direction of Maya, and squeezed out one round that sailed over Maya's head. The box fell to the pavement, and the man doubled over in pain. The revolver flew from his hand and clinked onto the concrete pavement. Maya approached the man in lightning speed and planted an upper cut to his jaw. She gave him little time to recover, pummeling him with kicks to his head and stomach.

Maya knew that this professionally trained killer would recover quickly. Her expectations were painfully realized. He responded with powerful jabs to her face. She had to fight her natural tendency to retreat from the pain he was inflicting. Maya stepped up her resolve and called upon her hand-to-hand combat training. Her evasive moves saved her—the man's powerful thrusts to her face and stomach missed their target again and again. She grabbed his arm on the last miss and used his momentum to wheel him around so that his back was to her. She immediately jumped on his back, threw her arm around his head, and twisted with all her might. The stocky man, with Maya still holding on, fell listlessly to the ground with a thud.

Maya extricated herself from the crumpled form lying on the sidewalk. "Help me," she said to Frank. "Doorway over there," she panted, as they dragged the lifeless body to a doorway alcove.

"What will happen when he wakes up?" asked James, leaning against the brick wall to climb into an erect position. He received no answer.

"I'll get the revolver," said Maya, stepping back from the doorway. She stuck her hand in her coat pocket and pulled out a white tissue to grasp the silencer end of the firearm. She placed it on the ground behind the man. "Let's go."

"He will wake up?" said James. He was afraid to confront the truth, but he knew the crumpled body would not take another breath.

"Get in the car, James," ordered Frank. James stared at his friend, and Frank stared back. For the first time in their association of over ten years, James realized that they were now in deep trouble. "Now please, James!" he said. Maya unlocked the car, and James obliged by crawling into the backseat. This time the enforced banishment to the backseat was welcomed. He wanted to run away, but the backseat of Maya's vehicle was as far as circumstances would allow.

The roles were now reversed. Their old patterns were broken. Maya would follow Frank's orders unflinchingly in the old order. Now, at forty-seven, he was obviously not as agile and powerful as the thirty-year-old Maya. She was unquestioningly in control, but Frank was unsure where she was leading.

Maya crouched down at the driver side rear quarter panel of her rental car and reached behind the sheet metal. With a slight jerk of her hand she dislodged a small disc-shaped object. "So predictable," she whispered. Maya placed the object carefully in the gutter.

She suspected another device. It was lodged under the front quarter panel. Maya carefully placed it on the ground. She quickly got into the car and pulled into the street.

Maya checked the mirrors constantly for any sign of movement.

Four more people outside the web of the government's national security state saw aliens walk on earth. Unfortunately, they were now prime suspects in the affair of the stolen film. It would take a few hours to redeploy dozens of agents to St. Louis. Maya knew she had less than that to get her team safely away from St. Louis.

The shadow government originally had twelve directors. As bureaucracies evolve, they generally expand to meet the needs of the people they serve, or at least that is their justification. The hidden government currently has nineteen American directors including Adam Baines. Created in the 1950s by elected officials, the shadow, hidden, or invisible government was not created, as the conspiracy theorists claim, to be the real government behind the scenes. It was created to keep hidden the things that the career public servants and elected officials determined was far too destabilizing to the status quo. After World War II, the world needed America's stability. Stability did not include disclosure of the alien presence. It did not embrace the recognition of technologically advanced societies on this planet from ancient times to now.

The shadow government was once an anomaly of only America's needs and demands for secrecy. This was certainly a myopic viewpoint of some in the secret American government. However, the world recognizes the US hegemony in relation to the alien presence. Additional directors were added from other countries for the same reasons America chose this route.

The American directors met once each month, more if a crisis was perceived by any one director. The international directors joined the American directors at the quarterly meeting. Despite the ability to video conference, the directors met for an audio connection only. The audio of each director's voice was filtered to disguise their voices. Anonymity was paramount, protecting each director from purges, retaliation for uncomfortable decisions, and public exposure.

Barbara walked into her boss's office with a grim face. She had to report the worst—something that he vehemently opposed. It would not be a good meeting, but they would get through this. She opened the door.

"Come in, Barbara," he said from his chair.

"Good morning, Mr. Baines."

"What? Now that violence has been breached on this operation, it's Mr. Baines?"

"You know already? Well, of course you know. No . . . how do you know? My link to the operative is *my* operation," said Barbara, shaking the report in her hand.

"Yes, it is *your* operation, but the entire planet is narrowly focused down to this one person, and she is in a lot of trouble now. I'm not too pleased with Broadhurst now either. I don't know if he is up to the task."

"He's a good soul. He will come through for us," said Barbara. "He doesn't know this yet, but this is just the beginning for him."

"Do we have clean operatives for support?"

"Yes, Adam, we alerted six more excellent people along their way, just in case."

"That should probably do it, though nothing about this little adventure is for certain. The analysis has given it the best chance of success—the best scenario we've ever had."

"I'm optimistic," said Barbara, flashing a bright smile. Her smile reflected her relief that Adam wasn't yelling at her. She'd had very little experience of that in her ten years with him. "I'm surprised you're not angry at the violence and death at the hands of our operative."

"I was up very early this morning, and I had a notion to tap into the feed. I saw it live, Barbara," said Adam, showing signs of being emotionally distraught. Barbara got up and walked behind him and gave him a hug. "I know people die every day and people are murdered every day. This was a defensive measure, to be sure, but it still resulted in death. It was regrettable and it will have complications with our adversaries, but if my reports are correct, they still do not know who they are dealing with yet, and that's a good thing." Barbara walked to the side of the desk.

"We picked new recruits who have no trail to us. Even the additional six operatives will be unknown to them. A full-scale operation, and up to now we have absolute deniability. It may jump to plausible deniability, but even that is manageable."

"Thanks, Barbara. This is working out. Keep me posted."

"Yes, Adam," she said and turned to leave the office.

Maya drove for blocks without saying a thing, and her passengers were silent as well. She swiftly made it to an intersection with the freeway. "Nothing like the safety and anonymity of early morning traffic," she said, not expecting a comment. They arrived at their destination: a four-story parking garage that was ten miles from their hotel. Maya drove in, took the ticket from the automated dispenser, and drove to the third floor. In the middle of the ramp, she pulled into an angled space farthest away from an elevator or stairwell. She motioned for all to get out of the vehicle. They did so without question. Maya motioned them over to the concrete wall alcove near the elevators and stairwell, about fifty feet from their car. The waist-high concrete wall was topped with a steel lattice screen.

Maya stood at the wall and looked out at the lights in the surrounding office buildings. She turned and spoke to James. "James, the man I fought with back there is not going to wake up. He's dead."

"I suspected as much. You need to come clean here. I for one am not going further with this dark plan without knowing the truth—if there is any to be had."

"There is and it's important that you know. I have been authorized to answer your questions. You're right about knowing. You shouldn't go forward unless you do."

"What's with this 'authorized' stuff, Maya? Who are you working for?" asked Frank.

"I'm not with the FBI or CIA, if that's what you think."

"I don't know what to think, so suppose you tell me," said Frank, folding his arms. "You've been particularly cagey on this mission. Who's giving you orders?"

Maya turned to stare at the lights of the buildings in the distance. Without turning back, she answered him. "You and your fellow researchers are right, James. There is a shadow government and I'm a part of it. When I left the military five years ago, I was recruited by the NSA. I did a lot of things, good things for my country there for about two years. I met some individuals who introduced me to some special programs that they were working on. It sounded interesting, so they told me more. Soon I was leaving there to join a secret group that works on specialized technology."

"What does that have to do with a dead man back there?" asked James.

"The specialized technology is developed from captured, stolen, and gifted extraterrestrial technology. Yes, James, it is true. The secrets that you allude to in your talks are mostly true. There's some disinformation there, but you have found the kernels of truth. The secret has been maintained at great cost for over sixty years now. The shadow government controls all of this stuff."

"But you still haven't said why you terminated that operative," said Frank.

Maya turned to face the two men. "I'm getting to that. In the fifties and sixties, the shadow government was pretty homogeneous—no dissention at all. Now there are two factions, and an easy analogy is the white hats and the black hats—the good guys and the bad guys. The good guys want to stop all this secrecy and disseminate this information. The bad guys want to suppress it forever, and they want to do much worse in some factions. As an American and a citizen of this planet, I cannot allow that. I am working with the white hats to help disclose this to the world—something that should have been done since the beginning. Our attacker was one of the black hats. If he had been successful, we would probably be dead and the film and copies would be safely in some vault again."

"So, what have we signed up for? It seems that we're pawns in this operation," Frank lamented.

"Fred Willow, the man you met in the alley in San Antonio who gifted you the film, was a sympathizer to disclosure. He was working on a project controlled by the black hats, but he had white hat aspirations, if you take the hat analogy to its extreme. So, we built a scenario based on his access to ultra-classified materials. Through our agents we created openings in the firewalls, and we directed him to you, James."

"Why me!" shouted James. Maya nervously looked around the deserted garage.

"Lower your voice," whispered Frank. "We safe here?" he asked Maya.

"Relatively speaking. We're over ten miles from the theater. We might raise some suspicions—three people standing around jawing in a parking garage at four in the morning. Eh, we're okay here."

"Again, why me!" he echoed in a heavy whisper.

"You already know the answer to that. You believe in this stuff, and you have the means to get it out. We have assisted you with that too."

"If you and your 'white hats' are so powerful, then why don't you just steal that movie yourself and send it out?" demanded Frank. "Why bother us?"

"It's complicated," said Maya quietly. "I don't know it all yet either. I demanded to be let in on as much as they could tell me without making me a security risk."

"What do you know about '*why us*'?" asked James, showing some signs of calming down again.

"Your disclosure plan is well thought out. The white hats are convinced your amnesty for all of the belligerents is the only way out of this mess. It's workable and they believe it's the only plan they can use to convince the black hats to stand down. They have plans for you. That's all I know."

"So, what do we do now?" asked Frank, resting his back against the concrete railing.

"You led our team back in Iraq, Frank. What would you do now?" Maya had a weak, relaxed smile, more a response to the pressure but still genuine.

"You don't have contingency plans for this?"

"I don't want to lead you both around. We know where we have to go and by when. I have one important stop to meet someone in Pittsburgh, but little else is fixed. Because of the death, we have fewer options, but we have additional resources that we can use."

Frank was connecting the dots. "Wait a minute. You were with us until this very minute. You didn't call anybody, and I watched you drive the whole way. You didn't pull out a cell phone or anything. How do you know that you have new resources? Was this anticipated?"

"Okay, I'll give you one more piece of information. As a preparation for this mission, in addition to months of physical training, I've had some enhancements." Maya waited for her words to sink in to their brains.

"Are you some kind of robotic soldier?" surmised Frank.

"In a way, that's correct. The people I work for have access to alien technology and alien medical devices. Behind each of my eyes are transmitting devices. They are like a camera that sees what I see. They do not impair my vision but give my handlers a front row seat to what is happening. Imbedded in each earlobe is a listening device. That's it."

"You say that as if you could have had much more," said James.

"You're right." Maya offered nothing more.

"Okay," said James, drawing out the word.

"So, they're watching us right now?" said Frank.

"Probably. I think they want to know how you are reacting to all of this."

"What doctor performed this operation on you? That's an incredible skill set to do that," mused Frank.

"It was an alien team of doctors, Frank."

"Christ! What have you done?" yelled Frank.

James smiled. "Now it's my turn. Lower your voice, Frank. I think this is amazing—a hybrid of alien technology that increases the capability of the senses. I know it's only surgically done but wow, double wow!"

Frank shook his head and turned to stare out into the night. "We can't go back," said Maya.

"To the hotel? Yeah, that's a given," answered Frank without turning around. "Got an escape plan in mind?"

"It's being prepared now."

"That's good," said Frank.

"That's not good," said James. "What about the conference? I made a commitment. They paid me—well, not a whole lot, but I'm expected there this afternoon."

"First, James, you need to come to grips with your destiny here. Your days as a researcher of UFOs and aliens are over. In the words of one of your heroes, Paul Hellyer, former Canadian Defense Minister, disclosure has occurred, it's done. It's time to move on to the next steps.

"Right now, you have a more pressing engagement. You need to come to grips with that. Edward has been asked to pack up your room contents and prepare the bags to be shipped to your home. The announcement that you have taken ill has been prepared and will be delivered to the conference organizer. I suppose they will read it in the morning and get a lot of heartfelt murmurs from the crowd."

"You're enjoying this aren't you—being able to manipulate events and people? A little too much power maybe." James held up his right hand with thumb and forefinger creating a small gap.

"It's important that you get this, James—all of it. It's very important. You're going to be called upon to do more and accept more responsibility for this operation. It's hardly over with."

"I can do that. I understand that. Just don't ask me to kill anyone. There's been enough killing of humans in the name of God knows what. I'm not going to be a part of it. This is damn important to me, and I'm talking to you—yeah, you—behind these eyeballs," said James, raising his voice and pointing in Maya's face. "I'll do this and then we'll see what's what." James turned away, walked over to the concrete railing next to Frank, and stared silently out into the night sky.

"We need to change into our street clothes," said Maya. "You guys go first. Get your duffel bags out of the trunk and change in the car." James and Frank resolutely turned and did as she asked. When they returned, Maya returned to the car, changed clothes, and picked up her purse and some things from the glove compartment. She checked the seats. She picked up the film box and locked the car. Maya dropped the car keys and some cash into a mailing envelope.

"It is time. Our ride is here," she said, arriving at the concrete railing again. The two men turned and followed Maya to the elevator. They filed out of the elevator on the ground floor and walked toward the garage entrance. All three were done talking and physically drained. The color of the sky was changing perceptibly. A faint glimmer of light in the east heralded the new day. *Maybe if they get some sleep, things will be better. A good night's sleep, or at least a couple hours' sleep, will improve their attitudes*, thought Maya. She wondered if Adam and Barbara could use the implanted devices to read her mind too. She didn't ask and they didn't offer.

Maya looked to the left and then to the right. "This way," she said, walking in the middle of the deserted street. A half block down was a large motor home parked at the curb with its parking lights lit. Upon seeing the three approaching, the driver started the engine and pulled into the street. Maya and her partners made way for the approaching vehicle and stopped next to a parked car. Maya unconsciously stuck her hand into her purse clasping the cold steel pistol.

"Welcome aboard, my friends," said a white-haired lady as she propped open the door on the passenger side. Sitting next to her was a white-haired man at the wheel of the vehicle. The three of them looked up at the extraction team a little stunned. "I know. I know you weren't expecting Ma and Pa Kettle, were you?"

Maya slowly shook her head from side to side. "It's okay. We're close friends of Adam. We were camping about fifty miles away, and out of the blue he calls us and he says that some friends needed a ride. He joked about something like it was about national security or some crap. He always was a jokester. C'mon up here. Let's get a good look at you."

"It's okay, guys," confirmed Maya. One by one the three new travelers boarded the camper and stood for a moment while the old woman conducted her inspection.

"I'm Mary and this is Jonesy. We've been on the road now how long, Jonesy?"

"Forever!" exclaimed her husband. Mary promptly smacked him on the shoulder with the back of her hand.

"We've been traveling for about two years now," said Mary. Behind Mary's head Jonesy mouthed the words *two hundred*, bringing a smile to Maya's bruised cheeks. "We haven't seen all of the country yet but been in most of the lower forty-eight."

"I'm Maya, and this is James and Frank."

"You I recognize," said Mary, pointing at James. "From where I can't remember; it will come to me."

"We're here to drive them somewhere not interrogate them," said her husband.

"He's right. Okay, Adam said you've been up all night and need your rest. We've got sleeping accommodations for four back there, but its two-by-two. I get that you're all separate here in that way, but you'll have to make do. Feel free to crawl under the sheets. I just changed them. Or grab an extra blanket under the big bed. Adam said you want to go to a truck stop east of Indianapolis on I-70. It's about six or seven hours from here."

"Is it out of your way?" asked Maya with genuine concern.

"No, we have no commitments this week. We're going to meet up with our daughter in Georgia by the end of the week, but that's it. Jonesy will keep it steady as she goes so you can sleep. You can all sleep in one of these, can't you?" she asked, opening her hands to encompass the recreational vehicle.

"I slept through the whole Gulf War," admitted Frank.

"I can attest to that," interjected Maya, raising her right hand in affirmation.

"This will be wonderful," finished Frank.

"Frank needs to sleep by himself—he moves around a lot. So, it looks like we will be sharing a bed," said James with a slight smile.

"Okay," said Maya hesitantly.

"Why don't you two guys get settled? I want to ask Maya something," said Mary. She flashed a broad smile that disarmed any concern. The men sauntered off to the rear of the RV. Maya sat down on the bench seat just behind Mary. Jonesy put the vehicle into drive and proceeded down the street.

"You have two, maybe four bruises on your face, honey. I know it's not my business, but did one of those men hurt you? We can help you if you need it," whispered Mary, placing her hand on Maya's knee.

"The reality is they saved me from the man who did this. I needed to get out of St. Louis fast, and they are helping me."

"Those guys are helping you? Honey, you're clearly the leader of this bunch. I would find it more convincing that you got in a fight to save them from something. Anyway, at least they're not responsible for these," she said, passing her hand close to Maya's face. Maya gently took Mary's hand and pressed it to her bruised face. She tried to hold back her emotions, but one tear cascaded down her cheek. The old woman moved forward in her seat and hugged Maya. The tears flowed copiously down her face as the two women embraced. Maya and Mary hugged for two blocks as Jonesy concentrated on navigating the wide RV through the narrow streets.

Maya pulled back and took the tissue that Mary pulled from her small jacket. "Thank you for the hug." Maya felt something, something deep and broad, expressing great importance, great knowing. Her facial pain eased a bit as well.

"Hugs are always free here, honey, and freely given," said Mary, her smile the smile of a sincere woman of simple purpose.

"How do you know Adam anyway?" said Maya, touching her face to verify that the bruises were still there.

"He lived down the block from us in Joliet. We would go camping together."

"Adam was going camping? That's hard to believe," said Maya.

"He was elected to the House of Representatives for one term in Congress. Everyone liked him. For some reason, he chose not to run again and took some government job, something he never talked about. One time we scheduled a four-day trip, and he calls us and says he can't go. Then he gives us the reason— 'a matter of national security.' Well, we knew he worked for the government and all, so we were real quiet on the phone thinking there must be something big going on. Then he laughs and then we laugh and ever since then it's a running joke—this national security thing. So, if he hasn't called in a month or two or he can't stop by when we're camping near DC, he gives us the old standby—national security."

"National security," said Maya in mock amazement. The two women shared a laugh. "Mary, I need to mail this envelope from somewhere in St. Louis. Can Jonesy look out for a mailbox for me?" Maya held up the envelope with car keys and cash in it.

"I'm on it," announced Jonesy. "So how do you know Adam?"

Maya thought for a moment. "Well, we only go back about three years. I was in the military. When I got out, he helped me find employment. He's a real peach of a man—a real straight shooter. You always know the truth when you're working with him."

"I agree, except for that 'national security' stuff," answered Mary with a laugh.

"We're in luck, Maya. There's a box over there," said Jonesy.

Jonesy pulled the RV over near the curb, and Maya jumped out, dropped the package in the box, and bounded back on the RV.

"Now you join those boys back there and get some sleep. All things look better the next day after a good night's sleep."

"Thanks, guys, we really appreciate this." Mary smiled and offered a thumbs-up to her passenger. Maya walked back to the small bedroom.

"Everything okay?" whispered Frank.

"Yeah, Frank, everything is just fine. Where's the film?"

"Under the bed in the compartment," answered James. "Why did we stop?"

"I had to mail the keys to the rental back to the local rental office. I added some extra money for them to pick it up. The 'black hats' will be on our tail by morning, but fortunately, thanks to Mary and Jonesy, we will be long gone."

"Can we trust them?" whispered Frank.

"They are indeed good friends of my employer. I think Adam found my surprise at who was picking us up particularly delightful. It's just like him. Things that shouldn't just happen seem to happen for him, and I haven't quite figured him out completely even after years of working with him."

"I want to hear more about this employer of yours," said James.

"In the morning, James—in the morning I'll answer your questions," Maya said, grabbing the blanket that was left out for her. She curled up next to James and promptly fell asleep.

"Looks like Adam really needed us this time," whispered Jonesy.

"We get so few chances to help. I'm glad he asked. Could you feel the nascent power in those three?" said Mary.

"Sure," he said, pointing unnecessarily to the on ramp for Interstate 70. "Maya perceived something in you, a great knowing?" Jonesy looked intently at Mary—a lot longer than an old man should when merging onto a freeway.

"Well, I can say no more than that," said Mary.

The old couple whispered in unison, "It's a matter of National Security!" In suppressed giggles, they segued into the early morning traffic out of St. Louis and into the rising sun.

"Try to watch the road, honey," said Mary, clicking on her seat belt. Jonesy smiled and focused his gaze down the highway.

Chapter 3

Sunday, September 10

Don Petrulio took his orders very seriously. He didn't ask the "why" question when receiving an assignment from his supervisors at Langley. He just did it and moved on to the next challenge. However, his current assignment was not working out very well. The perpetrators he was seeking were eluding law enforcement agencies, left and right. He surmised that some very powerful people were assisting Broadhurst. It brought up all these secret government conspiracy theories that he just hated. He was going to do his job, meet the responsibilities head-on—and may the conspiracy nuts be damned! The only flaw to this scheme was that his agents and analysts seemed to be more than just one step behind.

Don Petrulio could handle that; honest efforts would sometimes not resolve a case. What he couldn't stand was bumbling on the part of his staff.

"Is Broadhurst still in St. Louis?" asked Don Petrulio, sitting at the large conference table. The core team of federal agents had moved to St. Louis to collaborate with local officials to find Broadhurst.

"Well, he's got a presentation late this morning, and he hasn't come out of his room today," said Harold, sitting at the far end of the table.

"Are we sure he's in his room?" asked a woman at the center of the table.

"I can answer that," said a young agent opposite her. "We have a tape from last night." He typed in some commands on his laptop, and the screen behind Harold lit up with a view of a hallway. "Here at 8:22 PM is the last time we see Broadhurst. He's taking towels from the maid." The agent pressed a button on the remote to fast forward the tape. "And here we see him go back into his room."

"He never came out again?" asked Don.

"No," said the agent.

"Who was that maid?" asked the woman across the table.

"I don't know. It was just a maid. We have a full tape of her going down the hall offering more towels and toiletries to the guests."

"Isn't 8:00 PM a little late for that?" she said, pressing the young agent to explain.

"Is there something here?" asked Don.

"I don't know. I'm not profiling, and I hope I don't offend anyone here, but aren't all maids at hotels recent immigrants, like Hispanics, eastern European, or some Asian nationality? This woman was clearly not Hispanic or Asian."

"Rewind the tape," ordered Don. The agent complied and brought the tape back before the interaction with James Broadhurst. The agents watched the maid from the side. At each doorway, only a profile view was seen of Maya as she made her rounds.

"Seems odd to me," surmised the female agent.

"Can someone check this out and find out who that woman is?" asked Don.

"We'll get right on it, sir."

Barbara, the thin, elegant, middle-aged woman dressed in a black sport coat with matching pants, sat up straight at the edge of the leather chair and laughed. "So what did she do when she saw Mary and Jonesy?"

"Mary looked down at her from the passenger side of her big rig and said to Maya, 'Well, I suppose you weren't expecting us.' Maya's head moved back and forth, and back and forth," laughed Adam, struggling to keep his coffee cup level.

"I wish I could have seen her face," added Barbara. "That would have been priceless. How did you ever find these people?"

"They're old family friends. When Ruth was still with us we went camping together."

"You went camping! Well, Ruth maybe, she was always somewhat of a tomboy adventurer. But you? I find it hard to believe that you would sit around the campfire and tell ghost stories."

"It was alien invader stories," said Adam in his best deadpan delivery.

"Really?" she asked.

"No, of course not. It was a lot of fun. It wasn't just a lot of drinking and cards, though we did play cards on some rainy nights and drank a bit. It was more of getting away and out of contact. This was before cell phones. Anyway, we had some great discussions, long into the night."

"So, in a couple of hours they will be getting up from a long nap and meet our contact at the truck stop. I believe we are ahead of them," said Adam, bringing the discussion back to the mission.

"I think you're right. You didn't answer my question. How did you locate your friends?"

"Who?"

"Godzilla and Mothra," said Barbara, looking askance at her longtime friend and employer. "We were talking about Jonesy and Mary."

"Oh. Well, we do have a covert network, and their rig was configured for our eyes a couple of years ago."

Barbara slumped a little in her chair. "I'll never get used to this—never. They're your friends. How could you do that to them?"

"Barbara, it's precisely because they are my friends. Most of this is just business. Because of my affiliations and—"

"Power," interjected Barbara, careful not to accuse him of anything.

"That too. I have used these capabilities to further our goals and look after my friends. They think they have a guardian angel out there. I've been able to get them out of a number of close calls and brought police within minutes when they were in trouble and conversely smoothed things over with law enforcement before Jonesy got a ticket for that lead foot of his. It's all good. I love them. I don't want anything bad to happen to them."

Getting an answer about Mary and Jonesy, Barbara came back to the mission. "Our team is ahead right now, but I'm afraid of what the others will do when they discover their man is dead. Do we know who the asset was?"

"Yes, unfortunately he had a family that will be devastated. This killing must stop. Even when the good guys perpetrate it, it gives me no comfort. We will contribute to the family. All of us will provide for them. As usual, they'll have no clue about how many murders were perpetrated by their husband, their father. This is a wretched business we're in, Barbara, but I really see an end in sight."

"Aren't we, in a way, throwing the dice here? What if they are right and these secrets are just too secret to reveal?"

Adam walked over to her side and placed his hand on her shoulder comforting her. "After ten years you still have doubts?"

"Yes, Adam, I still have doubts. Don't you?"

"Not about the outcome, not even about the timing. I believe that this country, actually this world, was ready for it fifty years ago. We were just too afraid, too paternal. Now we will have a measured approach after one big wallop."

"Then, what do you doubt?"

"It's the methods over the years. We are such a violent people. We capitulate to it every chance we get. Broadhurst's concept of blanket immunity must be realized for this to succeed."

"You won't get any arguments from me. Well, I have to get back to work. We're expecting an escalation due to last night's death. I need to make sure our plausible deniability is convincing. They're going to be armed to the teeth now, and I'm afraid if Broadhurst surfaces they'll take him out. This neat little extraction bought us some time, but I don't know if it will be enough. Can I get a link to eyes on the camper?"

"It's already set up at your workstation. The link is JONESY." Adam mustered a confident smile. He was worried, and they both knew the stakes were very high.

"So, it's confirmed?" said Kathleen, sitting at her desk in a darkened basement command center in Fredericksburg, Maryland.

"Yes, ma'am," said the agent, his hands nervously clutching a file. The death of an operative on assignment in St. Louis was a serious blow to the shadow government faction attempting to recover the top-secret film. All of the directors were notified at once.

"Is that his file?" she asked, looking at his fidgeting hands.

"Oh, yes, here," he said, attempting to control his stammer.

"Did you know him, Charlie?" asked the woman as she opened the thick folder.

"No, ma'am, I did not."

"He and I started in the Agency together. His dad and my dad were good friends. They both were members of the same fraternal organizations."

"The Masons, ma'am?" interjected the young agent.

"Yes. But that wasn't what they were about, not really. They were Americans who saw a need. They were both in the military, and they encouraged us in the same path. I haven't regretted one day until now."

"I understand. Maybe our cause is not worth the number of friends and family that we have to lose. My mom always told me that family is the most important."

"Yes, Charlie, your mother was right. We're your family too. I know some of you young guys don't understand why we keep secrets. You want everything to be revealed, and we'll all just get it."

"No, ma'am," said Charlie, stiffening in his stance in front of her.

"We started down this road because we had to do so. The American people were not ready for this, and they still aren't. Yes, surveys say that over half of the people in this country 'believe' in UFOs. What does that mean, 'believe'? It means that they really don't understand. It's some kind of mythology or religion to them that you have to believe or you don't believe. It's one thing to believe in something that's far away and out of sight. They also say they believe in God. If the Supreme Being, unmasked, appeared in their immediate presence, they would be mentally burnt to a crisp. They would fare no better if aliens landed in their backyard. They don't have a clue!"

"Isn't it our job as the leaders, those with the knowledge, to give them a clue, ma'am?"

"Yes, and slowly we are doing that, but the UFO fanatics want to open our files, put it all on the six o'clock news, and tell the world that they're here and they've been here for a hell of a long time. Have you forgotten your training, Charlie? You've seen the analysis and some of the history of what we do here. Your clearance is high enough to know that we have knowledge of dozens of species of intelligent travelers from out there. Do you really think that America and the world are ready for this?"

"No," he said, staring down at his shoes.

"Some of it, maybe in a hundred years, can be revealed," added Kathleen. "The problem with revealing things is that people are smarter than we think. They may not be able to take the whole story at once, but little by little it could work. The difficulty is if we said that we suppressed this knowledge with force and deception and this person or that person suffered for it—"

"As our agent did," he interjected.

"Then we may sacrifice the trust that our people have in the American system."

"Didn't that all get blown away with Watergate, ma'am?"

"I remember Watergate. I was in the army then. You, Charlie, weren't even born. How can Watergate be a seminal point in your life?"

"A President's resignation is now part of history. Before Nixon no other President did that. Yes, I read about it and saw some videos. I guess I studied it in college a bit more. I want you to know you don't have to worry about me, ma'am. I am committed to this program."

"That's good, Charlie. We need good people like you who think, who have a good head on their shoulders and can follow orders. That's very important. Our agent was murdered. From all signs, it looks like a professional attack. We are committed in getting that film and all copies back in our possession." Another agent knocked on the jamb of the open office door.

"You wanted an update on this as soon as we got it," said the agent.

"Yes, come in. What is it?"

"Broadhurst has taken ill and will not be attending the conference. The conference organizer just read a statement. Connors is gone too. We got access to his room and there are no clothes, no suitcases. Everything is gone."

"That's it!" yelled Kathleen. "I suspected that smiling bastard all along. Broadhurst is too old to overpower and murder our agent. He must have accomplices."

"We were watching the room all night. He must have sneaked out last night, though for the life of me, I don't have a clue," said the agent at the door. "No matter, we'll catch him."

"We have every resource in the world, and these amateurs gave us the slip. I want to talk to our agent in San Antonio. He was supposed to be coordinating with our St. Louis team. What went wrong?"

Charlie's eyes brightened. "We need to figure out where he's going. We haven't seen this film on CNN yet. We need to get a list of possible end games for these guys and be there when he surfaces."

"Excellent, Charlie, get the team together. We need to set the objective and then break into work groups and brainstorm possible ways he may try to get this artifact to the public. One team will pursue them from St. Louis, but the rest of us need to get that 'end game' of yours going. Fifteen minutes in conference room B."

Kathleen dropped her eyes to the file in front of her, and the two men quickly exited the room. She opened the file and stared at the picture of the dead agent. She lightly passed her forefinger down the side of his face. A single tear welled up in her left eye and cascaded down her cheek. "You won't be forgotten, my friend. Your life had meaning. We will find your murderer and make this right."

"I believe this is the right place," said Jonesy, pulling the RV into a crowded truck stop at just short of the noon hour. "Should we let them sleep some more?"

"I don't think so. Their ride is here. They are going east."

"We're going east; we could have taken them."

Mary looked down the aisle and then resumed the conversation. "They're in a bit of trouble."

Jonesy caught Mary's attention. He looked down the aisle to the partitioned anterior of the motor home. They looked back at each other, communicated wordlessly, and resumed their conversation, now at a volume audible to the guests awakening in the bedroom. "Yeah, you said that about six times last night." Mary jabbed his shoulder. Jonesy fabricated a moan for the nonexistent pain and flexed his shoulder backwards.

"I'm serious! It isn't over. They have many challenges ahead of them."

"And we have been taken off the list as the responsible party.

Adam said that we are to let them off here, and that's all we can do."

"You've done way more than enough, you two," said Maya, padding toward them in her bare feet carrying her shoes.

"Oh! I didn't hear the door open," stammered Mary, rotating the passenger seat to face her guest. "Did you sleep well?"

"I didn't wake up until you pulled off the interstate." Maya sat down in the second row of seats.

"Are your friends awake?" asked Jonesy.

"They're starting to move. I told them to get up. They have paid showers at these truck stops, don't they?"

"I think so," said Jonesy, scratching his close cropped grey beard.

"We're all going to need it."

Mary looked into Maya's eyes. "Where are you going, Maya?"

Maya was taken aback by her forthright question. She looked away out the window and answered her indirectly. "We're in a bit of trouble, but not with normal law enforcement. I wish I could tell you more—you've been so kind to us, to me."

"We're old people but we still recognize the signs of trouble. At first, we thought it was abuse from your travelling companions, but you cleared that up. Someone else is after you, aren't they?" said Mary.

"Mary!" said Jonesy, shaking his head side-to-side.

"No, I understand. I have an aunt who is just like you, always wanting to protect, to rescue. I loved her so much that I became just like her. I'm doing the protecting. I'm the rescuer and protector for these gentlemen," said Maya, putting her hand on Mary's knee.

Mary sat back in wonderment as this young woman took charge of the situation, portrayed a sense of entitlement to an order and purpose for the three travelers.

"Boy, am I hungry for some breakfast," announced Frank, stepping forward and sitting down in the seat next to Maya. Maya looked at him and rolled her eyes.

"What? A guy gets hungry after a long sleep."

"Yeah, you did all that work chasing naked babes in your dreams, and you need some more fuel." Maya patted him on his paunchy stomach.

"That's a great idea," interjected Jonesy.

"What, chasing naked babes in your dreams?" asked Frank.

"No, breakfast; is your roommate back there awake?" said Jonesy.

"Yeah, he's getting there," answered Frank. "So, what's the plan for this?" He looked at his watch. "It's after noon—already?"

"We have a contact to make. I hope the support team thought to bring a change of clothes. There are showers here we can use."

"More friends of Adam?" asked Mary.

"More friends of Adam," confirmed Maya. Out of the corner of her eye she saw James starting for the front. "Did you pick up after yourself back there?"

"Yes, mom," he answered.

"Did you get the package?"

"No, mom, but I will," said James, turning back to the bedroom.

"He's adapting well," laughed Mary.

"Both these guys, I've got them wrapped around my little finger," added Maya, thrusting the little finger of her left hand in the air. Frank rolled his eyes and shook his head.

"What did you say?" asked James.

"Nothing," said Frank.

"Do you want to leave that big box here until you meet up with your party? No sense in carrying it around with you until you're sure you have a ride," offered Mary.

"My wife is hoping that you'll not make your contact and you'll continue on with us."

"I know," said Maya, giving Mary a hug. "It's safe, James; put the box back where you got it, and we'll come back for it."

"But?" protested James.

"Listen, are you going to put that on your lap while you eat and then take it in the shower with you? Besides, we're going to look quite suspicious lugging that thing around."

"It will be safe here," confirmed Jonesy.

James stood there watching everyone look expectantly at him. After a few moments of silence, he relented, "Oh, alright."

"The sign says they have three restaurants here. Do you have a preference?" said Mary.

"No, I don't," answered Frank, without looking up to see if he was expected to answer.

"Let's just take a walk. We'll go exploring," said Maya. Everyone got up and followed Mary out of the RV. Jonesy pulled up the rear, locking the door as Maya watched the process.

"Do you want to take the keys?" asked Jonesy. "I trust you. It's okay."

"Are you sure?"

"Hell, yeah!" Jonesy handed the keys to Maya, and they proceeded to the complex of service stations and restaurants.

James pulled Frank aside leaving Maya, Mary, and Jonesy to walk ahead. "After all this, and the death of maybe two men, we're just going to leave the package in that motor home?" whispered James.

"You know my sister Anabelle, don't you?"

“Yes, Frank, I know that your sister is precious, but what does she have to do with the most precious of films ever in our possession?”

“While in college, she had a part-time job working for a jewelry store chain. She wore jeans and a sweatshirt in the winter and cutoffs and a T-shirt in summer at this job.”

“I’m sorry, what does her dress code have to do with anything that we’re talking about?”

“She was responsible to pick up jewelry at any of the ten stores in the tristate area and move it to any other store. She carried the stuff around in a beat-up gym bag. It was nothing for her to transfer one or two million dollars’ worth of jewels, watches, and gold chains. She once was told that she had transported eleven million dollars’ worth of stuff in one run. The point is, anonymity is more effective than an armored car. A beat-up motor home is the perfect place to store a priceless historical artifact. Get it?”

“Yeah, yeah, I got it,” said James. “You have some wardrobe maintenance to attend to. You’re untucked in the back.” James reached the front of the truck store complex and held the door for his trusted associate. “And Frank? No more talk about priceless artifacts and where to find them.”

“Oh darn, I was about to run to the public-address system and make an announcement. What is that license plate number?”

“Very funny,” said James.

The group entered through a main entrance. Once inside Maya and Frank checked the surroundings carefully looking for entrances to restaurants, hallways, and service doors as well. It was a habit these two found hard to break even when things appeared safe.

“Pit stop,” yelled Frank, pointing to the restroom sign. Everyone nodded in agreement and split up for the restrooms. One by one they returned to the crowded hallway and waited for the others.

"Why don't we go to this one?" said Maya, nodding in the direction of a full-service restaurant. "It's busy and it looks like it would have something for everyone."

"Call it done," announced James, with a thumbs-up of his right hand.

They stood for only a short time while a table for five was set up for them. Maya and Frank took up the rear as they weaved through the restaurant to their booth. The two security authorities insisted on sitting on the outside of a large circular booth, putting James, Mary, and Jonesy in the center.

"So how do we hook up with our ride?" asked Frank.

"He'll meet us here when we are leaving," said Maya.

"I know you're a smart girl, but how would you know that? You've never been here before, and there are three restaurants and other facilities. That's more than just a little scary," said Jonesy, tapping his fingers on the table.

His wife gently put her hand on top of his. "Read your menu, dear." He complied, but the extra wrinkles on his face and furrowed brow did not go away.

"The best way to describe our little 'master of ceremonies' is that she's psychic and leave it at that," suggested James. Jonesy continued to read his menu in silence.

"Just a little special," added Mary, placing her other hand on Maya's. The two women smiled at each other. "Honey, I see they have chicken fried steak on the menu. You like that, don't you?"

"I do but you never let me have it," whined Jonesy.

"We have guests, and you've been so good on your diet lately. You can splurge a little."

"How about the chocolate cake? It's on the menu too."

"Maybe we'll split it." Jonesy's spirit brightened a bit, and he forgot the previous dialog. The meal proceeded with good conversation around the table and sharing of food. From time to time, Maya and Frank scanned the room and quickly returned to the discussion. Mary seemed to accept the unusual behavior of these two people even though she hardly knew them.

"I got it," said James, snatching up the check.

"Okay," said Maya slowly. "How are you going to pay for that?"

"What do you mean?" he asked indignantly. "I have money."

"I know you have money, James. I'm asking *how* are you going to pay for that?"

James reached into the pocket of his sport jacket and pulled out his wallet. He quickly pulled out a credit card and set it on top of the check.

"I'm sorry, James. You can't do that," said Maya.

Frank knew it was time to intercede. "Look, my friend, we're on the road away from situations we left in St. Louis. Don't you think they could find us, rather easily I might add, with your transaction using that?" he asked, pointing to the plastic card on the table.

"Let us cover this," offered Jonesy.

"No, let Adam cover this," suggested Maya.

"What, is this Adam going to pop up in the next booth?" queried James. His indignation over Adam's control of everything rose, concurrently with his frustration over his inability to pay for lunch.

"No, I came prepared," said Maya, reaching into her purse. She pulled out a thick folded wad of bills and peeled off a hundred dollar note and put in on top of the check. Maya picked up the card and lazily handed it to James. "We're cash only from now on."

A thick silence descended on the table. The waitress took the check and the payment and disappeared. "I'm not sure if I can keep this up," said James, staring at his plate.

"I know, James," said Frank, patting him on his back.

"Just what kind of trouble are you in anyway?" blurted Jonesy.

"It's a fair question, Jonesy. I'll answer it outside," said Maya quietly.

Frank called Maya's attention to a television screen in the nearby bar. Maya saw the image on the screen. Within a few seconds, she was standing in front of the bar listening intently to the news report.

"Today in St. Louis, state and federal officials are looking for James Broadhurst as a person of interest in connection with the death of a federal agent last night. Mr. Broadhurst was a speaker at the Extra-terrestrial Conference taking place in St. Louis this weekend. Mr. Broadhurst is missing along with his longtime associate Frank Connors. If you have any information about these individuals, you are instructed to contact your local FBI office."

The segment ended, but Maya stood motionless staring at the television. She turned and scanned the room once more. No one seemed interested in the television, nor was anyone interested in her abrupt arrival at the bar. She sauntered back to her seat to expectant, worried looks from her lunch mates. Jonesy and James exhibited the most distress.

"Well, what did they say?" demanded James. "I saw my picture flash on the screen and Frank's too."

"I don't believe it. I don't believe they went public. They couldn't possibly defend that agent's actions in a court of law. They're out on a limb—way out!" exclaimed Maya in a hoarse whisper.

"What the hell is going on here? Who are you people?" exclaimed Jonesy. Mary tried to quiet him down.

"I'm not going to be quiet about this. I want an explanation," he demanded.

"Let's go!" whispered Maya, pulling Jonesy out of the booth. Maya locked arms with the old man and hustled him out of the restaurant. The others followed in close order behind them with Frank bringing up the rear. Out in the covered hallway, Maya turned left with Jonesy. A thin, tall man with dungarees and a grey T-shirt, unknown to everyone except Maya, ambled up alongside Jonesy. "Hello, Mr. Seth Jones. I want to thank you first of all for your service to your country today. You will eventually know what this is all about, but for now I can tell you that you have been helping us with a matter of national security."

"National security," repeated Jonesy with a laugh. "I didn't believe it when Adam joked about it, and I don't believe it now."

The thin man stopped in the middle of the hallway and stared into Jonesy's eyes. "Adam has never lied to you."

"He couldn't go camping with us because of 'national security.' He couldn't go to the races with us because of 'national security.' All true, huh?" said Jonesy.

"Yes, all true," said the thin man, still gazing into Jonesy's eyes. "We really can't stay here." The insistent tone of his voice activated Maya. She pressed forward with Jonesy, reaching the outer doors in seconds, and went out into the midday sun. "I have placed your vehicle next to the RV. You cannot stop for showers now," he said, turning to James and Frank. "You will need to keep going to your destination, pick a safe motel, and pay cash. Maya will handle the transactions. James and Frank must stay out of sight."

They walked across the pavement in silence now. James thought to himself, *How could a day with such bright sunshine and an easy breeze be filled with such potential doom? It couldn't be.*

The party of six reached the RV. Parked adjacent in an open space was a large SUV. "First, I want to get Seth and Mary safely on their way," said the tall, thin man.

"No arguments from me. The sooner I get away from you people the better," said Jonesy with a fearful shudder.

"Again, Mr. Jones, our country thanks you for assisting these three people. Maya, will you retrieve the package now?" Maya unhooked her arm from Jonesy, then stepped over and unlocked the RV.

"How did you know they had a package in there?" asked Mary, pointing to the RV.

"We wanted to be sure that it was still there," said the tall, thin man.

"But no one told you it was there." Mary looked exasperated and confused. James put his hand on her shoulder attempting to comfort her.

"We have ways of knowing these things. We have provided you some compensation for your time and effort here. You will find an envelope in the glove compartment. I know you initially did this out of love for your friend, but clearly, things have changed with your vision of this mission. Do you see that dark blue car over there?" The tall, thin man pointed to a late model sedan parked over next to a clump of trees in the parking lot. As soon as Mary and Jonesy found the vehicle in their sights, two men inside the vehicle waved to them. Mary tentatively waved back with a small movement of her hand.

"These people will follow you to your next camping spot tonight. As soon as they are convinced that you are not followed, they will leave you—but not until then. They are for your protection."

"Do you think this is necessary?" said Mary worriedly.

"No, but Adam has ordered it, and it will be done," he said in response.

"I knew that guy worked for the government, but I always thought he just pushed paper in some office somewhere," surmised Jonesy.

"I can assure you, Seth, Adam does more than push paper."

Maya stepped out of the RV with the box under her arm and bounded over to the others.

"Let us not detain you further, Seth and Mary. Once again we express our extreme gratitude," said the tall, thin man.

"Yeah, yeah, let's go, Mary," said Jonesy.

"Jonesy, you fire up the beast. I'll be there in a moment. I want a word with Maya," said Mary, gently grabbing Maya's arm and pulling her out of hearing range of the others.

Jonesy turned back and presented his right hand to Frank and James for a handshake. "Actually, you weren't bad travelling companions, and lunch was nice up until the end. I hope you're on the up-and-up and you do well. I just can't stand this cloak and dagger stuff. It's not in my nature," said Jonesy. Frank and James said goodbye to Jonesy, and the old man boarded the RV.

"Somehow, Adam is following what is going on, isn't he, Maya?" whispered Mary.

"Yes, Mary, he is."

"Is he listening now?"

Maya paused for a moment. "Yes, he's listening now, and he can see you too. If you want to say something to him look into my eyes and speak normally. He will see and hear you."

Mary appeared to waver a bit at the impact of what Maya was telling her. Maya held her arm and steadied her. "Adam thought you could handle this."

"So that's how it works? I just talk to you, and he sees and hears me?"

"Yes, and if he responds, I can tell you what he said. Go ahead and speak to him, Mary."

Mary positioned herself right in front of Maya and spoke. "Jonesy didn't think you had a very important job, but I knew you were a very smart man. I knew you knew more than most of us. I want to know if it will be alright for Maya. Will you keep her safe?"

Maya was taken aback by Mary's question. Of all the things she could ask, she asked about her. Moisture welled up in Maya's eyes, and she let out a little laugh. "Adam says that if I start crying, he won't be able to see you clearly."

Mary held her hand to her mouth in shock. "He sees me through your eyes. What have they done to you, Maya?"

Maya stood silently for a moment and spoke again. "Maya volunteered to help her country, Mary, just as I have. I want you to know that I trust her implicitly. She is a good woman, and you were right to take her under your wing, just like you did with me years ago." Maya was silent for a moment as the new transmission came through. "I will keep her safe, Mary. Don't worry about her."

"Will you come camping with us again sometime, sometime soon?" pleaded Mary. Maya stood silently looking directly at Mary. "Did he not hear me?"

"I think he's thinking about what to say. He's not saying anything," said Maya. Maya looked puzzled, then she held up one finger to wait. "I am sorry, Mary. I will not come camping with you again. I am going far away."

"To Europe—I always wanted to go to Europe. We'll meet you there," said Mary excitedly.

"I'm not going to Europe, Mary. Please understand. My long

weekends with you were the best times of my life. Choices that I have made lead me in another direction now. I love you and Jonesy very much." Maya stopped to wait for more. "I wish you a long life, my friends. Take care of each other. It is people like you who make this all worthwhile. Goodbye, my dear Mary."

Maya closed her tear-filled eyes and dropped her head towards the ground. Mary threw her arms around Maya and screamed, "Is he going to die?"

"On the contrary, Mary, he's going to live." The two women held their hug for a few moments until Jonesy called for her from the RV.

"I'm wasting gas here, Mary," he said, coming one step down to the open door. Mary ended the embrace with Maya, kissed her cheek, and walked slowly to the RV. She looked back once to small waves from everyone. Mary boarded the RV; the door quickly closed, and the large vehicle slowly pulled out of the parking lot followed by the dark blue sedan.

"Remarkably good people, Seth and Mary," said the tall, thin man.

"Your man has filled us in on what's in the SUV. I think we have everything we need," said Frank, not trying to hide his excitement.

"Okay, thank you for your help," said Maya in a detached voice. "Adam is off the grid now. Tell him I appreciate your calming effect on our friends, and thanks for the supplies. Are there any last-minute instructions?"

"No, these guys have heard it all. Maya, please be careful. Now that they are running almost unmasked, they will be more ruthless. I fear there will be more violence. Stay low, very low. Hang out separately in crowded parks and public events during the day. Drive in late afternoon and evening hours. Sleep in your vehicle late at night. You know the drill."

"Alright, thanks again," said Maya, shaking his hand. "Do you need us to drop you somewhere?"

"My transportation is all arranged. Here are the keys."

"Frank," called Maya. "You drive." She flung the keys at his outstretched hand. "I would like the backseat, but they will be looking for you two men and putting you both in the front seat would be ridiculously imprudent. I'll take shotgun only if James can sit back and not bob his big head in my view."

James was about to take offense at her put down, but he happened to look at Frank who shook his head to discourage him. "I think I can do that," he said. The three got in the vehicle after final handshakes and pats on the back from the tall, thin man. They took the same direction taken by Jonesy and Mary. It was uncertain if their paths would cross again.

Chapter 4

Monday, September 11

"So, Charlie, your idea brought us to this meeting. Can you start us off?" said Kathleen.

"Sure, I just thought that we may be spinning our wheels with Broadhurst here. We know he's got the film—our deceased agent proves that," said Charlie, looking at his supervisor.

"Go on, Charlie," she said.

"I think we need to explore where he's going. He could have pushed this out on the internet at almost any time. He could have offered it to any number of media markets along the way. So far, we have two points on the map—San Antonio, where Broadhurst and Conners received the film from Fred Willow, and the other city is St. Louis. The obvious goal is somewhere on the east coast, but it may be anywhere. We've been lucky up until now in that we haven't seen this on the news yet."

"So, this is a brainstorm session to profile his *likely* destination?" asked a woman at the table.

"That's the idea. The St. Louis team will continue to push from that end. I heard that they're having some luck," said Kathleen.

"An abandoned rental car was found in a parking garage leased to a Maya Jablonski. She has some history with Frank Connors in the military. She worked for the NSA but disappeared a few years ago. She might be one of us—we're checking our various projects now, but if she's in deep cover, we may not be able to locate her," added the woman.

"I think he's on his way to a major news outlet. Our operative at CNN is not as strong as we'd like. I think if any news service will give this some air, it will be them," said an older man with a salt and pepper beard at the end of the table.

"So, they have what, a big reel of 1950s era film. I don't think all media outlets have old projectors and equipment for someone to run a clip of that," said a young man sitting next to Kathleen.

"I worked in television five years ago. Television stations have basements. There they have stacks of old film and the projectors to run them," said the man with the salt and pepper beard.

The young man shook his head in defiance. "It takes some sophisticated hardware and software to make a broadcast ready clip. Besides, wouldn't the TV station, upon seeing the raw footage, freak out at what they saw? Wouldn't they come crawling to the FBI and say 'I think you lost this' and hand it over?"

"I think that depends upon the market," said Charlie. "If it was somewhere in the south central states they might do that, but in New York or LA the competition is fierce. The station that releases this could boast about the scoop of the millennium for weeks or months. I don't think that Broadhurst is interested in enriching one news outlet over another."

"Then where do you think he's going?" asked Kathleen.

Charlie had eight pairs of eyes staring at him. He briefly fidgeted with his notebook and answered Kathleen's question. "What about presenting this at the UN? Doesn't the General Assembly start in New York in less than a week? What if they were to get it to the UN via some sympathetic delegate? Do you remember what the president of Grenada did a while back?" he asked, not expecting an answer.

"Hold on now, isn't the security tighter than a drum there?" said a woman across from Charlie. "Broadhurst isn't going to walk in with a DVD and say, 'Look what I got for you.' It isn't going to happen."

"I'm not so sure, JoAnne." Kathleen twirled her pen. "These two UFO guys are getting help. Wherever they're going, they're receiving assistance at the highest level. I'll be looking at our likely suspects. We break in to everything and anything around the world. That's what we do. Why not the United Nations?"

"We haven't had an operative in the UN administration for at least five years now. I heard the rumors that a director level person has an 'in' to the UN, but the rumor mill is mighty thin on that. Anyway, what's some grey-haired director going to do to pull that together?" said the young man at the table.

Kathleen cleared her throat. "I have grey hair, and some of it gets seen from time to time," said Kathleen, flicking a strand of her close-cropped hair style for effect. Others around the table laughed appropriately. Kathleen continued, "Some of us more mature members of this organization still have the wherewithal, the chops, the chutzpa to take on the disclosure fanatics."

"We would be going in as any other alphabet agency," said the bearded man. "It's like another country on that piece of ground. They don't want the CIA or the NSA walking in as if they owned the place. The UN doesn't care whatever fake badge we flick at them, they want no part of us."

"We can pose as tourists if we have to do so. I still think this is the logical venue for Broadhurst. Maximum exposure. Everyone covers the UN at this time, and all those diplomats are going to hear about it. Some of our friends, current democratic administrations around the world, are very supportive of releasing UFO files. This will be right up their alley."

"I think there's enough here to support Charlie," said Kathleen to muffled groans around the table. "We're going to divide and conquer here. Fernando, I don't trust our man in Atlanta. Will you focus your team on collecting intel on the CNN possibility? I want you and your best two operatives to go to Atlanta. I want feedback twice a day. And keep our man in the dark, but watch his actions and communications."

"Michael, I think the LA venue has some real possibilities. We have lots of people there—some I trust, some I don't. I'll give you a brief rundown tomorrow. Get a flight out for you and at least one other member of your team. You'll need a lot of help tracking down leads. The LA staff is on a need-to-know basis though."

"Thanks, Kathleen," said Michael, giving his supervisor a thumbs-up.

"JoAnne, I sensed you have reservations about the UN angle." JoAnne quickly nodded affirmatively. "I'm sending two teams to New York City. I want you to follow up with as many of the news outlets as you can. I think the easiest venue for getting this film out is a major news outlet or a Web outlet of any kind. Our New York team is solid. I'll put you in touch with Brad. Tell him what you need, but the less people who know about this the better, even among our people."

"The second team is yours, Charlie. The UN General Assembly is an intriguing option for Broadhurst, albeit a difficult one. If this is it and he makes it past security, the whole world will know—immediately. This is your first team lead, so I want you to pick some senior people to help you. Make no mistake about this, they will report to you. If something is going down, you have JoAnne's team in place across town. Call her and she will assist you. Okay, JoAnne?" Kathleen asked.

"Of course, and the first thing I'll say is 'I apologize, you were right!' and then help you get Broadhurst and the film," said Joanne, speaking directly to Charlie.

"Thanks, JoAnne." Charlie turned and faced his supervisor. "Thank you, ma'am, for supporting me on this; I hope one of us ends this protracted nightmare."

"I want everyone to follow standard protocols. We have one departed operative. We cannot afford another. Use your judgment on this. We must retrieve that film and any copies. Frankly I'm afraid that even if we retrieve the film, there will be copies floating around out there.

"I want twice daily reports from each team. This is not a holiday, folks. I expect your best work. Those of you who are heading out tomorrow, I expect to see half hour appointments on my calendar before you leave tonight. Schedule an evening flight tomorrow. Figure two weeks, everybody, so spend some quality time with your families tonight. See you all in the morning."

Charlie got up out of his chair carrying a tablet notebook with him. He turned into the main hallway and walked a few paces with Michael. "See you tomorrow, Michael. We'll get him now."

"I hope so," said Michael, getting into the elevator. Charlie waved goodbye and proceeded down the hall alone to a small room on the left. He entered the room, closed the door, and immediately disappeared.

“We need to stop for fuel again,” said Frank.

“Okay, there’s an exit up ahead that has services,” said Maya.

“You know, this is an extremely comfortable vehicle, but gas mileage is not its strong suit,” said James, propped up in one corner of the backseat with a pillow against the blacked-out window.

“I’ve heard we’ve retrieved power sources from alien space ships that are table top size and put out tremendous amounts of energy,” said Maya, staring out the side window.

“Where did you hear that!” asked James, getting excited at her pronouncement.

“From you, of course,” laughed Maya.

“Oh,” said James, slumping back into his pillow.

“Don’t sound so let down there, ace,” said Maya. “You’re one of only a handful of researchers out there working on this. You alone addressed the amnesty issue, James, and that’s why we’re in this car together. Without amnesty for those involved in these black projects there would be no incentive for disclosure. Disclose, go to court, go to jail would be the sick three ring circus for nearly everyone behind the scenes on these hidden programs. I certainly wouldn’t come forward if I was going to jail for what crimes they could summon.

“Going back to the technology part of the program, this effort is to bring the hidden mechanisms, tools, and equipment out fast enough so that it saves the environment but slow enough to not totally destroy the economic system.”

“I don’t know that the economic system is that beautiful right now. I’m not sure we need to save it. Maybe a good jolt and change of direction is what it needs,” said Frank as he slowed down on the exit ramp.

"Why, Frank, I'm surprised. I never figured you to be an economic terrorist," said Maya.

"Economic terrorist, huh? You know I don't support that socialist/communist crap. I had some friends in the service who worked on gas wells in Texas. They had some very powerful gas wells that when they turned them on they forced all the other wells on the grid to produce nothing. The gas from this mega well was under so much pressure that it pushed the gas from the other wells right back down the pipe. Sometimes the practices of conglomerates in this country are so powerful that they push the little guys in Central America and Africa right out of business. They can't compete. With everyone having cheap access to a limitless power source, the playing field is leveled; the big power grid obsolete. If that's economic terrorism then, brother, sign me up." Frank held up a clenched fist as a coda to his proclamation.

"Tell us how you really feel," said James, jumping into the discussion.

"I think he has a point," said Maya. "That reality may come to pass."

"Right on! Right on!" said Frank as he pulled into a truck stop. "Can I interest anyone in a restroom?"

"Yeah, just one moment," said Maya. She checked mirrors and scanned the pump area and the convenience store. "It looks okay. You go first, James. I can wait."

"I'm in total agreement with that." James quickly opened his door and headed for the store, followed by Frank.

Maya rolled down the passenger's side window. "Do you want me to drive, Frank?"

"Yeah, that would be nice," said Frank, turning back momentarily before heading to the store to pay for the gas. "That pillow Jimbo cuddled with back there looks appealing. I could use a little rest. How about we get some food too?"

"Sounds good to me. We could all use some fuel," said Maya, resting her head on her arm in the open window. "I see a table with some benches over there," said Maya, pointing to a collection of three picnic tables sitting on a hillock of green grass at the edge of the payment. "It will provide good cover from the parking lot. I saw, from the freeway, where the staff park their vehicles off the service road. I'll park the SUV next to theirs. The GPS shows a rural entrance back on the freeway five miles down. Less exposure for us with that access to the interstate," said Maya.

Frank smiled and trotted off after James.

"She's pretty nice, isn't she?" asked Frank.

"Yeah, I guess so," responded James, hunching his shoulders a little as he adjusted himself on the bench seat. It was a warm summer evening an hour before sunset. The truck stop in Ohio was their last road stop before retiring at a motel selected by Maya near Pittsburgh. They followed the thin man's instructions. Sunday after leaving Mary and Jonesy they acted like tourists in Indianapolis, taking in a local Irish Festival and lounging at a crowded sports bar. Late Sunday evening they drove to Columbus, Ohio, spending the next day in public parks where Maya challenged Frank to an impromptu wall climb in Bicentennial Park.

Late summer fireflies were momentarily sprinkling bits of light in an open field of uncut hay behind them. In the distance, the interstate growled with trucks that would lumber through the night to ensure early morning delivery to points east and west. Frank envisioned himself sitting shotgun in one of the bigger rigs that passed. *To be carefree and only have the next destination on our minds. Deliver those canned goods to Indianapolis by morning. Yes, sir, I can do that.*

They shared a few stories on the way, but no one was ready to talk about the really important things on their minds. Maya volunteered to pick up dinner at the outdoor window service at the convenience store. The burgers and fries on the menu suited them just fine.

"C'mon, you're warming up to her," said Frank.

"Hey, I thought she was hot when I first met her."

"And now, where's she on your top ten list?"

"My top ten list is filled up by my wife—in every slot."

"That's nice, but really, James," said Frank, waxing sarcastic.

"Really, Frank, here she comes," said James, looking up to watch Maya stride across the paved yard.

"Don't either of you get any ideas," said Maya.

"About what?" asked Frank.

"About expecting me to get the food for you boys. Consider this a one-time deal."

"I wouldn't confuse you with a homemaker. No, the image is not coming through," said James, stroking his forehead with the fingertips of both hands. Maya offered a smile to his attempt at humor and set the bags of food on the rough wooden table.

"This is a good spot to eat. From here we can see most of the parking lot. Because of the location of those shrubs and trees by the entrance your eyes don't wander over here," said Maya, reevaluating the security of their picnic table for James. Maya waved James out of his seat so she could sit facing the parking lot.

"Once again, security has the day," said James, fishing through the white paper bag for his order of French fries.

"Once again, we get another day to live and fight for what's right," whispered Maya. She haphazardly raised her hand in a clenched fist. James offered Maya a blank gaze, chomping on his first fry out of the bag. "Oh, I've received an update. The rental car company documented my car for nonpayment even though I sent them the money. They sent someone out to pick it up, and federal agents were there to see who would retrieve it. The rental car dude got thrown against the vehicle. They roughed him up a bit. They tied me to you guys. Adam said there are teams out to intercept us at multiple locations."

"Is any one of those locations 'the Big Apple'?" said Frank. He nervously jabbed three fries into a mound of ketchup.

"Not only 'the Big Apple,' but one team with a new guy is going to case the UN."

"We're sunk. We might as well give up now," said James. He dropped his sandwich in its wrapper, and the bun rolled off careening into his diet soda.

"It's not over yet, James. It's just a little more interesting," said Maya, sipping her drink.

"This is some kind of game for you, isn't it?" said James, clenching his sandwich with enough force to eject two ketchup soaked pickles into the burger's paper wrapper.

"Not a game, but a challenge. We have one unwavering goal here, and it's the release of this video. Nothing—and I mean nothing—is going to deter us from achieving that goal. I am not without resources here, James. There are literally hundreds of people working on this for us."

"This sounds like some super hero scenario where these hundreds of people expect us to thwart all of the adversaries and come out on top. You of all people know that it doesn't really work that way," said Frank, slurping his milkshake.

"I'm not saying that the Red Sea is going to part for us and we just sashay into the General Assembly meeting. This is just so important for us to not take every opportunity, every reasonable risk to get the job done."

"Okay, you told us in the car that you need to see someone at the University of Pittsburgh. I know you said you went to school there. Is this really the time to stop and have a nice social visit with some professor you had in college?" asked Frank.

"I'm not authorized to say why I need to see him, just that he is vital to the success of this mission," said Maya, adding a coda to her statement with a staccato chomp of her cheeseburger.

"We're rather vital to this mission, at least Jimbo here is. You can't let us in on the 'how and why' you need to see this dude?" continued Frank.

"Is this Adam's plan?" said James, wolfing down some more fries.

"No, actually it's our plan, and those who are listening are saying, 'Go for it.' I need to connect with this . . . man and let him know the how and why of our mission."

"It's that important to convince him to work with us?" asked James.

"Yes, James, it is," said Maya, holding her sandwich in abeyance to answer him.

"I think the question here is: are *we* going to 'go for it.' More and more I feel this is your agenda and your mission. We're just the tagalongs in this little adventure of yours."

"On the contrary, James, you and your ideas are the key to making this all work after the video goes out to millions. I'm just the muscle on this 'adventure,' as you call it." Maya took a big bite of her sandwich, hoping to still eat her dinner despite the fact that she deferred to James and his questions.

"So, what am I going to do after disclosure, huh? I want to know now. I'll eat my burger and fries, and you tell me how it's going to be." James proceeded to pick at what remained of his sandwich.

Maya sipped her drink. She seemed to be listening to something for a while. Looking at Frank and then to James she began to explain. "We have been looking for an opportunity like this. As I said earlier, the guy who identified himself as Fred Willow made the move, and we facilitated his success. You were selected to be the recipient of the package. There was no other."

"You say that as if it was some divine plan or something," said James, waving the remains of his burger towards her face.

"Listen, James, do you remember my statements about the 'white hats' and the 'black hats'?" James nodded his agreement. "There are about equal numbers of them. My associates, led by Adam and company, are part of the 'white hats.' We need to get more of the 'black hats' to change sides. That's where you come in. There are men and women sitting on the fence here. They aren't opposed to disclosure, but what they need is immunity. If you head up this change and we ensure immunity for all, then we tip the balance toward general disclosure."

"What does it mean to 'head up this disclosure'?" asked James.

"It means supervising a corporation size workforce. Like your Judy Davenport, half of the couple of Christopher and Judy has signed up. She has already gone into deep cover and is studying alien species. If she keeps up with it, she will work as liaison with new arrivals. She'll help select the venue and the way certain species are introduced to the public."

"Judy . . . the same Judy who took the film out of San Antonio to mail to Henry?" said Frank.

"The very one," said Maya, rummaging through the paper pouch for the last few French fries. "We approached her, and she did not hesitate. She has already met with my doctor and another race from the edge of the galaxy. She didn't freak out like she did when she realized back in that San Antonio hotel room that she handled our film."

"Really, no kidding?" said James.

"In some ways, she's ahead of you on this journey," said Maya with a flick of one of two fries left in her hand, sending it higher than the other as a visual aid for James.

"Judy," said Frank, musing about the woman he had pegged to barely assist on anything after disclosure.

"Judy," said Maya, verifying that it was true. "On the political front, key senators and congressman have already written the legislation using your guidelines for immunity. Believe it or not, all of us keep up with what you guys are saying. Some of the 'black hats'—or should I say the 'grey hats'?—have said they will support all of this if you work with Congress to push through this legislation. We have already talked to the President, and he'll go along with this; he'll sign the amnesty legislation first. He agrees with you on the detailed agenda that you wrote in your second book. It was easy to adapt to legislation. We're getting some back-channel support and ideas from those that will directly benefit from the blanket amnesty."

"The President of the United States knows about me?" exclaimed James.

"Yes, James, we've provided him summaries of your ideas, and he's onboard. Without immunity for all of us, the court cases would tear the nation and likely the world apart. The President has developed a Presidential Commission, with you as the head, as a venue for you to bring these ideas forward."

"Presidential Commission? No one listens to those, Maya," said Frank.

"It's just a vehicle, Frank. James will work with the 'white hats' to get this legislation through Congress. We want to get this technology out into the public sphere. The military industrial complex that Ike warned us about is very real. That's the power base for the 'black hats.' We need to get these alternative energy devices out without bringing down the entire economy."

Frank saw them first. Two men getting out of their black SUV parked near the middle of the lot. Dressed in dark blue suits, they looked as irregular as an unmarked police car.

"Again, ideas and concepts that James has promoted will be the key in convincing the corporate titans that this is good for society," said Maya, looking at Frank, who touched the outside of her leg.

"What?" said Maya.

"Middle of lot, eleven o'clock, walking toward the entrance," said Frank.

"James, you will not turn around," whispered Maya, grasping his hand across the table.

"What is it? Have they found us? Oh Christ!" said James, starting to move too much.

"Don't move, Jimbo!" ordered Frank. "They haven't seen us. Just a little more, please," said Frank as he watched the men scan the area on their way to the front door of the convenience store and restaurant.

"As soon as we say so, James, we are going to bag up everything and fly out of here through that field behind us. I parked the car down at the service road entrance. We are going to run as fast as we can without stumbling. You got that?" said Maya, squeezing his hand hard.

"And . . . and . . . we are out of here," said Frank, monitoring the methodical movements of the two agents as they moved past the vegetation shielding the front entrance.

"Good evening, sir. We are federal agents," said the first man to arrive at the counter.

"Good evening, federal agents, booth or table?" asked the elderly proprietor.

"Ah, neither, we are looking for—"

"Some dessert, maybe?" interjected the proprietor.

The second man in the dark blue suit pulled a photo out of the inside of his coat pocket and thrust it into view of the old man. Displayed in a triptych of three separate photos were the images of James, Maya, and Frank. "Have you seen any of these in here today?"

"You know most people stop in here just to go to the bathroom. I guess they'll never know how good our apple pie really is. I can wrap up a couple of pieces for you in a jiffy," said the proprietor expectantly.

"We don't want any pie, old man. Look again. Do you recognize any of these people?"

The proprietor took the photograph and studied it for a few moments. "That photo in the middle."

"The woman? Have you seen her?"

"A woman that looked cuter than this photo came in to buy some food and took it outside."

"Outside where?" said the second man, the one with the gravelly voice. "How long ago?"

"We have a lovely little picnic area just around the corner. Perfect for a couple of young guys to eat a piece of pie and watch the fireflies. You know we have very few mosquitos here."

"How long ago?" pressed the first man. His insistent, threatening tone of voice finally made an impression on the proprietor.

"About an hour ago," said the proprietor. The two men quickly turned and bolted for the door.

"You weren't supposed to stumble," said Frank in a heavy whisper.

"How was I to know that there would be fricking stumps in the middle of that field?" said James in almost a normal voice.

"You're supposed to lift your feet, not shuffle. Especially in an open field at night," said Frank in an elevated voice.

"Shut the hell up!" whispered Maya. "I promised that I would not take out any more men for this cause. I will do it if you bring them down on us!" Maya had led them through the open field that cascaded down to a drainage ditch built decades ago when the interstate was constructed. The ditch was forty feet wide at the culvert end. The ditch and the culvert were obscured by a natural vegetation of sycamore trees, alder, and a few rhododendron plants that had survived the decades.

The entire drainage ditch was surrounded by a four-foot stone wall crumbling in parts. Maya had hustled her charges down through the field to the base of the stone wall. Two flashlight beams frantically panned the field from the picnic area above. Maya crouched below the undergrowth, untying her black sweater from her waist and affixing it over the head of James who lay on his belly. Frank positioned himself deeper into the ravine. "Here we go. Remember what I said," whispered Maya.

The federal agents made their way down through the field, stumbling on the occasional rock or tree stump. "We're here at the bottom," said one of the two men. "They're not here. Maybe they weren't ever."

"But the old man said . . . said she was cuter than her photo," said the other man continuing to scan the drainage ditch.

"What the hell difference does it make if she's cute? I swear, if she were here we would drag her back in along with her lackeys Broadhurst and Connors. One of our agents is dead because of her. I swear, she's going to take a bullet first, and then we'll drag her ass in."

"I'll bet she has a nice ass," said the first man.

"There you go again—thinking any woman in the world wants you. We would hog tie her along with Broadhurst and Connors. I don't care what her ass looks like."

"Is that their van over there?"

"Hardly," said the first man. "Three vehicles neatly parked on this service access for the place up there. They would have left an hour ago. We stumbled down through that field for your cute ass friend that was never here."

"What are we going to report about this?"

"About what?" said the first man. "Come on, let's hike along this wall to the service road. It'll be a hell of a lot easier than going back through that booby-trapped field."

The men picked their way along the top of the wall inches from the heads of the three people they sought. They carefully walked across the crumbling stones, sending chunks of sandstone and granite into the drainage ditch. They turned off their flashlights and started walking up the road to the picnic area. "No report?" asked the second man.

"Nope," answered the first, their voices drowning in a particularly loud burst of trailer trucks passing each other on the interstate. The uniform blanket of vegetation in the drainage ditch remained undisturbed.

"Now?" whispered James. Maya and James hunched over facing each other in a crumbled section of the wall that was thick with undergrowth. Heads positioned side-by-side were covered by Maya's dark sweater. Maya reached up and pressed her index finger to his lips. They waited.

"Now," said Maya after an eternity of moment-to-moment fidgeting of the man next to her. James was never so close to Maya. She smelled nice for a woman after a couple of days on the lam. Maya pulled the sweater from their heads. She carefully took in her surroundings. "Frank, it's good." Deep in the brush, the plants rose with a human magically attached.

"How does he do that?" asked James. "I was fighting beetles and spiders crawling over my hands and legs."

"When you're presentable, Frank, verify that they're gone," said Maya. Frank detached branches and underbrush from pockets, shirt, shoes, and pants. He carefully followed the top of the wall to the service road.

"Frank," said James.

"Yes, boss," answered Frank.

"You're untucked, as usual, my friend." Frank looked down at his pants. The tail of the blue shirt had escaped his beltline. Frank shook his head and stuffed the shirttail into his pants and walked onward. Maya and James slowly moved off the wall towards the SUV.

"Does Frank know that you love him?" asked Maya after Frank had reached the top of the service road. "Yes," said James, the word coming freely and confidently to his lips. "Does Frank know that you love him?"

"I think so," answered Maya.

"There's yet another who loves him too," said James, watching Frank's head disappear over the crest of the hill.

"Your wife Susan," said Maya.

"How did you—? Oh, I don't want to know. I'm finally getting it here. Finally feeling not so bad about all this stuff. Thank you for not 'off-ing' these men tonight."

"You're welcome," said Maya, pulling out a key fob from her pocket. She pressed one button, and the car unlocked. Maya pressed another button, and the door opened silently with no interior light.

"Let me brush you off before you get in," said Maya.

"I'm crawling all over with bugs!" said James, doffing his shirt.

"Of course, you're not. I'll brush you off, and you'll feel clean," said Maya, using his shirt as a dust mop.

"Hey, what's going on here? Can I play too?"

"Nothing's going on here," said Maya, handing James his shirt.

"Gee, James, I thought you came to agree with those guys that she had a nice ass," said Frank. A hard to suppress giggle gushed from the corners of his mouth. Maya's sweater came fluttering in the air and whopped Frank on the side of his face.

"Everybody in the car, please," said Maya, ignoring any and all comments to do with her posterior.

"Maya, I never—"

"Just get in the car, James."

"Okay, Harold, who is he?" asked Don as he pulled out his leather office chair and sat down.

Harold pulled up the chair in front of Don Petrulio's desk. "He was apparently not one of us."

"NSA?" asked Don, taking the manila file folder from his agent.

"No, they're mystified too. It's some black project. What amazes me is that black projects don't stick their heads above ground like this. It would be like us saying on network news, 'Oh, the CIA had this covert project on native territory and it failed, and we're after whoever screwed us over—just wanted to let you, the public, know. Have a nice day.' It sounds like desperation, or they're in an all-out push to get Broadhurst and gang in custody at all costs."

"I suppose if we pick them up, the black project will surface long enough again to apprehend these guys and go to ground again. I don't like it. We do some nasty things at times, but if these guys get ahold of Broadhurst, I can guarantee we'll never hear from them again." Don sat back in his chair and squeezed the leather arms.

"I agree, sir. This has a bad odor to it, and the odor is getting stronger by the hour. If we apprehend these two—or should I say three?—we should keep it quiet for as long as we can."

"The rental car lead is a good one." Don began skim-reading the file in his hands. "A Maya Jablonski rented it in St. Louis. She was signed up for the conference, but few people saw her."

"The conference never really got started, and our three musketeers had already vanished," added Harold.

"Musketeers, that's good. 'All for one, one for all.' That's probably how the three see themselves. I wonder if they know how much deep trouble they're in?"

"They might. This Maya individual has special military training and worked for us for a while and then the NSA and then nothing."

"Another black ops character?" asked Don.

"It looks that way. There's a picture from our files in the back.

She has a good face for undercover work. She is pretty but not with any striking features. She would receive a pleasant smile from those she would encounter, but very little would be retained. I wish she was still working for us."

"She's not just another pretty face, Harold. She's kept us at bay for days, and whatever black ops team she's working with, they really have her back." Don handed the file back to Harold. "Get this picture out to all of our field agents."

"Already done, sir. We've added her mug shot to the others. Our agents have all three musketeers now."

"Great work, Harold. I want you to lead the meeting tomorrow on where these three are headed. Meeting is set for 9:00 AM in conference room 710. Do you have any problems with that?"

"I can do that. You're not going to be here?"

"They've called me back to Washington to report in person on this."

"That's kind of unusual in this day of video conferencing and cut-backs."

"Yeah, kind of unusual is an understatement. Good luck tomorrow."

"Good luck to *you*, sir," said Harold, standing. He quietly repositioned his chair and left the room.

Maya inserted the key into the lock, and the motel room door opened easily. Through Indianapolis and Columbus, they were apprehensive about indulging in the luxury of an overnight lodging. However, the utilization of cold water sinks in public park bathrooms was wearing thin. With the confluence of Maya's meeting tomorrow at the university and a cautious optimism that they were successfully unnoticed by their pursuers, they stopped for sleep in real beds. The unanimous assertion that their personal hygiene had slipped into the groaty category tipped the scales in favor of hot showers.

Maya walked into the darkened room while James fiddled for a wall switch. "Where's the damn lights in this place?" he muttered. Maya found a table lamp on the dresser that illuminated the room in a soft yellow light. The simple accommodations included two double beds, a dresser with a television, and a small bathroom.

"Nothing but the best for my James," boasted Frank, patting him on the back.

"Well, before the arrival of Frank Connors, James Broadhurst saw the interior of many of these rooms. Back in the day when I was struggling to get a gig—any gig—accommodations that looked like this were configured for a king, except that carpet stain over there." James pointed to a multihued dark stain on the otherwise light blue textured floor covering.

Maya went over to examine it. "Not a problem. It's not blood, so nobody died here. Just looks like somebody lost their cookies. How's that burger sitting right now, Frank?"

"Just fine, Maya, just fine. We could never compete with Maya in a gross out contest. She would always win. She's very useful when you're on a long mission and the food is low. Just fire up the gross out rhetoric, and no one wants to eat—yes, very useful."

"I'm glad I'm always good for something," said Maya with a laugh. "Okay, shout out ages here."

"What?" asked James.

"Just do it. Tell her your age," said Frank.

"I'm forty-five," answered James.

"I'm forty-seven," answered Frank with a knowing smile.

"And I'm thirty, so Frank wins. You hit the shower first. By the way, I've already checked. There are just three towels. We each expect a dry one for our turn." Frank saluted and pivoted on his right foot for the bathroom. "Wait a moment. Are you going to come out here just wrapped in a towel?" asked Maya. "Don't answer that." She fumbled through the packages they'd brought into the room from the SUV. Maya selected one and ripped off the clear plastic wrapping. "Well, I don't care if you are a brief man. Tonight, you're a boxer man." She handed him the shorts. "One more thing, gentlemen—neither of you is sleeping in the nude, no matter how much you protest. We're all adults here, so that garment I just handed you is the minimum. Got it?" she said.

"Got it," answered Frank. He disappeared into the bathroom and closed the door.

"Throw me my package, Maya. I want to check out how fashionable I'll be tomorrow," said James.

She found his clothes and pitched the package to him. "I'm sure it will be nothing but the latest from GQ."

"Let us hope," he said, carefully opening the package. "I suppose I shouldn't ask how they got my size correctly," he said, laying out the clothes on the bed.

"I suppose not," answered Maya as she did the same to her package. They explored their new clothes in silence as the shower ran in the bathroom.

"Not bad—a sport jacket with two pairs of pants, two shirts and enough underwear to go a couple of days. Probably more than we need." Maya didn't respond to his comments. He tried on the jacket. "So, what do you think?"

"Looks good on you," she said.

"Is your stuff going to work for you?" he asked in an attempt to prolong the conversation.

"Yeah, I think it will be just fine," she said, holding up a powder blue blouse.

"You know, I'm glad we sent him in first. I've never noticed he had a problem, but after a couple of days now . . ."

Maya laughed and sat down by her outstretched garments. "Back in Iraq we went on a long mission that kept us from facilities for eight days. On the fifth day, as we passed a mountain stream, we staged a mutiny of sorts. Two of the sergeants confronted him with everyone watching. They said they were willing to risk a court martial by throwing him into the stream with a bar of soap."

"I've heard a lot of stories from him, but not this one. What did he do?"

"He knew he had a problem, and he certainly didn't want to court martial his two best sergeants. He stripped down to nothing and took the bar of soap and stood in the stream as requested. The water was so cold that he couldn't stay in for more than a few minutes. He stood on the shore, and after he soaped up, the men emptied their canteens to rinse him off."

"You were on patrol with him. Were you watching all of this?"

"No and yes. We volunteered to turn around while it was going down, but the three women couldn't resist taking a peak once in a while. All in all, it was good team building. He earned a lot of respect from everyone that day, and during future missions he always found a way to clean up somehow. It takes guts to stand naked in front of your team and go through that."

"He does have some very good qualities. He's very loyal."

"Yeah, that's why we loved him. He always looked out for us. He put us first."

"The same guy is still here with me. I don't know how I would have survived these last ten years. He really comes through again and again."

"What are you two talking about?" asked Frank, standing in the bathroom alcove wearing just his boxers. "What?" he asked, noticing that Maya was staring at him.

"It's just that I said boxers are the minimum." Maya started laughing. "It reminds me when you were forced to dunk in that stream."

"So that's it. Well, you have to do what you have to do sometimes. Anyway, next," he said to James.

"I'm on it," said James.

"Are you forgetting something?" asked Maya. Maya walked around the bed and picked up his boxer shorts and threw them at him. "You men, not only do I have to feed you, I have to dress you too! Is this how your wife takes care of you?"

"And his man servant," said Frank, pointing to himself. "His valet gets to pick up after him where his wife leaves off." James waved his hand down in disapproval and entered the bathroom.

"I was thinking of taking this bed," said Frank. "I move around a lot when I sleep. You two slept together in that motor home. I just made the assumption . . ."

"Relax, Frank. Due to the condition of this floor, I wouldn't want any of us sleeping on it. There's not enough space in this little room to take the mattress off of the bed, unless one of us wants to sleep in a hotdog bun."

Frank laughed at the analogy and realized it was aptly used. "Okay, are you sure you're okay with this?"

"I briefly spoke to James on the way to the room while you

brought the car around. He's okay with it. I could tell in his voice that he's a little nervous about it, though he's warming up to me, and that's good. He sees that I'm on his side. We need to get some sleep, but a little conversation now with him will clarify where we're going with this. It's 'pillow talk' without the sex."

"Talk all you like. I'll be out in five minutes or by the end of your shower, whichever comes first. James is giving up a lot in his current life not knowing what it will be if we succeed."

"When we succeed, Frank, *when* we succeed," said Maya. "We were a bit overly confident this evening about our status after those guys left saying they wouldn't file a report. The entire project almost ended tonight."

"I may be an optimist here, but I don't think anybody out there has a clue where we are. You're taking it a day at a time—that's good." Frank got into bed and propped up the pillow behind his head.

"You're probably right. What I'm worried about is New York. The place is crawling with police, agents, guards—you name it. Adam has a good plan for getting the film in the building, but getting us in is still a little dicey. I'm counting on you, Frank, to take charge of some of this." Maya sat staring at her longtime friend with an impassioned look on her face.

"I'll try, Maya. I'm not as fast and agile as you, but I think I can still handle myself in most situations."

Maya changed the subject. "I'm going to put your clothes over on this chair."

"Okay, just keep it in a bundle until tomorrow."

"We have a rendezvous with some team members in New Jersey. We'll get the final plans at that time. Again, I really want this to work. Adam is counting on us."

"James is counting on us. He really wants this to be successful—lifelong dream and all."

"Do you think he's up for it? I'm not just talking about this current mission that ends in a few days but the long-term goal of seeing his ideas come to fruition? Most Presidents of this country are not world leaders when they start—they grow into one. We need him to visualize himself in a leadership role with the 'after disclosure' world."

"I really think he's coming around, Maya. Day by day I'm seeing a change in him. I think he recognizes this is an issue for all of us, not just for him. Feed him more of the plan as we go along, so it's not too daunting for him."

"What about you, Frank? Are you still going to help him?"

"If he wants my assistance, he has it, Maya. What are you going to do after this, the mother of all missions?"

"I have some promises made to me. We'll see."

"Always keeping your cards close to your vest—you were a formidable poker player back in our unit. Do you still play?"

"I haven't been able to put together enough people to fit around the table lately."

"Maybe we can put something together before we break up," said Frank, sliding further down into the bed.

"What makes you think we are going to break up?"

"You're not likely to stay in one place. Your career shows that, but even if I didn't know your history, I know you. You're an adventurer, always thinking about the next mission. Too bad. Based upon your domestic duties today, you have a shot to make some bloke a good wife."

Maya grabbed a pillow on her bed and threw it at Frank. "Go to sleep, Frank."

"Yes, dear," he said, turning out the light on his nightstand and rolling over to face the wall. Maya carefully folded her new clothes and stacked them on the dresser. She began to undress and placed her outer clothes in a plastic bag that came with the new bundle. She walked over to the door and looked out through the security lens, then returned to sit on the bed. Within minutes Frank was asleep, and the water in the shower stopped.

James opened the door. He was dressed in the boxer shorts and still drying his hair as he walked into the room. He stopped and stared at Maya. She was wearing a white T-shirt and white cotton panties. He was transfixed at seeing his fully clothed travelling companion so disrobed. Maya quickly walked over to him, pressed her index finger to his lips, and whispered, “He’s already sleeping. Did you find the toothbrush and toothpaste that I set out?”

“Ah, yeah, I used the yellow one like you suggested. The green one is yours.”

“Thanks, James,” whispered Maya. She gently clasped his upper arm and gave it a gentle squeeze as she passed by him.

James surveyed the room. One single light was still on at the nightstand. His clothes were half in the bundle and half on the bed. He picked up his new sport coat and hung it in the small closet next to the bathroom. James could hear the water splashing in the tub. He pondered the proximity he would have with this young woman under the covers.

He took a few moments to disburse the remainder of the clothes bundle and stacked it neatly next to Maya’s on the dresser. With no tasks left to do, he crawled into bed and waited for his bedmate to arrive. He folded his arms behind his head and thought about what had transpired in the last few days. Accepting the role that they wanted him to perform was mindboggling but seemed just a little more achievable each time he put his attention on it. *They want me to be a leader, devise plans for the whole country, maybe the world. Simply incredible*, he thought. That they wanted to build it all around his ideas was both humbling and an incredible ego rush. *A second-rate UFO researcher has some ideas that will lead us out of this morass, and even more incredible—it's me!* He shook his head from side to side at the bewildering thought.

"If I'm going to do this, I've got to get my shit together," he said out loud. James was distracted from his thoughts by the inception of silence from the bathroom. He remembered that he never thanked Maya for saving his life. *I'm going to start now mending fences*, he thought. He continued to listen and wait.

Maya opened the door and stepped quietly over to the unoccupied side of the bed. "How did you know I wanted this side of the bed?" she asked with a warm smile. She was wearing a pair of panties in some soft pastel color and the white T-shirt. She leaned down to lift up the bedding.

"I assumed you wanted to be next to the door, being in charge of security and all," he whispered.

"Good thinking, James. Last thing on our agenda is setting the alarm for tomorrow. We're about an hour out, and we should be there about nine, so set it for seven, James. The guy I'm going to meet has office hours tomorrow from nine to eleven in the morning. Maybe we'll have time for breakfast. I know just the place, if it's still there."

Maya was sitting up in bed looking down on him. He smiled and sat up, bumping her arm slightly as he positioned himself to set the clock. "Sorry," he said.

"Sorry for what?" she whispered.

"For bumping into you," he said, not turning to face her. He immediately focused on the clock, getting the buttons set properly. "I think that will do it," he said, turning out the light and slumping down in the bed next to Maya. She did the same, bumping him this time.

"Don't worry about bumping into me, James. I'm not made of glass. I won't break."

"I know. I just don't want to offend you."

"That's not in the cards, my friend." Maya felt his thigh next to hers under the blanket. She patted his leg with her right hand and turned over.

"Maya, I never thanked you for saving my life . . . twice. You've done so much for us on this mission. We would be sitting in some jail cell now or laid out on some metal slab. Whatever happens, you and your helpers have brought us further than I could have imagined."

"You're no longer upset about sharing this mission with, probably fifty other people?"

"No, no longer upset. It's all good."

"You haven't mentioned your wife at all, James. Is everything okay?"

"Yeah, after the San Antonio conference I talked things over with her. She was worried, but I told her something like this might happen."

"Good, I wouldn't want her to worry about you." Maya patted his thigh again. "Now let's get some sleep." Maya moved a little closer, and her bottom touched his thigh. He thought about moving away but decided against it. "James, can you sleep like that?"

"Why?"

"You're fidgeting. That night in the motor home you put your arm around my waist, and you fell asleep within minutes."

"I did? I put my arm around you, around your waist?"

"Yep, that's an affirmative, sparky. Come on, bring it. Seriously I felt so relaxed and content with you holding me, even though you didn't remember it."

"You sound disappointed."

"Only a little bit, now that I know you did it unconsciously. Come on, I'm waiting."

James slowly slid his arm around Maya's waist. She then pulled on his arm, bringing him in even closer. Their bodies were spooning in close proximity. "Ah, that's better. Goodnight, James."

"Goodnight, Maya. I'm glad that you and I are friends."

"Makes things smoother, same objectives. We care about each other now."

"Yes, yes, we do," said James, drinking in her scent, his head at her soft earlobe. Unknown and unseen, the woman and the man who would change the world forever fell asleep together.

Chapter 5

Tuesday, September 12 – Early Morning

“Do you want some more coffee?” asked Kathleen, getting up from behind her desk to retrieve the pot brewing on her bureau.

“No, I’m wired enough with that last cup,” said JoAnne, tapping her empty cup on the arm of the chair facing her boss’s desk.

“Okay, we have the formalities of this trip under control.” Kathleen stepped out of her way to close the door to her office. With her fresh cup in hand, she sat down at her desk. “What do you think of our little rising star?”

“Do you mean Charlie?” queried JoAnne.

“None other. He got high ratings when he got assigned here.”

“Do you mean you had no control on whether he came here or not?” asked JoAnne, failing to hide a note of anger in her voice.

“No, I could have refused him, but on what basis? He comes

from a good family, and his record is squeaky clean. His scores on all testing are first rate. It almost seemed like he was answering some questions wrong just to show us he's human."

"Really?" asked JoAnne, leaning forward.

"I mean, we all missed answers on the DD1572."

"Tell me about it!" said JoAnne, rolling her eyes.

"Here he answers all the really tough ones with the correct response, and just to show us he's a little normal, he misses a few. But the few he selected to miss were no-brainers. If he was a plant and he wanted to fit in and be normal, he should have missed some of the hard ones like us normal dunderheads."

"I'm not sure I trusted him even before you told me this. And by the way, why are you telling me this?" asked JoAnne, tapping her empty cup again.

"Because you're going on the biggest mission we've had to date. Remember, it's not the usual collection of information or planting disinformation. It's all about the retrieval, and you may have to work with him. I wanted you to know that we're not sure about him."

"Does *not sure* mean he may turn on us, like in 'traitor'?"

"Something else," she answered, looking at JoAnne for a reaction. JoAnne studied her boss's demeanor looking for clues as to where she was going. "Did you hear his response to what we needed to do yesterday?" she asked with heightened interest.

"I don't remember it. It was vague, whatever it was."

"I remember it clearly. He said, 'I hope one of us ends this protracted nightmare.' He didn't say he would capture Broadhurst or even retrieve the film. It seems he wants to make it clear that the 'nightmare' must end and that's that." Kathleen set her china cup down hard on the pad of the desk with a disregard for the probable spillage of the liquid inside.

"Do you think maybe you're reading too much into this, Kath?" asked JoAnne, getting up to get more coffee in spite of her former decision.

"I don't know. I sure hope so," she said, leaning back in her chair.

"Do we have contingency plans if Broadhurst is successful?" asked JoAnne, turning around at the bureau.

"All setup. We have protocols in place for just such an eventuality. We have key office people who will begin shredding documents, and we have more shredders in storage. At our warehouses, we have preparations for disposal of artifacts."

"I read the protocols when I was hired. They were scary then, and they're scary now."

"Why scary?" asked Kathleen, following her friend's eyes as she reacquired her seat while negotiating a filled cup of coffee.

"Just the thought of all those records and those beautiful devices being destroyed makes me shudder. And—and!" said JoAnne, getting excited. "I remember that one report of four scientists forcing some device forward, to make it work. The hole in the ground was enormous. Twenty people died that day. And they're going to destroy something so it doesn't get discovered. Really? The world will be ready some day for that stuff, and we did a good thing here protecting the public and all. They sure as hell aren't ready for it now."

"With no records and no artifacts either, no one can make a case against any of us. We have plausible deniability. We will be under scrutiny for a while, and unfortunately, we can't show a good chain of command. But without hard evidence, we have much less to worry about."

"Is that what it comes down to, saving our asses?" asked JoAnne, setting the cup on her boss's desk and throwing both hands towards her chest.

"I don't want to go to jail. Do you?" threatened Kathleen, pointing a finger at JoAnne. "We've stolen technology out of the hands of inventors, we've murdered citizens of this country, and we've kept this secret for decades. Even I've seen the signs that this is getting increasingly negative. JoAnne, whatever you do in whatever organization, there are always people above us and people below us."

"Above us? Who?" asked JoAnne with a worried look on her face.

Kathleen got up, slowly walked around her chair, and pulled up the second guest chair positioned in front of her desk. She repositioned it to face JoAnne and sat down. "Below us is the CIA, the NSA, the DOD, and some more unnamed agencies."

"No argument there," said JoAnne.

"JoAnne, people around here have a tendency to disappear. I don't mean men and women like our agent in St. Louis who give their lives in battle for our cause, but people who just disappear. Their families are never heard from again. You've heard all of the claims from the wacko UFO guys. They talk of fleets of back-engineered space vehicles, of human bases on Mars?"

"Yeah," answered JoAnne, nervously drawing out the word.

"I can't confirm any of it. I suspect a lot though."

"But we've had this stuff for decades, and we still can't figure it all out. I've seen the reports. Some unit that they extracted from a ship without it blowing up in their faces gives off tremendous amounts of energy from God knows where, but we still can't understand it."

"If you read those reports carefully, you'll see some great ideas on how to utilize this power, all theoretical of course, but some idea how to make it work. The authors of some of those reports disappeared too.

There's a guy I knew years ago. His name was Adam Baines. He hung around with a woman—what was her name?—Barbara something. I once went to Adam's home, had dinner. He disappeared. Barbara disappeared too. I did some poking around. Adam sold their house, but there was no forwarding address. Someone miraculously wrapped up their lives and—poof!" expressed Kathleen with an open hand gesture. "I may be meeting with him by conference call—we meet with directors once a month without video—and I probably wouldn't even know it. It's really weird here."

"I don't know about all of this."

"Who signs your check every other week?"

"I assumed it was some guy in accounting, like the CFO."

"We don't have a CFO, JoAnne. Never did and probably never will. The guy who signs the checks is Tom Bradenton. Have you ever met this man?" Kathleen didn't expect an answer. "I met him and his wife. They got divorced about five years back, and—poof!—he disappears too, and he didn't move to some corporate office somewhere. That's not our structure."

"So, where is he?"

"I assume he's here on the planet somewhere, working with the higher-ups. The higher-ups," said Kathleen with a laugh. "My position here is director."

"Okay," said JoAnne.

"I know that I'm a junior director. There are senior directors. They're given all of the information. The seniors would know the extent of our artifacts, contacts with aliens, and whatever is being back-engineered to build a fleet of our own interstellar craft. But who manages the directors? Do the senior directors do it as a group, or is there one managing director? I've heard rumors that, early on, when there were only twelve directors, they found that they were butting heads, couldn't agree on something or other. What they did was enlist—get this—an *alien* to make the final decision."

"An alien?"

"An alien. I tell you, JoAnne, there are a lot of unknowns here, but we know our mission and we will carry it out. I really don't think the UN venue will pan out, but because I'm more than a little suspicious of Charlie, I'm sending you to New York as well. Keep in touch with him. At the first sign of trouble, I want you to come running."

"I can do that," said JoAnne confidently.

"We'll monitor things from here and keep you informed. Any questions?"

"No, I'm good."

"What's up?" asked Frank. James and Frank were seated at a table for three at a small restaurant in the Oakland section of Pittsburgh.

"What do you mean?" asked James, taking cash out of his pants to pay the bill for breakfast.

"You know, the little bickering and one-upmanship you two love to do. You're courteous to each other, smiling at each other, patting each other on the back. If I didn't know better—" He stopped. James looked up at him and smiled. "Tell me, please," said Frank. "Tell me you didn't get lucky last night."

"I don't know what you mean," said James, studying the bill for some hidden charge.

"Oh, Christ, it's true!" Frank exclaimed.

"Keep your voice down, you old coot," said Maya, returning to the table. Frank fell silent. He fiddled with the paper napkin on his lap for a few moments and then set it daintily on his plate. “What’s this about?”

“He’s upset at us.”

“And that would be because . . . ?” said Maya.

“He’s sure that I got lucky last night,” he said, staring into Maya’s eyes.

“No, he’s wrong,” she said, looking doe-eyed at James. “I got lucky.”

“Not only have you destroyed your marriage, you’ve turned our protector into a bag of mashed potatoes,” announced Frank, shaking his head from side to side.

“I’m being called out. Stay here,” said Maya.

“What?” asked James as he watched Maya get up, leave the table, and walk out the front door.

“I think she’s getting an important communication. It’s probably a stern admonishment for your dalliance,” surmised Frank, taking another sip of water.

The two men watched Maya through the front window of the restaurant. She paced back and forth on the sidewalk. “What’s she holding in her hand?” asked Frank.

“It’s her cell phone. It’s not turned on—just a prop to ward off those who would give her a second look for talking into thin air.

“Listen, my friend, we’re still sorting this out.”

“Oh, I’m sure Susan would like to hear that.”

“As I said, I’m not pleased at myself for last night. I took years of marriage and quite possibly flushed it down the toilet.”

“You got that right!”

“Okay, I’m done here. I have no defense. I’ll tell Susan, if we get through this alive, and beg her forgiveness.”

“You’re not sorry you did this, are you?” asked Frank, jabbing his finger at his friend. James refused to answer. He stared at Frank and then looked out the front window of the restaurant. Maya stood with her back to him facing the street. She moved slightly, balancing on one foot and then the other. After a few moments, she turned and walked towards the entrance. She was looking down as she walked the long aisle of tables to the booth in the back where Frank and James had fixed their gaze on her.

"Is everything okay?" asked James.

"No, let's go," said Maya. James could see tears on her down-turned face.

"Tell us what happened," pleaded Frank.

"No, let's go," she repeated, walking a few paces forward and staring toward the front of the restaurant. Frank and James looked at each other, then quickly gathered their things and followed her to the front. James paid the bill, and the three travelers left the restaurant with Maya in the lead.

"Now hold on, Maya," said James, catching up to her as she purposefully strode down the sidewalk. "You're obviously distraught. Are you in trouble?"

Maya stopped and turned to the men trying to keep up with her. "I'm to hand over the mission to someone else in New Jersey. They'll take it from there."

"Why?" demanded James.

"It's obvious, my friend. You couldn't keep your pants on, so she has to check out," explained Frank.

"Not as crude as I would have put it but . . ." answered Maya. The light turned, and she walked across the street as the two befuddled men attempted to catch up.

"Now hold on," exclaimed James, catching up with her again.

"Was it Adam who made this decision? I want to talk to him. *We* want to talk to him," said James, grabbing Frank's shoulder.

Frank squared himself with Maya. "Listen, James has been a real ass lately, but Maya must stay with us. This is working out right for all of us," said Frank, placing a reassuring hand on her shoulder.

"What's the point?" she fired back.

"We want you to see this through to the end. I trust you, Maya," said James, giving her a hug.

"Okay, but not here in the middle of the sidewalk. We'll find a bench on the university grounds." Maya turned around and continued her same pace for the two blocks to the Cathedral of Learning, the gothic tower at the heart of the University of Pittsburgh campus.

"Have you ever been here before, Frank?" asked James, trying to keep up.

"Nope. I've stopped at the airport once or twice changing planes but never into town. This building coming up looks impressive."

"Looks like our destination." The two men dropped back a little letting Maya deal with her problems with a vigorous workout. She stopped at each intersection to let them catch up, and then she would head out ahead of them with the change of the walk signal. Finally, they were on the cathedral's site. Maya left the sidewalk, striding directly for an open park bench under a large shade tree. She slowed her pace, taking in her surroundings. A few students in short pants were sitting on the lawn taking in the morning sunshine. Others were ambling slowly while talking intently about some subject. *How easy it was when I was a student here*, she thought, sitting down on the old wooden slats. Frank and James finally caught up and sat on the warm ground in front of Maya.

"Did you enjoy your days as a student here, Maya?" asked James, folding his legs under him tailor fashion.

"Very much so. Life was simple then. Sometimes I think these people are better off not knowing too much—better to think it all fits together with no uncomfortable interventions from outside our little world."

"That's probably what Pope Paul the fifth thought when confronted by those irritating heliocentric theories of Galileo," said James.

"Sometimes you can be downright irritating in your own right, Mr. Smarty Pants," announced Maya.

"Smarty pants, can I use that?" asked Frank. "It fits so well sometimes."

"Enough already! I have Adam with me now."

"Right now!" exclaimed Frank.

"Yes," said Maya. "From now on I'll only speak what he says. You wanted an audience. Here he is."

"Hello, Adam, it is a pleasure to talk with you. Maya has done her job well, and we believe you should not relieve her of this important mission. We trust her implicitly," said James.

"You have compromised your protector. The detachment that she needs to do her job has been corrupted." Maya paused. "I would like nothing better than to continue as before, but this mission is too important."

"You are going to punish her and us for being human. I have demonstrated that I'm human and have weaknesses, but you still must have some faith in me to keep this mission alive."

"I have my doubts now," said Adam.

"I want this project to succeed more than you realize. At first you were not sure of me, were you, sir?" asked James.

"No, I was not."

"Thanks to Maya, I understand my role more clearly now. Frank and Maya and I are a team. It may have some rough edges now because of my indiscretion . . ."

Maya shook her head. "I've got to intercede here. It's not all his fault. James was compliant with my wishes here. We did this together, whatever you want to call it, Adam."

"It's called adultery," whispered Frank. James glared back at his friend.

"What! What!" exclaimed Maya. A panic-stricken look coursed across Maya's face.

"What's going on?" asked Frank, getting to his knees.

"End transmission! Abort! End transmission!" screamed Maya.

"Something he said?" asked James. Maya closed her eyes and slumped down on the bench.

"What was that? Are you alright?" asked Frank.

Maya let out a brief wail. "Someone, somehow was tapping into our conversation. I could see them! I could see them!" she shrieked.

"How is that possible?" asked James, coming to her side.

"Some kind of feedback loop. I saw an older woman standing in a grey business suit and some geeky young man sitting beside her, and they were staring at me—at *me*!"

Frank looked up and scanned the scene from Maya's viewpoint. The Cathedral of Learning was squarely in Maya's field of view. "Whoever they are, it won't take them long to figure out where we are. I'll bet that that building is one of the most recognizable structures in Pennsylvania. We may not have long before everybody and his brother descends on this place. We've got to get out of here."

"Frank's right," said Maya, shuddering from the experience. "We're going in there."

"Why in! Why not away? Are you still insistent that you have to meet with some dude in there? The film is in the locker at the Student

Union building. We've got to make it back there, get it, and get the hell out of here," said Frank.

"I have a plan."

"She has a plan," said James, quickly shifting his reaction of incredulity to unabashed excitement.

Frank thought, *There's no fricking way, no logical support for that emotion. Two against one—crap!* They helped Maya up and proceeded quickly across the lawn to the cathedral.

"Tell me you got that!" shouted Kathleen.

"I got it! That wasn't much, but what you heard and saw was captured," said the bespectacled young man.

"I got the distinct impression that we were looking at each other. How is that possible?"

"I can only throw out a theory, just speculation."

"Hit me with it."

"This is a sophisticated listening device we have here. It searches, via our satellite, for signals on certain frequencies that agencies like us use in our communications."

"You're putting me to sleep here, Gavin," said Kathleen, faking a yawn.

"You want me to skip to the good parts of this story?"

"Sometime before lunch, if it's okay with you," she said, laying down a thick veneer of sarcasm.

"Our subject, the woman we both saw, has an audiovisual system hardwired into her head. Her system is so powerful that it fed back a signal through this Web camera."

"But why did we see her? A feedback could occur from a camera.

Where's the camera?" asked Kathleen.

"As I suggested, it's in her head . . . behind her eyes. The microphone is built into some other part of her head probably in her ear lobes. She's enhanced with a two-way communication capability," said Gavin.

"Incredible! So, what we saw first was her communicating with the two men in front of her. But there was someone else, wasn't there?" Kathleen surmised, gaining understanding of the phenomenon that they had just witnessed.

"Quite possibly there was. Let's say you send an agent into the field. You equip him or her with one of these systems, and they can report back in real time right to you at your desk. Damn convenient, don't you think?" said Gavin.

"Where was that? Can we triangulate the spot?"

"I don't think so. I've been doing a lot of work on tracker waves and harmonics in data transmission. I suspected that ordinary cell phone towers can be used by these sophisticated technologies to kind of surf along these pathways with a piggyback signal. The cell phone user has a little extra hum, and the cell company pays for the call in unrecognized traffic," explained Gavin.

"That's how it works, and I appreciate you letting me see the fruit of your work. No way to find this site?"

"It looks like a college campus. The top of that building in the background is not visible. The structure was gothic. There aren't too many sites like that," said Gavin.

Kathleen and her IT assistant stared at the screen as he replayed the brief video over and over. The faces of James and Frank were clearly visible.

"Who's in Pittsburgh?" asked an IT employee walking by.

"Oh, just some friends," responded Kathleen quickly before

Gavin could answer. "I've never been there. They sent me this little video from their digital camera, but they didn't tell me where they're sitting. Do you know?" asked Kathleen.

"Yeah, my wife's sister did her undergraduate work there. That's the Cathedral of Learning on the University of Pittsburgh campus. Pretty impressive gothic structure, isn't it?"

"It sure is," exclaimed Kathleen. "Thanks for the location—Jeff, isn't it?"

"Yes, ma'am." He continued on his way across the room.

"Who are these guys, and why are they hanging around a freaking cyborg?" asked Gavin.

"Like I said, just some friends, Gavin, just some friends. Send me this video in an e-mail attachment immediately. Keep up the excellent work." Kathleen walked away quickly from Gavin's workstation with a confident smile on her face.

Adam and Barbara, in Washington, DC, had a crisis on their hands. Communication was severed with Maya, their mission specialist. The protocols determined an extraction point, but there was no guarantee that Maya and the guys could get there in time. Another small but pertinent issue was the film itself. It was no longer physically in her possession. Maya reported that it was safe and that they could easily retrieve it.

As a senior director, Adam knew the importance of contact with the university professor. Was she going to see him now? Would that part of the overall plan fall apart? Maya could always just use the telephone, but everyone knew that the NSA was listening. The NSA would gather the data, immediately inform the shadow government, Adam and Barbara would be outed, their operation shut down. The primary building blocks of the shadow government were secrecy and anonymity of the directors. Once a director was unmasked, they completely lost effectiveness.

Barbara and Adam had to wait.

"Barbara, we need to get them out of there."

"What happened to the video? Who was that woman we briefly saw on the screen?"

"An old friend," said Adam.

"Did Maya see her? Did she see us?" asked Barbara frantically.

"You need to get a grip here, Barbara. The answers are definitely yes and no. The image feedback was all on her end, not here. Besides, we don't have a webcam on this machine, but apparently our grey-haired woman and tech guy do—that was the connection."

"I'm guessing they've figured out where she is."

"I'm sure of that," said Adam, rolling up an open chair at the telecommunications console and carefully dropping his bottom onto the faux leather material.

"They have about—"

"Ten minutes, tops, is my guess, before all hell breaks loose at the university."

"You don't seem too concerned?"

"You're the one who outfitted her with all the features. She still has some neat tricks in her bag."

"Look, she repeated the security codes in the right order to shut down her system. Maya received the automatic extraction protocols, but she still has to get there. The pickup is way out in Moon Township. How does she get out of the university area and out near the airport when all of the agents in the Pittsburgh area are going to descend on one gothic tower?"

"I love that—Moon Township. The pickup is even at Moon Park!

There's someone with a sense of humor in our organization, don't you think?"

"This thing is going down the tubes, and you're finding humor in all of this?"

"Serious you want?" he said in his best Yoda imitation. "The thing that gets me is we have no eyes. Maya is going to have to use her jumpers."

"They're prototypes! They're not fully tested!" exclaimed Barbara, pushing her chair back from the telecommunications console.

"They're gifts from our friends. They work flawlessly for their anatomy."

"Hence, my concern stands for their cavalier use on these three."

"There's nothing cavalier about this situation. Maya's surgically implanted jumper works fine. I saw the results of the tests. There's no reason the external temporary ones will fail us. Trust your operative here, Barbara. We can't match agent for agent. We don't need a freaking war on the grounds of a major university. She'll have to be resourceful."

"Well, if we don't have eyes on the situation, we need to carefully pick up on all of the private and public cameras in the area," said Barbara, keying some commands into her keyboard.

"I agree. At least it will keep us busy until we're sure the team is safe. Barbara, I want you to go and meet them. I want you to handle the extraction."

Barbara stared intently at her boss. "Me, in one of those?" she asked.

"You might as well get acclimated. It's your operation soon. I've had the protocols upgraded. When the message went out to Maya, the teams were informed that you can direct this without any backup from me. I want you in Maryland by midnight. Call your husband and tell him you're called away on an emergency."

Chapter 6

Tuesday, September 12 – Late Morning

Frank opened one of the heavy wooden doors and ushered Maya and James into the entryway of the gothic structure. The short entrance area opened to a high vaulted ceiling. "This is a university? It looks more like a church."

"It's the gothic design that is giving you those clues," said James. "I must admit this is pretty screwy as the start of a plan. We should be going away, not holed up in this medieval fortress."

"I'll explain, but not here. We need to find an open nationality room," said Maya. She pressed forward, leaving Frank and James looking at each other with perplexed expressions. Recognizing their protector had left them behind, they quickened their pace to catch up.

The nave was crowded with tables and chairs illuminated by decorative lights hanging on cords attached high in the arched ceiling. The space took on the feeling of a library filled with students reading or engaged in quiet discussions. There was no time for thoughtful reflection of college days gone by for any of them. There was only the thought of survival. How the books these students were reading would change was the only diversion James permitted himself as he followed Maya weaving through the crowded tables.

They hurriedly climbed some stairs at the end of the nave and then turned left down a long hallway with rooms on the outer wall. Maya looked in the small window of the first room. "No, I don't want to learn Lithuanian today," she whispered, discovering a class in progress. She walked on. The next door was locked. "Closed for renovation," Maya said, reading the sign. She looked from side to side in the darkened room, appearing to study the layout, to quizzical looks from her friends. Satisfied that she had collected whatever information she needed, she was on to the next room. "Ah, the Polish room is open for business!"

James and Frank slowly followed Maya into the decorated room. The walls, ceiling, and floors, even the window frames and the glass in the windows, were decorated in ethnic folk art themes. Frank and James twisted and turned around in the room trying to take it all in. "This is quite amazing, Maya! This is your heritage, isn't it?" said James, generating a broad smile.

Maya physically examined the rear wall of the room, rapidly running her fingers along seams of smooth carved wood panels, slate blackboard surfaces, and cabinet interiors as she verbally responded to James. "A couple centuries ago my ancestors might have sat in a classroom similar to this. This is probably over the top with decoration. My family came from a rural area. We might have had maybe just a few intricate designs painted here and there, but it would be the same concept. Decoration of living spaces, work environments, and schools was very important. It was a mark of pride of heritage, a celebration of life. I wish we had time for a tour, but the black hats are on their way here."

"What are you doing, and why we are still here—apparently waiting for them?" asked Frank.

Maya stopped her probing of the wall adjacent to the closed room to face James and Frank. "Now is the time you must trust me implicitly. We are waiting for them to come here specifically so that they will focus their attention on this building. We will slip away, but not before I convince them that we are definitely here. I have other enhancements that I have not told you about. Just listen so I can get through all of this before they get here. In one eye, all I need to do is focus my attention, and a floor plan of whatever building I am in will pop up like a see-through fighter pilot's display.

"These parts of my enhancements continue to function properly. The system will inform me when deadly weapons arrive, and I can follow them as they move through the building. My objective is to be out in the hallway, for them to identify me and let them give chase. Do you understand?"

The men silently nodded their heads. "I am going to get you into the locked room next door. You will sit on the floor, and you will remain quiet. You will also sit under this sort of blanket. It will nullify your heat signature." Maya yanked a silvery material out of her purse. "Yes, Frank, don't worry. It folds out to be big enough to cover both of you."

"Okay," said Frank, drawing out the word making no attempt to suppress his skepticism.

"These are jumpers." Maya held two round, silver small hockey puck sized devices. "These, believe it or not, are transport devices. I have an implanted one similar to these. These require training to use, but we don't have a lot of time for that. We're going to muster a group effort to get out of this building. These jumpers have a limited range, so we'll have to choose our destination carefully. For the first jump, such a short distance, we won't need them. I can just put my arms around you and with a small amount of visualization all three of us will all be in the next room."

"Simply incredible," mused James.

"It's not too incredible, James. It's not reported well, and science definitely frowns upon this, but there are mystics and holy men who have mastered this skill on their own—no device needed. The hard part, and why we need the devices, is our ultimate escape. After I get the pursuers to follow me and I lose them once or twice, I will come back to the locked room, and we will need to use these devices to get out of here. You will feel like you're being pricked by multiple needles when I attach them. It won't really hurt much. I'll put my arms around you for added support. James, we passed that greenhouse structure in Schenley Park when we came into town. You said you would like to see inside. How about we go there?"

"That's about a mile away. I thought you said those things had a short range," said Frank.

"It will be well within parameters. Did you both look at the structure when we passed?"

"Yes," they answered in unison.

"Good. I want you to think about the place while I'm gone. I don't just mean think about it, I want you to visualize yourself being there. Standing inside looking at the leafy plants and feeling the humid environment—that is how you must think about it. When I come back, I'll attach the devices and assume a group hug position. We will all visualize being there and in a moment, we will be. Our pursuers will continue to search the building, maybe they'll get permission to lock it down and evacuate. It will take hours to search this structure. I'm counting on that.

"So, Frank, what do you think of my skill at formulating battle plans now?"

"I'm impressed. Do you know how our armed forces could use these devices?"

"This was why the black hats held sway with disclosure. All the new devices would be used as one more escalation in the relentless activity of man killing his fellow man. I'm not interested in that, my friend, not at all," she said with a sigh.

"Let's do the first phase. Come close to me and let me put my arms around you."

Frank and James slowly walked toward Maya. "Come on, James," said Maya, giving him the green light to come close to her again.

"Yeah, Jimbo, you didn't hesitate last night."

James elbowed his friend and strode to Maya's side. "I mean it, you two. You must not talk about anything but concentrate on standing in the next room. It means the success of our teleportation." With Frank and James closely tucked in her arms, she spoke again. "Now close your eyes. Come on, close them." Maya looked at each man to confirm that they had complied. "Now open them," she directed. They were in the next room. No sound, no movement—they were just there standing in the darkened room.

"Oh, my gosh!" exclaimed James.

"I had no idea. I thought that I would feel something. It happened with no mental or physical indication—just like that!" Frank snapped his fingers.

"I wanted to give you this first experience to convince you that what we will do next will also work. Humans understand by demonstration, by example. It is a crude way of learning but very effective for how our brains are wired. Take this blanket, sit down on those desk chairs, and get started on your visualization."

"Maya, don't take too many chances. Get them to see you once, and then let's get out of here. I'm worried about you," said James.

"I know, James."

The men were already seated in two school desks placed side by side at the back of the room, well out of view of the door's small window. They unraveled the thin silver foil material to cover themselves. No matter how thin it got, it still held together. It was big enough to cover them completely and still descend to the floor. Maya lifted the material, leaned down, and kissed James softly on his lips. She then moved her head slightly and kissed Frank on the cheek. "Be good and visualize." She paused and stood straight up. "They're here."

"Be—" started James, but before the word "careful" left his lips, she disappeared. The thin fabric cascaded onto their shoulders. Frank and James looked at each other for a moment and then fixed the blanket tightly to the back of the chair.

"Did you see two older men and a young woman enter the building?" The question, posed to two young students sitting on the steps of the Cathedral of Learning, was asked by a stocky man in a blue suit. His pleasant conversational style set one of the students at ease. "I told them to meet us at the Hillman Library, but they never showed," continued the stocky man. "I think they're lost. Did you see them?"

"They didn't look lost to me," answered the young man.

"Don't tell them anything. You don't know who they are," admonished the young woman sitting next to him on the steps.

"Thank you, son," said the stocky man. He waved his hand and another similarly dressed man joined him on the steps. In a moment, they were in the building. From the inside of their coats the men retrieved small headsets with microphones and earbuds. They quickly affixed them to their heads, and the stocky man began speaking orders into the device. "I want one man on each door. We want them alive, and we want the package. Team Two, start a ground floor sweep from the north entrance. We'll meet in the middle."

Team One started walking into the main nave. They drew stares from many in the room. Their dark blue suits and small listening devices caught the attention of a number of students. Muffled conversations followed the team as they visually scanned the room from side to side as they walked. They reached the center of the room and proceeded left and right to the outer hallways and the international rooms. Methodically they checked each room. If the room was open and empty, they tried the doors to large closets, looked behind the instructor's desk, and moved on to the next room. Ongoing classes got a brief, close look through the small access window. For locked rooms, they pulled out handheld units that scanned for heat signatures.

"Stop! Federal agents!" called out a member of Team Two. Maya ran down the hall and turned the corner. The agents of Team Two gave pursuit. They reached the end of the hall and carefully turned the corner and entered the nave. None of the students raised their heads until the two men breathlessly arrived at the entrance.

"Where did she go?" asked one agent.

"I don't know. She must be here somewhere," responded the other agent, trying to catch his breath.

"Did you see a young woman run through here?"

"No, dude, the only person out of breath is you," answered a young man.

The men of Team One ran up to join Team Two. "You saw them?"

"We saw the woman only."

"Did she have the package?"

"Negative. As soon as we told her to stop, she ran away. I don't think she even had a purse."

"Exits report in. Is there any action?" called an agent, turning his face to the wall and speaking in a hushed voice. By reading the facial clues, the others knew that the agent was hearing "No activity."

"Alright, she's got the men stowed somewhere, probably on an upper floor somewhere. Let's divide up and each man take a hallway and a direction. We'll try to flush her out. You two go through the nave and look in those nooks to the left and right. Divide up at the north entrance and work down the halls."

They started weaving through as instructed and made their way to the north entrance. Team One retraced their steps back along the east and west hallways. They continued to recheck rooms along the way. Along the west hallway, one man from Team Two progressed slowly down the hall checking rooms as he went. From the safety of a locked room only a few feet away, Maya studied his movements.

In and out of the rooms he went, sometimes leaving the hallway unoccupied. Maya jumped from the safety of the darkened room to the door recess. The agent in front of her entered a classroom thirty feet from her position. Maya chose her timing carefully. She appeared at the side of the open doorway and grabbed the man's arm, twisted it, and threw him against the polished block wall. The thud of his torso hitting the wall temporarily knocked the wind from his chest.

As he struggled to recover, she kicked his stomach repeatedly. One uppercut sent him smashing to the stone floor. His head bounced, and blood oozed from his nose. Maya stood up and jumped to a safe, deserted classroom on the opposite hallway.

"Man down! Man down!" repeated an agent, running from the opposite direction and touching the device in his ear. Within seconds, the others came running to the west hallway.

"Well, we can rule out that she's a projection," said the lead of Team One, helping the downed agent to his feet. "What's her game—picking us off one by one?"

One of the agents listened intently to his earpiece. "The Pittsburgh police are here," he said, vocally informing the others.

"Who called them? Hell, we're going to lose control of this."

"As if we had it to begin with," said the beaten and bloodied member of Team Two.

"There's a bathroom at the end of the hall. Get yourself cleaned up. I'll go out and talk to the police. What do you think? NSA credentials for Pittsburgh's finest?" he asked, readjusting his wallet to display the NSA ID.

"Sounds good to me. Win them over with your wit and charm."

"You and Ed from Team Two get out there and find that woman!"

Maya had jumped to the thirty-eighth floor of the Cathedral of Learning. "I couldn't get up here as a student. Now I can," said Maya, standing in front of a rough-hewn door in the center of the elevator lobby. Doors to the left and right had "Electrical Room 3" and "Mechanical Room 6" in faded white lettering about chest high.

From inside the room, a muffled voice said, "Come in, Maya Jablonski. You're late." Maya slowly turned the knob and entered the room. An odor familiar but more potent than remembered flooded her nostrils as her eyes carefully inspected the surroundings. The room resembled an old two-story library with rolling ladders on two sides of the room to reach the books perched on the top shelves. Maya observed that each wall of books was punctuated with standard height windows every three feet.

The back wall had no bookshelves, but the repetition of windows persisted. A conference room sized table was positioned on a three-foot elevated platform. Sitting at the desk was the individual Maya had come to see.

"You know, Maya, throughout history kings and men of power always positioned themselves facing the entry door when seated at desks or tables," said the individual facing the wall and appearing to write something with his left hand.

"I remember, sir. I remember," said Maya.

"Are you nervous meeting me after so many years?" said the man as he continued to write.

"A little," said Maya. "You obviously see no need to face the door."

"That's because I don't need my eyes to see. If I had to rely on my five senses, I would have been dead long ago."

"How old are you?"

"That's what you came here to ask me?"

"No, it's not. Anthony Rittenhouse, I need you to support Adam and the other senior directors in favor of disclosure."

"Come, come now," said Anthony. "We must not be so direct. These are delicate ideas full of nuance and subtlety. They need to percolate, or marinate depending upon your gastronomic predilection."

"I'm rather busy at the moment. I'm a little short on nuance."

"Your boys are fine." Anthony swiveled in his chair to face Maya. "They are sitting and thinking so hard about that silly little greenhouse that I think they'll pop over there without your crude devices."

“You haven’t changed a bit, professor. You look the same as when I took Ancient and Medieval Civilization from you nine years ago.”

“Ah, but you have changed, my dear Maya. You are a woman now. You are on a mission. One of many for your government. Very nice. I’m proud of you.” Anthony, a man with a long, thin face and deep-set eyes, flashed a big smile for Maya. Smiling never amounted to much for Anthony as a professor. Maya was taken aback by the double canines on either side of his mouth—uppers and lowers.

“I almost forgot,” said Maya, staring at her former professor.

“You were unaware as a student. But now, filled with all that intel that they feed you, I am now an alien. How sad, but true, my dear, I never was of this earth world.”

“You hid it well, and you hid your position of Primary Nexus, the one who leads the shadow government directors.”

“There you go again, being so direct and all.” In an instant Anthony had transported himself and was standing nose to nose with Maya. Maya reacted to protect herself, launching her right hand in the direction of Anthony’s neck. As it ascended, fingers anticipating soft neck skin were subjected to Anthony’s open hand grasping Maya’s arm and flipping her onto her bottom.

“Now, let’s talk,” said Anthony, plopping himself down on the carpeted floor beside the prostrate Maya wincing in pain. The odor in Maya’s vicinity was palpably stronger. It was Anthony. His body reeked of a strong scent similar to moist earth.

“Okay, I perspire, and I’ve been busy. I haven’t been through a cleansing in a while. You guys have kept me busy lately.”

“How is that?” groaned Maya, choosing not to move just yet.

“Well, for one thing, I’m still convinced that Adam is wrong. Your fellow citizens of this planet just aren’t ready for what you want to foist upon them. However, you're not giving me many opportunities to keep the scales tilted in my favor. So, I took the opportunity to level the playing field with that transmission in your pretty little head."

"You, bastard! Don't you know that we are going to do this? It *is* going to happen! You're wasting your time. Game over! The public will know in a few days."

"And you're lying prone on my expensive carpet. I could terminate your weak body in less than a minute. Without you, there is no disclosure."

"You're not the only one down on this expensive carpet who can read minds. You could have sent a bolt of energy to my brain and spawned an aneurism. You didn't for two reasons. One you would have to dispose of the body, and two in the back of that three hemisphere brain of yours you are still wondering if we just might be right on this issue."

Anthony sat quietly looking at Maya for a few moments. "Where does it hurt?" he asked.

"My back," said Maya, freeing her left arm to point to the spot of localized pain.

Anthony focused his right hand over the area of Maya's back. Gentle was the movement of fingers and palm vibrating quickly in midair drawing the pain out, reducing inflammation, relaxing the muscles. Maya felt remarkably better within less than a minute. "Just some nerve damage, inflamed muscle tissue, and minor fractures to three vertebrae. You know you really should ask for a desk job, Maya. I've got one, and I'm perfectly happy with it."

"Very funny, Anthony," said Maya, looking through the top of her eyes with her head still tilted forward. "Speaking of jobs, how did you manage to get this gig anyway? I've heard reports that you were close friends with John Bowman who became Chancellor here in 1921. How have you maintained a position at the university without someone suspecting?"

Anthony's eyes lit up. This was what he wanted a chance to talk about himself. "I met John at an informal get-together at the university when he interviewed for the position. I saw in him the vision of a fantastic university in this thriving center of steel manufacture back in the day. I stood by him on the gothic tower concept when it was struggling as an idea, not unlike your idea of disclosure. Anyway, I presented my credentials as a history professor."

"All made up of course?" said Maya.

"Of course," said Anthony, matter-of-factly confirming the apparent falsification of records.

"I was hired with no objections from the department. I lobbied for this space in the upper floors along with my equipment. I wanted to integrate my equipment with the local telecommunications at the time, but with the obvious little twists here and there."

"Obviously," said Maya, priming the pump a little.

"I traveled to New York and showed Nikola Tesla what I had in mind. Good lord, I knew he was struggling to keep on an even keel after he fell out of favor with his backers. I might have pushed him over the edge in his final years. He kept openly talking about aliens," said Anthony, shaking his head.

"Well, I got the equipment installed and stayed here teaching for twenty years. I kind of disappeared at the time right after the war in congruence with a change in faculty and the department staff. I came back under a new name, changing my appearance enough that the old timers thought I was really new. I was lobbying the Majestic 12 group that was forming at the time and offered my services as a mediator for their disputes."

"Did they know you were an alien?" asked Maya, sitting tailor fashion facing her former professor.

"Yes, they did. In about five years' time, I managed to put myself in charge of the Breakaway Group, as they were sometimes called. With three other incarnations as a history professor and constant electronic upgrades paid for by the school, I am able to direct the worldwide group of directors who work hard putting the lid on disclosure."

"You should be very proud of your accomplishments. Back to the question that I asked before but didn't really want to know—how old are you?"

"In 1832 I was born to a wonderful mom, part of an exploratory landing party that arrived in Tibet that year. I'm under two hundred, if that's what you're looking for. You think I'm young and inexperienced?"

"On the contrary, I believe you are set in your ways. You have this space way up here where no one sees you. When you want to talk to humans, you get into your wheelchair and ride down to your 'real' office on the twenty-seventh floor. The wheelchair provides you cover. If you would try to walk with them on the sidewalks, they would either rush you to the hospital or start really looking at you.

"No, you have it good here, Anthony. You control the flow of information and artifacts in and out of Wright Patterson Air Force Base in Dayton, you monitor the local scene of Westinghouse, Alcoa, Duquesne, and this university. What I'm asking you here, Professor Rittenhouse, is to consider one of two avenues.

"When disclosure occurs later this week, and it will occur, I'm imploring you to get behind the disclosure faction. Where Nexus goes, the directors go. I want you to preserve any and all artifacts managed by you through Wright Patterson and these private and public companies with your daily and weekly contacts.

"And, Anthony, if you cannot stomach disclosure, then I hope you will abstain from any further involvement with the Breakaway Group. Go back to your planet. Adam says that your mother is still alive and would dearly love to see you.

"We could do some silly fruitless fight to the death on this. I'm willing to admit it would be me lying on the floor in a pool of blood. I don't think you want that. I certainly don't," said Maya with a shudder. "Will you at least consider it?"

"Yes, Miss Maya Jablonski. As a favor to my favorite student, I will consider it. How about I return you to that room with the boys at approximately fifteen minutes from the time you left them?"

"You are a fountain of many surprises, professor. Thank you for hearing me out and thanks for—" Maya was thrown into the darkened room, falling on top of the "boys" who were still visualizing their target destination.

"He brought me back to the exact place that I wanted," said Maya, stumbling to her feet.

The men threw off the blanket. "Are you alright?" asked James with concern.

"Yes, I'm fine. It's time, gentlemen."

"You were gone only five minutes—probably not enough time to foil your pursuers and talk to your professor," said James.

"Five minutes? Oh . . . uh . . . They thought I was a projection, so I had to make it real for one of them. Come on, it's time to go. Have you been visualizing?"

"Yes, mom," answered Frank.

"Okay, one by one, turn your backs to me." Maya grabbed her purse and selected one of the devices. She peeled off a sticker on one side of the cylinder. James turned his back to her. She tugged on the material of his shirt collar, exposing his neck. With one push, she affixed the device to his neck.

"Yow! That hurt!" bellowed James.

"You must keep your voice down. We have only minutes. Frank, you're next." He quickly complied, and she affixed the device to his neck as he gave a wince and a low groan. "Now we're doing the group hug. Close your eyes again and concentrate. I want you to think of the glass structure, the plants inside. Think of the humid temperature. See the excess water on the concrete floors where plants were recently watered. Smell the fragrant flowers."

James was convinced that he was succeeding at the visualization. He could feel the heavy humid warmth on his arms. "Open your eyes, men."

They were there. Maya had done it. James and Frank opened their eyes and pulled away from Maya. They unconsciously felt their arms and chests with their hands.

"Why does everybody do that?" asked Maya, unable to control her frustration. "If we had left your skeleton or your skin back there you would have instantly collapsed to the floor, and I would have had a real mess on my hands."

"Where are we?" asked Frank, ignoring her tirade.

"Where you wanted to go," answered Maya.

"Specifically," he asked. "How did we get here without anyone seeing us? There are people ahead of us on the path."

"Frank, the movement was instantaneous. We were there and now we are here. Do you want me to explain the quantum leap to you?"

"No, I'll catch the reruns."

"I don't think she's talking about the television series, Frank," added James, rolling his eyes.

"Come on, it looks like we can join this tour provided for school kids. I think these two women ahead of us are some parents on the tour."

"We don't look like parents," advised Frank.

"We can tag along. Listen up, Frank, you might just learn something about the flora around you," said Maya. "We'll be safe here. Right now, police and FBI are probably putting the Cathedral of Learning on lockdown."

"Our package is in the locker?" asked James.

"There will be time for that. I'll jump in and jump out with it later. We will need to abandon the vehicle as well. If there's something small there that you need, I can pick it up for you. Let's go. The tour is getting ahead of us." Frank and James dutifully stepped forward. As each one passed her, she pried loose the jump devices and stuffed them in her purse.

Relief and continued trepidation greeted Adam and Barbara in Washington, DC.

"I told you she could do it!" said Adam, slapping the palm of his right hand on the telecommunications console.

"How do you know they made it?" asked Barbara. "Since we lost the connection, I thought we had nothing."

"The energy signatures of the jumpers were picked up on our secure channel off the NSA satellite. Maybe someday we should pay them for all the times we used their equipment."

"Another one of those amnesties that we'll have James enact. 'Adam is excused from paying his NSA satellite bill.'" Barbara paraded her hand in the air over an invisible marquee. "Anyway, what do these energy signatures tell you?"

"The signatures are quantitative. They show three energy spikes closely cropped together, which means they used the devices and all three moved from one place to another. I'm assuming away from the university."

"Where did they go?"

"That I don't know, probably not far, maybe a mile or two. Until we get her back, we have no eyes, and we don't know where she is. The coded message cuts it all off, and she was wise to do so. If our sophisticated video connections are compromised, then the simple GPS and health monitoring features are also corrupted. The link was made for the few seconds. If she didn't end transmission and abort the connection, we would still be talking with her and know where she was. But unfortunately, they would know her location as well. She had no choice."

"How are we working on the overall plan?"

"The President is ready and waiting. The amnesty legislation has had some secret committee meetings, and key members of the State Department are informed. We also have our man in the FBI alerted to act quickly to prevent any deletions of core information or technology. We're plugging holes as fast as they develop."

"What kind of holes?"

"Remember those antigravity and spaceflight technologies that were spirited out to Argentina and Antarctica prior to World War II? Our German friends were into nationalism. We need to make this a global effort. We don't want a back door to this technology developing and the game goes on at another venue. Full disclosure with amnesty must happen, but as Broadhurst states, it must be managed. If we lose a chunk of it to God knows who, we just change the scope of the game instead of ending it. By engineering a wrapper of amnesty around this long-awaited disclosure, we think we can better control the escape of somebody's pet technological project."

"You're okay with Maya continuing?"

"I don't think we have any other choice. We'll have Charlie on the scene in New York, but his skill set is more intellectual. Maya has the highest level of alien technology integration, she's highly motivated, and she has the support of the guys we want to bring the truth out of the wilderness. Plus, she seems to be able to handle it emotionally."

"Well, not really. She did sleep with Broadhurst—and I don't mean just sleep." Barbara shook her head and stared at the floor.

"Don't blame yourself. She's the closest thing we have to a cyborg on this planet, and she surprises us all with a hot love affair. Maybe this will be good for her. I mean, leaving and all. I want her to work with Frank getting the video into that projection booth. He has military training, and he can still move well if he has to do so. I want James ready on the floor."

"Who are you going to use to assist him?" Barbara looked expectantly at her boss. He formed that quirky smile of his, and the answer was clear. "You're not!" she exclaimed. "There must be someone else to do this—not you!"

"It will be okay. I know every step of the plan, and I do have some influence with the Secretary."

"That's all well and good if you don't get your head blown off before you get him into the Assembly. How many years has it been since you've been a field agent?"

"Too many, Barbara, that's the problem. This is my final mission. There is none other more important. Kathleen is going to be there."

"And you know this because . . . ?" asked Barbara, getting angry with him.

"I just know."

"So this is all for you to experience some 'old home week,' some godforsaken battle of good and evil with your nemesis. God, Adam! This isn't some morality play where you're the troop captain bringing the cavalry over the hill tooting your little horn. This is the end of the world for some and the beginning of a new world for others, the rest of us. What's your game—you fight to the death with this Kathleen and somebody rolls the credits and the violins play?"

"That's enough! I have no intention of going out in a blaze of glory. This is a morality play to be sure, and all of us are going to play a part. We have already worked through many acts in this long script, and we're wrapping up the plot as we speak. Never, and I do mean never discount the connection between what you call reality and the play, the illusion. They are so interconnected, so intertwined at a level beyond man's comprehension. We can only get little glimpses of the connection from time to time."

Barbara sat perplexed and still angry at the man who was leading the world out of ignorance. *Ignorance is bliss*, she thought. "I don't know what to say to that," she said aloud.

"Just stay with me here, Barbara. I know the pressure is building. This is all very daunting for all of us. You know the reason why we imposed this plan on this planet and what we expect will happen upon its success. I have a meeting in about ten minutes, a conference call."

"With Kathleen?" she asked.

"With Kathleen and about a half-dozen directors. It's an emergency meeting. We're keeping up appearances on this. I just need to persuade them that a low-key approach is best; that way our guys can ameliorate the situation at the UN without anyone getting hurt."

"It is still incredible that we're fighting an all-out war with ourselves, a world civil war that no one knows is raging all around them.

One side is gaining ground, but the other side is getting more desperate."

Adam stood up to leave. "We are winning this battle, this war. We will win, and there will be peace."

"Funny, that phrase has been uttered so many times by so many despots on this planet."

"I'm not a despot, Barbara. We—you, I, and the rest of the team—are liberators." He patted her on the shoulder and walked out of the room.

"I've heard that little nugget too!" she said to herself after the door closed.

Chapter 7

Tuesday, September 12 – Afternoon, Evening

"That's perfect!"

"What's perfect?" asked James as they mingled with the school kids in a small lunchroom adjacent to the conservatory.

"See that bus out there?" she said, pointing to a yellow school bus in the parking lot.

"Yeah, it's a freaking school bus," added Frank.

"Well, it says 'Moon Public Schools' on the side of the bus. I was hoping for a tour bus, and I got one. If worse came to worst, we would have stolen a car. Now we not only get a ride, but we practically get dropped off at our destination."

"How do you know they'll let us ride on the bus?" asked James, trying to be more understanding than Frank.

"There are twenty-three students, one teacher, and three parents. That's twenty-seven, and that brand and size of bus has fifteen seats on each side of the aisle, which will accommodate the three of us nicely," calculated Maya.

"That tells us we fit. It doesn't tell us we can get on, does it?" pressed Frank.

"What's wrong, Frank? You've been irritable ever since Maya jumped back with the film. Is there something in the car that you wanted her to bring you? She offered, you know," said James, trying to assuage his despondent attitude.

"She 'jumped back.' You take this stuff like it's going to the corner store for a quart of milk."

"I usually get a half gallon when I go. Milk is good for you," added Maya with a wry smile.

"Oh, what? Now you're making fun of me? For Christ's sake, woman, you're a freaking cyborg, and you dematerialize whenever you want. What else are you going to lay on us? Are aliens going to pick us up in their spaceship and drop us off where we want?"

The three travelers sat silent with their thoughts. Frank was finally breaking. Even though he intellectually knew these things were possible, probable in fact, it was untenable for him. What would happen when disclosure took place? Some, like Frank, were not going to react well. From three different perspectives, they struggled with this impending reality.

Maya looked at James and he looked back, now with understanding. His tasks were mounting, but his grasp of the fundamentals of the project were keeping pace. Finally, he was getting it. Maya and James stared at each other for only seconds, but the communication bristled the understanding of the mission. He knew and she knew he understood.

"What? I rant about your inhumanity, and all you can do is moon-eye each other? Both of you, you're a piece of work!" Frank got up from the isolated little table, then walked over to the doors that led into the conservatory and stared at the tropical plants. He stood silently, watching the tiny leaves under a ceiling fan rock and sway with each passing blade of the slow-moving fan. It was an artificial environment, but it was still life as he knew it. "Life was a lot easier when I didn't know all this crap," he mumbled to himself.

"Me too, my friend," whispered James, coming over to his side. "This isn't easy for me either, Frank. I knew in my heart that all of these things were possible. But to see them demonstrated so smoothly in front of our eyes, well, it's more than a little disconcerting."

"How do you do all this? You seemed to be fighting it at first, but now anything that woman does, anything that happens to us you take it in stride. How is that?"

"I'm not quite sure, but I'm starting to get it. The technology is a bit scary, but all new big leaps in technology are. We wonder about the implications, how it will affect our humanity." James paused and looked through the door windows at the leafy foliage draped on either side of a smooth concrete path lined with rough-hewn stone. He marveled at the incongruity of the surfaces. One to meet esthetic preferences and one grudgingly adhering to the convenience of a modern walkway with no bumps, no out of place sharp edges. "I wasn't moon-eyeing our friend. I've been dragging myself kicking and screaming through this entire mission, but in those brief seconds just now, it all clicked. This is an awesome responsibility, Frank. I believe I know how this all works out. I can do this."

Frank stared at his friend with understanding eyes. "I'm not sure if I can."

"I need you. We're not together on this just by accident. You and Maya have experience achieving a mission, one that has a built-in scenario for harm to all three of us. You know how to keep going even when your comrades fall around you. That's a strength I don't have. If one of you got hurt, I think I would just stop, and our mission would not succeed. We need you. I need you." James gently put his hand on Frank's shoulder.

"I need you both outside," whispered Maya, handing the film to James. "I need you to stand outside by the exit and wait for me. I'll wave you forward. I'm going to talk to the driver and teacher, so wish me luck." Maya flashed a smile and followed the students out the door. Frank and James lagged slightly behind and stood outside the exit doors as instructed. They watched as Maya presented an ID from her wallet and talked for a few moments with the driver. He called the teacher over as she ushered the last student onto the bus. The teacher looked at Maya's ID and looked at Frank and James.

"Smile, Frank, unless you want to use those jumpers again to our next location," advised James. Frank wasted no time. He caught the teacher's eye and smiled pleasantly. She turned and nodded affirmatively to Maya. With a wave of her hand, Maya ushered her fellow travelers toward the bus.

In hushed tones Maya gave last minute instructions to her team. "I don't want you next to the windows, so say something nice to your seatmate and sit on the aisle. We will get off at a small shopping center and figure it out from there."

Maya boarded last, and the bus pulled out of the parking lot.

"We're on our way to Pittsburgh, sir. I have you on speaker phone." Harold sipped his diet cola while adjusting the volume on the telephone to compensate for the whine of the engines of the small charter jet.

"I read the brief from the Pittsburgh police to the FBI. The cops reported 'federal agents' on the scene. One got beat up pretty badly. Neither the FBI nor the NSA has an operation in progress, and we're not there either. The police said these 'federal agents' were looking for a younger woman and two middle-aged men. Sounds like our guys," said Don, his voice crackling on the telephone speaker that sat on the tiny table between two leather bound chairs.

"We'll be landing in about thirty minutes. We have a couple of our guys giving us a briefing on the way to the university. Are you going to join us?"

"No, I'm going to New York City tonight."

"How are things going in DC?"

"As you might expect—conflicting priorities and tentative politicians. I am constantly amazed how anything gets done around here. Harold, I want you to find the vehicle that brought them to Pittsburgh. It's probably parked somewhere in the Oakland area. Bag and tag everything you find."

"Of course, sir," said Harold, looking at his associate in the adjacent chair and motioning in the air with his free hand in a writing pantomime. The agent got the clue and pulled out pen and paper from a valise on the floor. "A few of us think they're going to the UN for the General Assembly meeting. Is that why New York is your destination, sir?"

There was a long pause. "I read your meeting minutes and summary, Harold. There's a lot of good support for multiple destinations. Good work in bringing that all out. Hey, I've got to run to a meeting.

Please keep in touch, Harold."

"Sure," said Harold as he pressed a button on the keypad next to the speaker. Harold sat back in his chair and looked at his two associates. One shrugged his shoulders, and the other raised his eyebrows for emphasis. It was clear that Don knew what was going on, but he clearly had no intention of divulging it to his team members.

The school bus got off the freeway and took an access road next to the airport. It lumbered along stoplight after stoplight arriving at a small shopping center. Maya, sitting up front near the driver, waved to her compatriots seated in the back. They each thanked the teacher and the driver as they filed out of the bus. It pulled away, and they looked about.

"We're in the middle of somewhere. But where is somewhere?" asked James.

"Well, we're standing across the street from the Moon Plaza, and Robert Morris University is right here," said Maya, nodding her head in the direction behind her.

"I was afraid you were taking us to the airport. That place is going to be crawling with agents. By the way, we're here in the town of Moon," said Frank.

"Moon Township, Frank," she corrected.

"Okay, Moon Township. We have a ride from here? What kind of ride is going to pick us up? You said that we have to be in New Jersey by tomorrow. We still haven't got the raw footage slimmed down to presentation length."

"Yes, we have a ride from here," answered Maya curtly. "The team in New Jersey is going to make the videos."

"Team?" asked Frank. "Ride from here?"

"I'd like to not stand here all conspicuous like, if you don't mind. I'm getting hungry with all this zipping around greater Pittsburgh. How about we go over there and get something to eat for an early dinner?"

"Excellent, Maya. I could use a bathroom break too. Shall we continue this discussion over dinner at that café?" asked James, looking at Frank.

"Oh, alright, you two are acting like carbon copies of each other. I can't tell which one is vaguer." He followed Maya and James as they negotiated the busy street.

"Is that a word, Frank, 'vaguer'? I can assure you 'Darth vaguer' will not be picking us up tonight," said Maya over her shoulder at Frank.

"Ah, humor. I seem to remember that, back in the old days before all this," said Frank, jogging a bit to get out of the way of an oncoming pickup truck.

"Humor is the only way to go. As more and more of this information became part of my day-to-day reality, humor was the only way to counteract the awesome seriousness of it all.

"If we are successful, and I have no doubt that we will be, our James will be hobnobbing with heads of state. What are you going to say to the President of the United States when you see him?"

"The President . . . oh, I hadn't thought about that," answered James.

"He's anxious to meet you. I believe he's read at least one or two of your books. Really!" exclaimed Maya. "You're going to meet a lot of important people, James, and in fact you'll be one of them. Frank, you too. James gets to pick a team to do this work after the initial disclosure. You two have a big, wide world ahead of you," said Maya as they reached the door of the small café.

"Aren't we getting a little ahead of ourselves?" cautioned Frank, holding the door for Maya and James. They stood at the front of the restaurant waiting to be seated.

"Three of you?" asked the waitress. "This way, please."

The waitress seated them, handed out the menus, and announced the specials for the evening before disappearing into the kitchen. "I want one at a time to the bathroom."

"Always secure, huh?" said Frank, putting down the menu.

"I've kept you alive and out of jail so far," said Maya.

"While you two solve the world's problems, I'm off to the head. Order me the chicken fried steak with a side of green beans and a draft beer." James set his menu down and turned towards the bathrooms.

"What kind of draft beer? They have half a dozen here," said Maya in an elevated voice.

"Surprise me," he said, turning fully around to answer her. He resumed his journey and disappeared near the kitchen entrance.

"What happened to you, Frank?"

"What do you mean 'what happened to me'?"

"You used to be up for anything. Now you seem to be shutting down."

"I'm up for the conventional stuff, honey, but you're freaking me out."

"Really, Frank, I'm still the same Maya. I can still drink you under the table. I can still hike for ten miles with a fifty-pound pack on my back, and I still know how to make breakfast the way you like it."

"You did have your way with a sausage and egg breakfast in that house in Mosul. It's a cliché, but those were the days."

"That's my point, Frank. These are the days. Now is what's happening."

"May I take your order, please? What would you like, miss?"

asked the waitress.

"I'll have the trout special and the side salad with French dressing. Our third party is in your restroom. He'll have the chicken fried steak, a side of green beans, and your best draft beer."

Frank rolled his eyes making sure Maya saw him do it. "I'll have the pasta special and a Caesar salad. I'll take the same draft beer he's getting."

"Thank you. I'll put your orders in right away."

"Sometimes you act just like a little boy, Frank."

"That's not possible, because I think I'm starting to feel the aches and pains of getting old."

"You're not that old," she said, reaching across the table to place her hand on his.

"I'm so much older than your recent lover. At least that's what he tells me. Anyway, who seduced who?" Maya abruptly pulled her hand away from his. She sat looking down at the utensils wrapped in a paper napkin and held together with a paper sleeve. She played with the paper sleeve tugging at the fastened end.

"I did."

"You did what?" he asked calmly.

Maya continued to look down. "I seduced him. I'm sure of it." She looked up and stared at her longtime friend. Of all people, she did not want to disappoint her commanding officer. She craved his respect now as much as she had a dozen years ago, and she was convinced she was losing it.

"He really loves his wife. Her name is Susan. Of course, you know all about her. They wouldn't send you on a mission like this without being fully informed."

"You're disappointed in me."

"Yes."

"You're not going to make this easy on me."

"Nope, probably the most important mission of your life, and you break out into a tryst with the man you're supposed to protect. Can you blame them for wanting to pull you out?"

"No," she said, unwrapping the sleeve and uncovering the silverware.

"What are you two talking about?" asked James, returning to the table.

"Just sharing good times back when we were stationed together in Mosul."

"The next old man is off to the bathroom," said Frank, getting out of his chair. "Unless, does the lady have a need?"

Maya shook her head no.

"So, what kind of beer did you get me?" he asked, sitting back down at the table.

"I got you the expensive one."

"And I'm worth it," said James, primping his hair for effect. Not getting the reaction he expected, he relaxed and focused on Maya. "What's wrong?"

"You know we never really talked about last night. It happened and then we got up and went about our mission. End of story."

"It was not my intention to brush it off. This was a pretty momentous occasion in my life. You're so beautiful and you wanted me. I couldn't resist you even if I wanted to."

"Did you want to resist?"

"No, I knew it was wrong to do what we did, but I was an active participant. The only thing I don't know is where are we going with this?"

"I want you to stay with Susan. Frank was right. I was fully informed about you and your family, why you never had kids, how many times you moved, what your wife does while you're gone on trips, everything. Still knowing it all, I may have ruined your marriage for an hour of intimacy with you." James reached across the table and caressed her hand. Maya stared at his hand moving slowly over hers. He caressed each finger of her fine boned hand. "I don't get out much anymore. I don't remember. Yes, I do remember. It was one of those things that happened when you drank too much and you catch a ride back to base with some young lieutenant whom you always thought was handsome. It turned out every other woman on base thought he was handsome too.

"I'm not saying I was just up for it. I really feel a connection with you. I knew you before I saw you in person at the airport. You didn't disappoint. You were charming and you appeared to be taken by me."

"I most definitely was," he said while gently squeezing her hands.

"I had to spurn you at the hotel. I didn't want the agents following us to think we were together. I wanted the mission to succeed, and it will."

"It will. It will succeed, and we will change the world."

"I'm so glad that you have come into this like you have. This is what we had hoped for, James. You're going to drop this shroud of secrecy and reveal the truth in measured amounts that we can all safely consume."

"But, what about us?" he said.

"Your place is with Susan."

"I'm a man who wants two women. One doesn't want me, and the other will surely not want me," he said with downcast eyes. "I was uncomfortable with myself in how openly I talked with you at the airport. We were like adversaries all this time, but all I wanted to do was kiss you and hold you in my arms. There was just some special spark between us that kept me focused on you."

Maya joined her hands together clasping his across the table. Tears formed in her eyes as she looked uncharacteristically doe-eyed at him. "Will you stay with me tonight?"

"Yes."

"Aw, do I have to go back in the bathroom again!" exclaimed Frank, approaching the table.

"Sit down, Frank," said Maya, unclasping hands and wiping her tears with her napkin.

"Ah, our salads are here," announced James as the waitress set down the plates on the table.

The meal service proceeded smoothly, but the conversation was stiff and stilted. Frank was clearly uncomfortable with the relationship developing between his old army buddy and his business partner. He could not understand how two of his closest friends who did not know each other only days ago had sunk into a well of emotional attachment at his expense—and possibly at the world's expense. He wanted to throttle James or send his army buddy away or both. He was not getting through to either of them, and the frustration was showing.

Maya said she would fill everyone in at the end of the meal about their transportation plans. While James dreamily finished his meal, Maya kept the conversation going, touching on one topic after another. Frank tried to listen politely. This was one time when the homily espoused by his commanding officer that 'if you can't say something positive, then don't say anything at all' applied perfectly.

"We need to get to New Jersey, to our rendezvous point," said Maya as Frank and James ate desserts and Maya sipped a cup of black coffee.

"Where is that in New Jersey?" asked Frank, twirling his fork with a piece of chocolate cake dangling.

"This is really cool. We're going to the Schiff Scout Reservation in upstate New Jersey. Were either of you Boy Scouts when you were little?"

"No," said Frank.

"I was in it for a while," answered James. "Why go there?"

"We're not actually going to the main buildings on the reservation but to a cabin up in the hills. It's pretty remote. It was once used by Jackie Kennedy as a retreat. It's a very special place."

"This is where you tell us how we get there by tomorrow. I'm getting tired, and it's getting chilly out there. I felt the chill in the air before we came into the restaurant. I'm not using those jumper things again, so don't ask," said Frank, folding his arms.

"We're not using them to go across the state of Pennsylvania. It wouldn't work. When I saw those people in my head back at the university, I caused a near complete shutdown of my visual and auditory connections to my contacts. I'm operating blind here."

"Just like us normal folks. How quaint," snipped Frank, violating his commanding officer's golden rule.

"Okay, Frank, you disapprove of us. Or maybe it's the way this mission is unfolding. Whatever it is, this young woman has our back, and we're not going to get through this without her. I trust Maya, and so should you." The compassion James felt for his friend had not diminished, but his patience was clearly waning.

"Yeah, I get it," Frank said, unfolding his arms.

"I'm worried about this next part—about how you're going to react," said Maya.

"Why me?" he asked unconvincingly.

"Because I think James here can handle it. I don't want you running out of here screaming."

"You can tell me anything, little lady. I can handle it."

"I'm going to hold you to that. You're a soldier, and you are used to taking orders. Do you see me as the commanding officer here?"

"Yes, yes of course," said Frank, accepting the switch in roles each of them were playing.

"Good. I can't be of optimum use to this team without getting my enhanced vision and hearing back. To get there, I need help. Because of that breach in communications, the others have found us. Getting out of here by any normal mode would be disastrous. With the last communication, I got a set of coded numbers that key into a pickup location."

"Moon Township, right?" said James.

"Yes, specifically Moon Park—a few miles from here. It will be deserted at midnight. Frank and James," she said, turning to each of them, "we are being picked up by a ship." Maya waited for the concept to sink into their brains.

"This park is on the water?" asked Frank. The last word of his question trailed off into understanding of what Maya was saying.

"Holy crap!" whispered James in exclamation.

"My doctor will be on board the ship. Our trip to New Jersey will only take minutes, if that. He will reconfigure my sensory array and beef up my tools so that I can function at optimum levels for us."

"We're flying in a UFO?" asked Frank in a hoarse whisper.

"Remember, Frank, I expect a professional soldier's response. No theatrics here," she whispered back. "It's not a UFO; it's identified, at least by some of us."

"Do we get to meet the aliens? Are they like the ones in the film?" asked James with uncontained excitement.

"One or more may introduce themselves to you. I don't really know. They will probably have limited contact with us. There will be a human or two on board. You'll get to meet them, of course."

"This is so incredible!" exclaimed James with unbridled glee.

"How do we get to the extraction point, and how do we not suffer hypothermia out there waiting?" asked Frank matter-of-factly.

"There are no agents able to help us here. The 'white hats' are putting up a good front going through the motions to find us. Some of them know where this extraction point is, but none will come near us to give us away. There is a clothing store in this strip mall. I have enough money for all of us to get coats, gloves, and hats. It's now 8:00 PM, and we need to get to the store before it closes. I thought we could hang out at the library at the university across the street. The library is open till 10:30 PM. After that, it's a three-mile walk, or we can use the jumpers to get us there."

Frank raised his arm immediately. "I vote for a walk. Three cups of coffee and we'll be good to go."

Maya smiled at her former commanding officer. She extended her arm reaching across the table touching his hand. "Are you really okay with all of this?"

"I'm trying," he said, recognizing that he fell short in convincing her.

"Good, let's get some coats." The three travelers, soon to be travelling in a spaceship of extraterrestrial origin, left the restaurant and departed for the clothing store.

Chapter 8

Tuesday, September 12 – Late Evening

Wednesday, September 13 – Very Early Morning

"Cold enough for you, Frank?" asked James, slowing his gait on the country road to take a sip of his hot coffee.

"It's doable," he answered. James and Frank walked side by side down the poorly lit rural road. Tall trees on either side obscured any view of the surrounding countryside. Once in a while, a break in the trees would reveal a single-story home with a long, wide lawn and then more dense growth.

"Are you sure you can find this place in the dark?" asked Frank.

"Maya showed me the map. It's just a couple miles ahead. She said there would be signs."

"I still don't know why she couldn't walk with us," said Frank, zipping his coat a little tighter.

"I understand why. Here we are two burly guys walking down a country lane with nice bright orange hats on our heads so no one mistakes us for a deer. The store only had hunting gear—getting ready for the day after Thanksgiving."

"If I hear one more thing about blowing away a deer on that Friday I'm going to . . ." said Frank.

"Hey, I get it, but you know, you're going to need to be a little more political here. You want to head up the energy reformation on this planet, you're going to do it by pissing off the fewest number of people. Understand where they're coming from, what's their stake in the vast energy grid? How can you help them succeed in this new world of revolutionary devices?"

"Uh huh," said Frank halfheartedly, knowing the diametrical change in political motivation required to do the work.

"Anyway, if Maya was along, it would indeed look like a parade and would certainly attract attention. In these getups, we almost look normal."

"You better check that. I believe you might have missed it."

"That's my old Frank back!" exclaimed James, slapping his friend on the back. "Do you think they found our vehicle in Pittsburgh?" asked James.

"I'm sure of it—hours ago. Just who are we working with here, James—Adam and Maya? Now they're picking us up in a freaking spaceship. What are we getting ourselves into here? Back when we 'thought' or we 'guessed' or we were 'positively sure' that aliens were flying about and the secret government was pulling all the strings, it just seemed pretty cool. And disclosure was out there—probably sometime way off—

life was easier, much easier."

"Now we have people chasing us and probably not too cautious about blowing us away. Yeah, it's a hell of a lot more than 'disconcerting,' my friend," said James.

"Can we get out of all of this?"

"Do you want to, Frank?" asked James, slowing down to turn his head to look at his friend's face in the low light of a half moon.

"I never considered it until now."

"I want you to stay with me on this, but I don't want anything to happen to you. You're right. Susan may divorce me for what I've done, but she will literally kill me if something bad happens to you, and I'll never forgive myself."

"Hey, remember, I'm the older one here. I was also your security man until Miss Cyborg came along."

"It appears you had little choice in the matter, but you contacted her, didn't you?"

Frank walked along in silence for a while not answering his question. A gust of cold wind whipped around their faces, a stinging reminder that this was the month of September and the seasons were changing. Small leaves caught up in a whirligig brushed against their faces, counterpoint to the cold, smooth brush of air.

"Not exactly," he sighed.

"Go on," demanded James.

"I'm not sure how she found me, but she did. She said she was interested in UFOs and knew I was working with you. She asked to meet you, and since I hadn't seen her in a long while and we had that St. Louis gig arranged, I figured she could help us out on the security end of this thing we're doing. I mentioned the conference, and she said she was free and she excitedly said that she would be there. I was pleased to see her really. She was always my best soldier—hands down. She knew she could take down any man in the unit, but she never showed off. Actually, for all the trouble we're in, I'm kind of glad she's still on the case."

"Me too, Frank, me too," said James.

"So, we've come to a fork in the road—which way Rand McNally?"

"That way," he said, pointing down a dark road.

"That road doesn't appear to have any street lights on it. Are you sure?"

"Why, Frank! Were all your night missions in Iraq nicely lit with halogen street lamps and paved with asphalt?"

"No, sir, but the last time I checked—we're not in Iraq."

"Point taken, my good man, but it's still this way." They crossed the intersection and proceeded down the dark road. They walked for a couple of hundred yards and almost missed the sign for the park. The gate to the park was fashioned from two horizontal bars that pivoted from either side of the park access road and met in the middle. A lock secured the two poles together. The gate only prevented access to vehicles; pedestrians could simply walk around the side of the road and easily enter the park. The closed gate included a warning for anyone trying to enter after dark.

"The sign says the park is closed. I guess we better go back," cautioned Frank.

"You are back in form, aren't you?" said James. "The only choice left to us is do we break the law going around the left side of the gate or the right side? Decisions, decisions. What's a UFO researcher to do?"

"Get real would be my suggestion." James and Frank were so embroiled in their conversation that they did not hear a car approaching. The vehicle's lights turned on only when it was two car lengths away.

Frank grabbed his friend's shoulder and, turning their bodies away from the park entrance, moved forward down the road. The vehicle moved along side and briefly flashed red and blue lights.

"Oh shit!" muttered James. His legs felt rubbery with fear as he tried to keep going.

"Calm down, I'll handle this," asserted Frank as they kept walking.

"You two guys can stop walking now," said a voice from inside the approaching police car. Frank and James reluctantly stopped. They wanted to run away but ultimately knew that was futile. The vehicle came to a stop, and after a few moments the officer got out and walked around the front of the police car holding a flashlight.

"You do know that the park is closed after dark?" asked the officer, holding the flashlight and splashing the beam on their faces.

"Yes, we do," answered Frank, making sure to not supply more information.

"You guys going hunting? You know there's no hunting around here."

"We're just out for a walk. We find these coats comfortable. We go hunting around Kinzua Dam each year—just trying to build up our stamina for all the walking we're going to do."

"I go hunting up there too. Do you hunt east or west of the dam?"

"Last year was our first year, and for the life of me, I can't remember where it was. I got to call the owner of the land and get directions again." Frank knew he was going out on a limb, but he thought he was still keeping ahead of the officer.

"Does your friend talk? Can I have your names, from each of you?"

"I'm James Drury," answered James. He was trying not to sound nervous, but he was afraid it wasn't working.

"And you?"

"Robert Johnson, sir."

"You're out for a walk wearing your favorite hunting outfits. My, my, now that I know your names, can you please tell me your addresses?"

"Okay, that's quite enough," said a familiar voice from behind the officer. "This is not a stiff finger poking you in the back. I would really hate to hurt you. Over here," ordered Maya, grabbing his shoulder and throwing him on the hood of the police car.

"You're making a big mistake, lady. You just landed yourself into years of confinement in a federal prison for what you're doing."

"Don't hurt him!" yelled James from the side of the road.

"Shut up, James Drury! Robert, get over here and turn out the headlights on this vehicle and get his coat. We don't want him to freeze to death."

Frank quickly did what he was ordered to do. "Put your hands to the middle of your back." Maya deftly unclasped the cuffs from the officer's belt and handcuffed the officer's hands together.

"You did that so well. You must have had some police training," said the officer, keeping the conversation going hoping to extract some useful information.

"One takes work where she can find it," offered Maya. She turned the officer over and pushed him back down on the hood of the car. "Are those cuffs comfortable? I wouldn't want to be chafing your skin."

"Just fine, ma'am. So what's next?" said the officer, focusing exclusively on data collection to effectively suppress any encroachment of mortal fear of this woman.

"You know, you ask too many questions. All four of us are going to break the law this evening. It will be easy, 'a walk in the park' as they say."

"You're the people they're looking for from the University of Pittsburgh, aren't you?"

"More questions. You're just not getting this, are you?" said Maya. She grabbed his chest and pulled him toward her. "Put his coat on over his shoulders," she said to Frank.

"It's a hard habit to break, these questions . . . Maya, is it?" asked the officer. "We don't get many terrorists here in Moon."

"March—that way." Maya pushed him along towards the park entrance.

"What are we going to do with him? We can't take him with us," asked James nervously. "Sir, I'm sorry this has happened to you. Please forgive us."

"I understand, but really you need to convince Maya here to uncuff me and let me go. That will go a long way in helping you boys out," suggested the officer.

"Notice he wasn't going to be charitable to me, even after I was downright concerned about how those cuffs fit."

"We don't want to hurt you. You must listen to us and follow our instructions," said Frank.

"We're going to the ball field at the extreme eastern end of the park. We have a nice walk ahead of us, so everybody save your strength and shut up! Now move!"

They moved across open fields not following the road. The four park vagrants negotiated drainage ditches, dusty ball fields, and the occasional parking lot. They eventually arrived at the large ball field. Maya looked for a picnic table. Not finding one, she led the officer to the short rise of bleacher seats behind the first base line.

"Sit," said Maya, pushing the officer down on a bench.

"You know I have to report in soon. If I don't, they'll send someone to my last location."

"That's fine," said Maya. She shined the officer's flashlight close in on her watch. "We're out of here in twenty minutes."

"A deserted ball field at night," mused the police officer. "You're expecting a helicopter landing this close to the Pittsburgh Airport? It's going to check in. We'll know all about it. You'll be tracked."

The men chortled. "Let me worry about that. Just sit there and think warm thoughts. You'll have a wonderful story to tell your children tomorrow," said Maya. "You guys want to share some of that coffee?"

Frank handed his cup to Maya. "Want some?" asked Maya, offering the cup to the officer.

"I had a fresh latte back in the car. I suppose you won't mind if I go back and get it."

"Unfortunately, I do," said Maya.

"You people don't look and act like hardened criminals, not even you, Maya. You're ex-military I'm guessing, and Robert Johnson is too. Of course, that's not your real name. What is it, Frank something? The other guy never handled a gun in his life. I saw those legs wobble around as I got out of the car. Pretty snazzy there, fellow. You're the UFO researcher that they want to talk to in connection with the death of a man in St. Louis, but I guess it was Maya here who did the dirty work. Still you guys aren't the usual terrorist types."

"Don't any of you give him any coffee; he's already talking our ear off," said Maya.

"What's our time, Maya?" asked James.

"Thanks for checking. Here, Frank, hold the gun on him while I check the time." Maya handed the gun to Frank, pulled the flashlight from her back pocket, and held it over her watch. "Ten minutes," she said.

"I'm just reminding you, we will find you," said the officer.

"Eventually we will surrender to authorities. That's not the point right now. You been to the bathroom lately?"

"That's a strange question to ask of your prisoner."

"You're not a prisoner. You're an uninvited guest. Our ride will be here on time, and I just don't want you to embarrass yourself by peeing your pants."

"I assure you, that won't be a problem."

"Frank and James, do you have to pee with all that coffee? Go behind those other bleachers and get it done." Maya took the gun from Frank, and the two men did as they were told.

"Okay, officer, what is your name anyway?"

"It's Tim," he said.

"Where do you keep the key to your cuffs, Tim?"

"It's in my right front pocket."

"Here's what we're going to do. When Frank gets back, I'll get the key and put it on the bench somewhere over there." Maya motioned with her left hand to the other end of the darkened bleachers. "As we leave, you may want to watch us go; everybody does in these cases. You can tell as much of this incident to whomever you wish. Just to let you know, the agent who died in St. Louis held a gun on us just as I have one on you. We fought back, he fired at us, a fight ensued, and I admit winning the fight by applying lethal force. I had no choice. I must protect these men at all costs."

"I think I understand," said the officer.

"You don't now, but you will. See, we are the good guys. I'm an agent of the US government, and I am escorting these men."

"To where?" asked the officer.

"Ah, the good officer doesn't miss an opportunity to ask a probing question! No, I can't tell you that, but you'll hear about it on the news."

"Frank, are you about done?"

"Yeah, I'm coming back up," he said from behind her. Maya transferred the gun to Frank, extracted the key from Tim's pants pocket, and did what she promised.

"Watch the skies, gentlemen. You two will get onboard first. Don't go fearful on me now. I expect you boys to comply with the program. Got it?"

All three men gazed upward for signs of movement. The night was clear with only thin, intermittent trails of high cirrus clouds to obscure their view. James saw it first, a definite movement of a star-like light.

"That helicopter must be way up there," said Tim. Then, "It's moving too fast! It's going to hit the ground!" he yelled as he tried to duck from the impending crash. Just as the light seemed about to slam into the hard earth of the ball field, it suddenly slowed and appeared to stop about two hundred feet above the ground. Slightly visible was a bell-shaped, circular spaceship. The ship wobbled as it silently and slowly descended to the center of the ball field. The disc-shaped craft filled the entire infield as it came to rest on the hard-packed earth.

"Damn you! Damn you! Who are you people! What is that?" yelled Tim, trembling violently as he sat on the bench.

"That is our ride, Tim. Frank and James, start approaching the ship. A door will open shortly." Frank and James were not faring much better. They were trembling but not as severely as Tim. Maya threw her arms around Tim to subdue his nervous gyrations. She put the gun down on the bench and grabbed his face and kissed him hard on the lips. His trembling subsided as his focus was temporarily drawn to the woman's lips pressing on his. She kept her eyes open, and when he noticed what she was doing, she pulled away.

"I'm sorry I had to do that. You might have passed out and hurt yourself," whispered Maya, staring into his eyes. "I'm going to leave you now, Tim. You have a good life, and remember this night for the rest of your life."

Tim stared at her with terror-filled eyes. She kissed him once more and climbed down to the lowest bleacher where Frank and James were still frozen to the wooden plank seat. "Come on, guys. See, the door is opening. They're here for us, and we gotta move, guys." With her gun stuffed in her pants at the small of her back, she placed herself between the two men, encircled her arms around theirs, and lifted them from the bench. "I can't carry you both. You are going to have to walk with me here." Slowly the immediacy of the moment sunk in to their consciousness, pushing out the panic-stricken fear.

Maya looked back over her shoulder. Tim was staring at the spaceship, transfixed by the arrival of an unearthly object. Maya prodded and cajoled her men to walk in the direction of the ship. An access ramp similar to the one they had seen in the film completely extended to the ground, and a woman dressed in a skirt and business jacket stepped out onto the ball field. Seeing Maya struggling with the men, she bounded over to them.

"Hi. Looks like you could use some help here," said Barbara. She took James and threw one arm over his shoulder. "Walk with me. It's really okay," she said, pulling him along.

The two couples walked side by side until they reached the extended ramp to the ship. James stopped, taking in the immensity of this foreign ship not of this earth, right in front of them. His focus returned, and he seemed to understand where he was. Barbara placed her free hand to a device attached to her ear. “We have army helicopters approaching, Maya. We must hurry.”

“Come on, Frank, show me what a man you are. We got unfriendly guys in our sector. We need to evacuate!” The words jarred his confused stupor enough to get him to walk quickly ahead of James.

“James! Now! We must go!” yelled Frank from the top of the opening of the ship. Within seconds they were inside and the doorway quietly closed.

Kathleen had just fallen asleep on a couch in an executive office across from the United Nations complex. It was 1:00 AM, and she had conducted two briefings since arriving from Washington, DC.

“Kathleen, you asked me to wake you if anything important developed,” said Eric, her aide, opening the door to the darkened office.

Kathleen stirred in the darkness on the couch for a moment. “Yes, what is it?”

“We were about to hit the sack too when a local report came in from a police station near Pittsburgh. It seems some officer was taken prisoner by a woman and two older men. Sounds like our subjects, don’t you think?”

“Yeah, yeah, what happened to the officer?” she asked, sitting up on the couch and letting the thin blanket fall to her side.

“They handcuffed him with his own handcuffs and took him to a park. This is where it gets interesting!” said Eric with unbridled excitement.

“Listen, Eric, this is good material, but I just got to sleep here. What the hell happened to the officer?”

“Sorry. He’s fine. They let him go. Kathleen, the officer had the guts to report how the three of them got out of there. The officer said they were picked up by a flying saucer!"

"Shit!" exclaimed Kathleen.

"It's not one of ours," continued Eric.

"Of course, it's not one of ours, you ninny! This complicates everything. Broadhurst needed an extraction, and *they* were accommodating." Kathleen leaned forward and held her head with her hands, elbows balanced on her knees. She sat there silently in the dark as Eric waited patiently in the doorway. "Get an e-mail out to corporate on a secure line, Eric, before you go to bed. Copy the news article into your e-mail and say, 'They clearly have off-world help—please advise us by 5:00 AM Eastern.' Do you have that, Eric?"

"Yes, ma'am, attach police report, say 'They clearly have off-world help and please advise us by 5:00 AM.' I'll send it right away."

"And, Eric," she said as he turned to go, "close the door and don't disturb me until 5:00 AM."

"Yes, ma'am," said Eric, quickly closing the door.

Kathleen fell back on the couch and moaned. "Oh, Adam, what *are* you doing?"

"It's time to wake up, gentlemen. We're here," said Barbara, tugging at the sleeves of their cream-colored jumpsuits.

"We fell asleep," muttered James.

"Where's here?" asked Frank.

"Upstate New Jersey," answered Barbara.

James looked up. The portal to the outside was open. He could see in the distance what looked like lights of a large residence. Everything else around the house was darkness. He looked at the jumpsuit that he was wearing. Somehow, he knew how he came to be wearing it, but the process could not connect in his brain. The film and DVDs were right where he had left them. "What about Maya?"

"The operation onboard to reconnect and enhance her capabilities went very well. I needed to assist at the end."

"Complications?" asked Frank, getting to his feet.

"No complications, they just needed an extra pair of hands. Thank you, James. You got Bastian's message. It was a critical time, and I could not get away. He sent the message in the hopes that you would receive it, and you did. We can talk about this later, but we must get off this ship now. Collect the film, and let's go."

Frank and James followed Barbara down the ramp and out on the ground. Frank could feel small branches against his ankles. They were crossing an open field with vegetation a foot tall. *It feels good to be back on earth*, thought Frank. He wondered if James could still hear his thoughts. There was no confirmation or rebuttal to his musing. *It must only work onboard*, he thought. *But what did we say to each other? Did we do something? How long was the trip?* Frank sensed a subtle impression flooding his mind, a warm wave of compassion followed by a bolder, higher wave of just one word—"relax."

The subtle darkness surrounding the structure burst into a flood of security lighting projecting from all corners of the lodge-like building. Even in the harsh light of spotlights, Frank could see Barbara's eyes make a connection with his. She had sent the calming message. A feeling of euphoria swept his mind, intense pleasure that he had successfully received the message. The euphoria melted into a tranquil confidence of understanding, though he couldn't quite capture what he actually understood now.

"Has Maya left the ship already? Did she get more enhancements?" asked James.

"No, she is still there, James," said Barbara, looking over her shoulder. Barbara paused as they reached the clearing, a well-manicured lawn illuminated by ground lights. James could make out shrubbery and flowers nestled in corners of the large two-story log structure.

"When you have a medical procedure that approaches the technical complexity that was applied in that operation and the intrusions into multiple bodily systems, you would expect at least a six-month downtime for the body to heal properly. With our friends and their special techniques, the healing will take about five to six hours. It's actually quite remarkable," said Barbara, proceeding towards the lodge and arriving at the bottom of a wooden stairway that led to a screened porch.

The juxtaposition of a brief ride on the austere and sterile alien ship with the primitive yet immensely comfortable lodge brought Barbara to a teary-eyed expression of wonderment. The seamless, pewter-toned surface of the alien ship protected its occupants from the cold of space. It had moved silently for a quick orbit around the moon before arriving in northern New Jersey. It worked like magic. This was life as she understood it. The warm glow of incandescent lighting streaming outward from the screened porch beckoned the travelers to climb the stairs and reenter the world she knew.

"Where did the ship go?" asked Frank, looking back in the direction they had come.

"Oh, I'm sorry, I failed to explain. It's still there; it's only out of phase with our physical world. Inside, they can see all of this," she said, parading her arm in an arc across the porch. "But to us and all of our conventional means of detection, it's invisible."

"They are so concerned about preserving all life that they erect electronic barriers to small animals, even small insects from entering that space, particularly when they come back into the physical. You cannot go there until it fully materializes."

"Fascinating!" exclaimed James, climbing the short flight of stairs to the porch.

"Hurry through the screen door entrance so that we don't let insects in the house. Adam doesn't like that."

"We get to meet Adam?" asked James excitedly.

"He's very excited to meet you, James. And you too, Frank."

"It's always 'and you too, Frank,'" said Frank wistfully. He held the inner door to the lodge open for Barbara. She pinched him in the ribs, sending his body forward into the large living room.

"We kind of expected James to control the ship as he did, but you surprised us at telepathy. You got it."

"Control the ship!" exclaimed James. "I just don't know. None of it is coming through."

"You were listening to us?" asked Frank. "I don't remember anything about the ship . . . nothing about what we did there," said Frank.

"Please, don't worry about this. It will slowly all come back to you. First timer's always go through this," said Barbara, entering the great room of the lodge. The explanation was not enough, but alternate stimuli filled their brains to capacity. The men were content for now. The room was tastefully decorated with medium brown leather furniture that was positioned in two conversation areas. Lighting was provided by warm, tan-shaded table lamps giving the room a comfortable earthy look—a stark contrast to the very other-worldly environment that they had just left.

"Most people who know of this site, remember how run down it was," said Barbara. "We took it over and practically had to rebuild it from the ground up. What you see is not what it was six months ago.

"It's two-thirty in the morning, and they have every light on in this room! These people have never heard of conservation," said Barbara as she left her guests and turned off a few table lamps. "Well, are you tired, hungry?"

"I guess I'd like to hear a short synopsis of our agenda. You say it's two-thirty in the morning on Wednesday. The original request said that we should arrive at the UN on Thursday. I think you have a plan of how we get this video to the delegates, don't you?"

"We do."

"I'm kind of tired, and I don't eat after ten at night, so a short agenda of our next couple of days to prepare would be nice. In all of this we, Frank and I, we feel we have been sort of pulled along toward this goal. Maybe it's time for a full explanation," James requested.

"How about I give you the twenty-five cent tour of our next two days now, you get some sleep, and Adam can give you the five-dollar full excursion package tomorrow."

"Works for me. How about you, Frank?"

"Yeah, I'm good," he said, leaning on the back of one of the couches.

"Tonight, Maya stays on the ship recuperating. We'll see her in the morning. After breakfast, which is at 9:00 AM or as soon as you're up, we're going into a morning meeting to work out how we get into the UN during a general meeting, get to one of the projection booths, and try not to get anyone killed or even injured. We're going to do more of the same in the afternoon after lunch. I think our heads will be full after that."

"I concur," announced Frank.

"Then, we will have a nice dinner here. It's early to bed and in the morning, it's off to the UN after breakfast. We will have contingency plans for as many scenarios as we can conjure up. We have the resources, James. This is not a cheap operation by any means. Take the film and the DVDs to your room. We're renting this place from our own LLC so it should be safe anywhere, but there is no fence around this place. Without the film or at least one DVD, we don't have a mission."

"We'll take good care of it," said Frank.

"Any questions?" asked Barbara.

"About half a million, but they can wait until tomorrow. I'd like a general background about this project, maybe over breakfast. I won't belabor things too much, but Maya has told me a lot, and I want to know how this all fits together."

"I'll give you a little on that before you go to bed. The man who gave you the film, Fred, came out of the blue. He had tendencies to want to do something about disclosure from what our operatives said. We jumped on it because he had Majic or Echelon access. Everything since then, including getting you out of St. Louis via Mary and Jonesy, has been a work in progress. As Indiana Jones said, 'I make this up as I go along.' And that's exactly what we're doing."

"Got it," said James. "Are you ready to hit the sack, Frank?"

"More than ready," he said. "Where do we sleep?"

"Up those stairs and the last room on the left," said Barbara, pointing the way.

"Thanks for the exclusive transportation, Barbara," said James, turning halfway on the stairs to thank her.

"You're most welcome, James."

Chapter 9

Wednesday, September 13 – Morning

From the top of the stairs James could hear a number of people conversing. A muffled sound of clinking glasses and tableware heralded that breakfast was underway. "I think we're late for breakfast, Frank."

"They can't do much without us. We appear to be the centerpiece to this operation," said Frank as they reached the landing. The conversation stopped, and after a sliding of chairs on the hardwood floors, a group of men and women of which they knew only one approached the stairs. An older gentleman with white hair started to clap, and they all joined in the applause.

James tried to smile at the impromptu praise, and Frank did his best not to look embarrassed. They stopped and scanned the faces of men and women who were genuinely glad to see them. "Thank you," said James, trying to be modest as the recipient of sincerely rendered heartfelt applause.

"Did you sleep well, gentlemen?" asked Barbara when the applause died down.

"Yes, most definitely," answered James with a big smile.

"Let me introduce you to our friends. This is Carol; she is a security guard at the UN. She is going to help us with logistics." Frank and James shook hands with a woman who had facial features that were very similar to Maya's.

"This is Charlie. Charlie works with the other side, what Maya has called the 'black hats.' He even has a mustache to go with it." Charlie toyed with his mustache and tried to look sinister. "He really works with us, as what you would call a double agent. You'll learn more of his role as we go through all this. Go ahead, you can shake his hand. He won't hurt you." Frank and James expelled nervous laughs and shook Charlie's hand.

"This is June. She works with me and makes my job simple. If you ever need me and you can't get in touch with me, call June. She can get it done—and I mean anything." June, a blonde, petite woman in her early forties shook their hands but for some reason held Frank's hand for a long time.

"This is Steve. He does those things that we want quietly slipped under the rug. But from what I hear, if you look under the rug, it's not there. He's very efficient that way. And, oh, if you want to play poker with him you better bring a lot of money." Steve, a broad shouldered muscular man in his thirties, offered a wry smile and provided powerful handshakes to Frank and James.

"Next is Jacob. He is your liaison. He has worked with us for the shortest time, but he comes highly recommended."

"I think I've seen you before. Have you been to one of my conferences?" asked James as he shook Jacob's hand.

"Yes, I go to many."

"Yeah, I saw you talking to Stanton Friedman for a long time at that conference here on the east coast," added Frank, shaking the hand of the tall blond man.

"It could be. In my work, I get to meet many of your friends. I hope we can work together well, well into the future," he said to James.

James continued to stare at this strange man. "Are you—" asked James, barely getting the first two words out of his mouth.

"Yes," answered Jacob, responding to his fully formed thought. "I am your liaison, as Barbara said."

James studied the alien standing in front of him. The long-lived hope of a brief close encounter of the fifth kind was overtaken by this promise of continuous interaction—a working relationship with a person not of this earth. This emissary, this human looking man was talking to him, sharing words, thoughts, and ideas with James Broadhurst! The immensity of the experience was whipping through his brain as the realization pressed down hard on him.

"Whoa there, James!" said Steve, coming to his side to hold James up when his legs started to give out.

"I'm sorry, everyone. This is a little much for me."

"No problem, James. The consciousness has difficulty collecting itself with heretofore incongruous information," said the man with the white hair.

"And last, but definitely not least, this is Adam," said Barbara, completing the introductions.

"Frank and I are very pleased to meet you, sir. I take it you organized all of this?"

"The pleasure is mine. I've read each of your books and papers.

I'm a great fan of your approach to disclosure and full amnesty. If UFO researchers have groupies, count me as number one." James and Frank laughed at the concept. "Come, sit down, rest your legs, and have some breakfast."

The others had mostly sat down after their introductions and re-commenced their breakfast meal. "Oh, and over in the kitchen are Rudy and Nancy. They're our personal assistants, drivers, cooks, and almost anything else—right, Nancy?"

"It's the 'anything else' that is always way above my pay grade. If you don't see it on the table, yell it out to us; we'll have it for you in a jiffy, boys."

"Thanks, Nancy and Rudy. This table looks great," said James, passing his arm over the table as he sat down in a chair next to Adam.

"Finally, someone who appreciates us," added Rudy.

"Everyone here has the highest security clearance. You can say anything in front of anybody . . . including Rudy and Nancy."

"Always an afterthought," muttered Nancy.

"What was that?" asked Adam.

"Nothing," said Rudy, bumping Nancy's shoulder as she stood at the sink washing dishes.

"First of all, I'm so sorry for turning your world upside down these last two weeks. From the point you received the film in San Antonio, you've had quite a time of it," said Adam.

"Yes, we have," said James, picking up a bowl of scrambled eggs from Barbara.

"Got any bacon here?" asked Frank.

"There's some here," said June. "Let me have Nancy warm it up for you."

"That's okay," said Frank.

"No problem," offered June, getting up with the plate and taking it to the kitchen.

"Is Maya okay?" asked James.

"Why, yes. She came in earlier this morning. Maya?" said Adam, raising his voice. "Can you come in now?" A door opened on the lower floor, and a woman walked over and stood behind Carol, who was seated at the end of the table.

"What's going on here? That's not Maya. That appears to be . . . Carol's twin sister."

"Looks like the operation was a success," said Frank as he smiled at June and accepted the plate of reheated bacon from her.

"What?" asked James, snapping his head to address his friend across the table.

"It's a good plan. I wish I had thought of it," said Frank, using his fork to slide some bacon onto his plate. "Find someone on the inside that looks like one of your agents, let the aliens do their magic, and—voilà! A very good job, I might add."

"Is this true? Is this the plan?" demanded James, still uncomfortable about not getting it as quickly as his friend.

"Yes, James, this is the plan. We need to get all three of you, plus one or two more for security, into the UN. Maya offered to go through this procedure to make this happen. With Maya's auditory and visual implants fixed, Carol will be able to walk Maya through every step of the way." As Adam provided the narrative, James pushed back his chair and walked over to Maya. She turned and looked directly at him with a knowing smile.

"Go ahead and touch my face, James," said Maya in a soft reassuring voice. James did as she asked and felt the soft face that he had kissed so few days ago. "It feels natural, doesn't it?"

"Did it hurt?" he asked.

"No, a little discomfort as the rapid healing agent worked its way through my body. A side effect is that if I get a paper cut it will heal up quickly."

He continued to touch her face until he realized everyone was watching the intimate moment. He quickly pulled his hand away. "I hope a paper cut is the worst that happens to you tomorrow," said James, looking into her eyes. She was still there behind the grey-green contacts and the high cheekbones. He touched her cheek once more and sat down again.

"I'm done with breakfast, Maya. You can have my chair," said Steve, vacating his seat.

"Thanks, Steve," said Maya.

"Do you already know all these people?" asked Frank, accepting a serving dish of fruit from June.

"Yes, I do," answered Maya matter-of-factly.

"How long has this operation been going on?" asked James, turning to Adam.

"Since the heist of that film you have upstairs. Well, a little longer—well a lot longer. You see, we had lots of pieces in the puzzle put together. Your piece was played early. It fit very nicely on all sides in our puzzle. We wanted you from the beginning, James. We couldn't just come up to you and say, 'Oh by the way, you've been recruited by a secret arm of the government to divulge that alien visitation is real, and you are going to bring all this out to the public, and the focus of the entire world will change.' We didn't think you'd buy that at the time. We needed this big piece, this artifact, to make it all work."

"I see. Let me take a skeptical approach on something for a moment. These extraterrestrials that brought us here last night are helping you out. Those jumpers we used to get out of the university were not manufactured by some semiconductor maker here on earth," surmised James.

"Well, they were. You see, we have been working with our friends for a long time, and the jumpers you used are a little crude in that they need direct contact with your body, hence the needles. They were manufactured here on earth with circuitry designed by our friends."

"Okay, still I have to ask. Why are they helping you? Everyone has an agenda. I think it was Stephen Hawking who objected to that plaque on Voyager, telling the universe where we are—kind of dangerous, he thought. In other words, to get right down to it 'what's in it for them,' and do we need to be concerned about their intentions?" asked James.

All eyes at the table turned to Adam. He was trying to maintain a look of calm, but it appeared he was not up to the task. Little nuances of a furrowed brow mushroomed into dark eyes uncontrollably darting left and right signaling the disconnection. *After all this, how could he not understand? How can we proceed? He's still looking for the bloody Bogeyman!* thought Adam. In a trembling, plaintive tone of voice, he barked a simple retort. "You watched the movie, James." Giving his best response with his diminished faculties, he recognized that he had failed to deliver the unequivocal response. He looked away. An uncomfortable silence descended over the table.

"I think I should speak on this subject," said Jacob, his words rippling a sense of relief around the table. "It matters nothing that you did not categorize me when we were introduced. It was quite refreshing, James. You obviously took me as human, which I am not."

"You have me at a disadvantage, sir," said James apologetically.

"No need to apologize. We are quite human looking in many respects. Some humans detect something about us and feel uncomfortable in our presence. Even now there are those on this mission in this room who are skeptical of our 'agenda' as you say. We are not here to dominate or suppress you. We are not here to even take advantage of you like some of the other off-world species have done.

"All is not much different from when first contacts were made that you saw in the film. You are still a very violent species. Your greed and lust for power is still unchecked throughout your culture. The spiritual development has yet to blossom, though pockets here and there are truly enchanting to behold. What has changed is a set of circumstances set about by the other off-world species with a group of what some of you call 'black hats.' They are setting you on an enhanced program of self-destruction. They think that if they can just dispose of some large portion of the population, then they would somehow bring them and what remains of society into some kind of golden age."

"I've heard about some of this," said Frank.

"They don't understand that through education alone the population bomb will diffuse in one of your generations. But this is not your question, is it? You want to know what's in it for us—the aliens. It's a complicated answer with a simple sequence of words. Simply said, this is a precious jewel of a planet. Life is ubiquitous on this planet. Farmers in some areas pound a fence post into the ground and it grows into a tree. Devastation wrecks your planet from time to time, and the irrepressible life stream begins anew.

"We assisted your species so many times before, nurturing it and bringing it back after global natural disasters. We truly want you to succeed." He paused for a moment and looked at the faces of the men and women around the table. "Some of you have children. You love them dearly. You want them to enjoy a happy life of fulfillment and progress. It is thus with us. In some ways, we feel a spiritual bond with you as a parent has with their child.

"Some of your people think that aliens from another world will eradicate them, the people of this planet," Jacob continued. "It is true that we have the physical capability to perpetrate such genocide, just as a parent has that power over their defenseless children. But we truly do not want to hurt you. We are your parents. We love you."

His words were filled with emotion but with no hint of sentimentality. It appeared that he had captured the room except for Steve, who grimaced at the perceived audacity. He approached the table in silence holding back until he arrived behind Carol's chair.

"Children grow up and leave their parents. That is the way with beings on this planet," he said thoughtfully. "I am sure that we no longer need parents."

Jacob gave Steve a knowing nod of his head. "The last time we directly interacted with you, the people took us as gods, god-kings as it were. Eventually they didn't need us, and we appeared to leave. Your people were quite adept at creating their own gods to worship. You have grown up over the centuries. You are no longer little children who see the world simplistically. You may not be children, but you are certainly not adults, to carry the analogy to the end. You are more like energetic teenagers squabbling and strutting to impress each other. Vast continents are at peace. Europe and America are stable and prosperous. Yet the oldest continent is still struggling to emancipate its citizens from violence. Your self-described 'Cradle of Civilization' has not enjoyed a level of sustained peace and prosperity in recent times. But you insist that you are all adults here and you have everything under control."

"Listen we make mistakes, and we make a lot of them. But we need to be in control of our own destiny," demanded Steve.

"I think that there is a role to play for our friends," said James, getting out of his chair. He started to walk slowly around the table. "The UN is a good place to start. Michael Salla believes we had a choice back in the fifties, and it's his assertion that we made a treaty with the *wrong* aliens, aliens that took advantage of us and made it even more difficult to have full disclosure. We need to talk and negotiate a new treaty with Jacob and his species. Maybe we can come to an agreement. Maybe we won't. The important thing about our options now is that we have options. If I may summarize what I am hearing, I perceive that the current state of affairs with our off-world contacts is not as productive as it could be. It may be that we are going in the wrong direction for our species. Also, the tide is turning with the 'white hats' and the 'black hats.' We need to take advantage of this opportunity now.

"The interaction with all off-world species must be managed. We also must manage the technologies that the secret governments are using," continued James. "We need to get this technology to the people in bites big enough to make a difference but still small enough for the average man or woman to chew. You talk about controlling our own destiny," he said, looking directly at Steve. "How can we do that when a small group of people hold all the cards and we don't have a seat at the table? Hell, we don't even know where the table is!

"You're right, Steve. We don't need our parents anymore," said James. "We're way past ready to move out of the house and live on our own but we're not permitted to do so. I welcome the support of those who have been holding all of the cards. As I've said over and over, the 'black hats' are at fault here, but we, the people they tried to protect, are also at fault for letting this happen. Amnesty is the hands down sole option to resolve this deception that has lasted over sixty years. Nothing will be gained by dragging anyone to court. It would be like flailing our own backs for all the bad deeds we have done to ourselves. For what? Some momentary satisfaction of saying ‘those guys did it to us’? Let’s punish them. Let’s sue them. Why not? Let’s bankrupt every nation on earth with multiple lawsuits, class action lawsuits ad nauseam. When we’re finally all destitute, we can pat ourselves on the back and say ‘right on’—right after we completely collapse as a society. No, amnesty for all involved is the cure.

“I think we have a better way,” said James, coming back to his chair and standing behind it. “Jacob is right. We’ll turn the population bomb into a firecracker with education. We’ll turn the energy crisis into a forgotten memory with inexpensive and revolutionary energy sources. Productivity will be up and waste will be down. This will work. We will succeed.”

James looked at the quiet faces around the table as they stared at him.

“What do you think, Steve?” asked Adam.

“Yeah, he’ll do fine,” he said flatly. “What do you think, Jacob?”

“A little emotional, but authoritative. Yes, most acceptable.”

James stared at each of them in succession. His eyes were as big as saucers. “You were playing me, weren’t you?”

“Of course, we were. Now let’s go into the conference room and get down to business,” said Adam, getting out of his chair. He patted James on his back. “Don’t be too hard on yourself. You weren’t the first human hoodwinked by an alien,” chuckled Adam. He put his arm around James and led him off to the meeting.

Don Petrulio arrived at a no name office in upper Manhattan alone. With the entry of a code in the door’s keypad, he entered the room of centrally located high walled cubicles and exterior windowed offices. With no receptionist to greet him, he walked down the corridor and into a small conference room outfitted with an oblong table.

"Good morning, Mark. What do we know now about their location?" asked Don, opening his briefcase.

"Good morning to you, sir," said the young agent who was sharply dressed in a crisp white shirt and tie. "The craft left the ground at 12:05 AM just as our helicopters arrived. It hovered over the playfield in the park and then shot straight away at tremendous speed. There was nothing much to do at that point."

"You couldn't dispatch a fast jet to pursue it?"

"We couldn't get authorization. As it was, we had to play the terrorist card to get those helicopters out there. You know the rules, Don: we're not supposed to be here," exclaimed the agent.

"Any thoughts or reliable guesses where they'll land?" asked Don, getting a little impatient with the answers he was getting.

"The UN General Assembly is our best guess. It's the biggest audience of notables around the world. But they're going to have a devil of a time getting in there. It's really restrictive at this time."

"Excuse me, gentlemen, you're going to want to hear this," said another agent who stuck his head in the door.

"Well, you're halfway in now, come *all* the way in," said Don, drawing out the "all." "What's so important?"

"I just got a call, an outside call—and it wasn't a sales call."

"Go on," said Don, encouraging him to speed up.

"This woman, her name is Kathleen Johnson, says she wants to talk to you, sir."

"To me, she wants to talk to me? How in the hell did she know I was here? Did you offer that information?" asked Don.

"Of course not. She knew you arrived here this morning, and she wants to come over and talk to you personally."

"Damn it! You gave her our address?"

"Again, no, sir. We never offer that under any circumstances, not even in conversations with staff at Langley. If they're supposed to know where we are . . . then they already have that info. We absolutely never give it out. She rattled off the address, floor, and room number. Of course, I confirmed nothing."

"She just wanted to talk, and she knows where we live, and I don't have a clue who she is. What the hell is going on here?" said Don, summarizing what he had just heard. He looked at the other agents in utter disbelief.

"When is she going to be here?"

"Momentarily, sir. She said that she was only five minutes away."

"Do we let her in?" asked the first agent.

"Let's just sit tight and see if she is cleared for the cipher lock out there. Do you have a revolver here?"

"Yes, sir. I'll get it for you." He quickly left the room.

"This is the damnedest thing I've ever heard. Someone at the Agency is compromising our cover," mused Don, sitting down at the far end of the table to face the door. Mark took a lateral position at the table, still with a good sight of the entrance.

The other agent returned with the revolver and handed it to Don. He placed it on the seat next to him. "Is there anyone else here?"

"No, the three other analysts are out to lunch, they get in at 5:00 AM. They'll be back in about a half hour."

"Let's at least look unconcerned here and try to get some work done." Don removed a bundle from his briefcase and unrolled a compact set of plans. "These are the entrances that we need to watch."

"I've alerted all of our staff. Any projects that they have are on hold and—"

"That won't be necessary," announced Kathleen, stepping into the room. The men quickly took stock of the situation and did a threat assessment on the intruder. Expecting them to enforce their protocol, she put them at ease. "I'm not a threat to you, gentlemen. You, you're the closest," she said, pointing her finger at the younger agent. "Come over here and frisk me. And do a good job. I taught it at Quantico for three years. I can tell if it's done right."

The young man looked to Don for approval. Getting a quick nod, he got up and started to pat her down. "And what if I had a gun in my purse? You're supposed to separate a woman from her purse first. That's destabilizing to her, and it gets any threat hidden there out of the way. Here," she said, shoving the cloth purse down the length of the table to the other men. Some of the contents spilled out on its slide along the polished surface. The men quickly disgorged the remaining items from the fabric bag.

"How in God's green earth did you get in here, and who in blazes are you?" demanded Don, stuffing the nonthreatening items back into her purse.

"I work for the government, just like you."

"No one—and I mean no one—knows about this place, lady."

"Oh, come now. I didn't exactly find this on an internet search, but it wasn't that hard, if you have the right sources. How I was able to get in here and how I knew that Don Petrulio was here is not important. I'm here to see you, sir." Kathleen looked expectantly at the other agents, attempting to send the message that this was to be a private conversation. "I'm sorry, gentlemen."

Don nodded to the first agent with a look of resignation on his face. "Okay, let's get out of here," said Mark to the younger agent. "We'll be right down the hall, sir, if you need us, sir." He slid the purse up the table to Kathleen and followed the other agent out of the room. Kathleen closed the door and sat in a chair positioned at the middle of the table.

"You need to stand down your operation at the UN," announced Kathleen.

"That's it? That's the big message? I suppose you're going to tell me why I would consider such a thing, or is that not part of your agenda?"

"I'm advising you for your own safety, Don. Another branch of the government will be staging an operation there to retrieve the film and incarcerate Broadhurst and his cronies."

"And just what part of the government is that?"

"The secret part of the government that crops up when you least expect it and cleans things up."

"Secret government, huh? Well, at least you're somewhat honest and forthcoming. I report to my director, and he reports to the President. Who do you report to?" asked Don pointedly.

"I have my superiors. You might know some of them or you might not. It all depends."

"Well, I have orders from my director that I need to monitor this UN business and take James Broadhurst into custody as well, and figure out just what's going on here."

"It's way too deep and dangerous for you, Don. If you get more involved, you will get the CIA into a heap of trouble. You're going to be held accountable for the operation here. How many agents do you have here, five maybe ten on this? What's going to happen when they get wounded or killed and your little clandestine operation on American soil gets exposed?"

"Are you threatening me, Kathy—or whatever your name is? At

least if any of my men and women got burned on this, I can say I was following orders, a chain of command. These people could be terrorists."

"Really, Don, you think they're terrorists? The only foreign nationals these people hang out with are aliens, and I'm not talking about émigrés from Romania. These are misguided people who think it's time to roll out the red carpet on the White House lawn for interstellar travelers. Have you thought of what will happen if they succeed?"

"It's not for me to say. These people have got themselves in a lot of trouble. By the way, wasn't it your agent who got a bloody broken nose from a little lady by the name of Maya Jablonski? And was it your guy who got his neck in a twist in St. Louis? Pretty sloppy there, Kathy; maybe you tell me the contingent of men and women you have and put them under my leadership on this operation. I'll keep them safe, and we'll get the job done."

"So, I take it that's a no? You're not willing to play ball here?"

"This is not a freaking game, woman! We have dangerous people coming to the UN to do God knows what. For all I know, you could be part of the problem, you and your secret government of yours. No, I don't want to 'play ball,' patty cake, or any other freaking game. We will be there to intercede and detain, and if you're in my way, then you can suffer the consequences." Don stood up and looked down on Kathleen. "We're done here."

"Suit yourself," said Kathleen. She grabbed her purse and left the room. Don hurried out behind her to make sure that she exited the suite of offices. The closing door quickly brought the agents into the hall to watch her leave.

"First things first. As soon as your guys are back, I want you to change that cipher lock. Next, we are going to find out—and fast—who that bitch was."

"I'm on it, sir."

"You," said Don to the younger agent, "retrieve your revolver in there. Wear it today. If she gets within five feet of this office, shoot her. You understand?"

"Yes, sir."

Chapter 10

Wednesday, September 13 – Evening

Warm mid-September days in New Jersey were a pleasant respite from the encroaching cold of winter. The sun had set. Dusk had settled through the mixed forest of pine, oak, and alder outside the lodge, leaving only residual light hanging high in the branches. The meetings were over. The scenarios were run until they were like worn footpaths around an open field. Everyone knew how important it all was. If they were successful, this meeting, this place just might be written about in history books, as Frank had said at one point.

Steve had corralled a quorum for a poker game for the evening. Maya, Carol, and Rudy had some money to lose and sought the diversion of a different kind of strategy. Maya stuck close to Carol, trying to capture every nuance, every habit that she could use. She didn't want to impersonate, she wanted to *be* Carol.

Charlie used a jumper to return to his office after lunch. He used it throughout the morning popping in and out twice to get maximum exposure to the mission plans at both ends.

Nancy brought books and was content to read in the living room with the backdrop of banter from the game. To the surprise of everyone, June and Jacob set out for a hike at sunset. Their destination was a rock outcropping that overlooked the valley to the west.

The remainder of the team had settled into the screened porch to watch the fireflies sail across the field in front of the lodge and listen to the incessant chirp of crickets as dusk disappeared into night. The guests occupied a collection of mismatched chaise longues and chairs facing the field.

"Do you think they'll find their way back?" asked Frank.

"Are you more worried about June or Jacob?" asked James, flashing a wry smile at his friend.

"I'll take that as a leading question—leading me into a trap no doubt," answered Frank, his eyes catching the momentary flash of a lightning bug in the field.

"Ever since this morning, starting with that plate of bacon, she's been doting on you. Her husband died in Afghanistan a few years back. She's single and so are you," said Adam, joining the roast.

"Well, Barbara, what do you make of this brazen matchmaking perpetrated by your boss?" queried James, trying to instigate a friendly argument.

"I have no comments about what an old coot will do—practically anything I guess," she sighed.

"June could just as easily find Jacob a compatible suitor," said Frank.

"Well, as far as we know, the species are sexually incompatible. A platonic relationship is always a possibility. I think she's just fascinated by our friends and wants to explore a friendly relationship before he leaves," said Adam, leaning forward on the chaise and turning directly to face Frank.

"I thought there was something there between Maya and Bastian. The way they looked at each other on the ship. It seemed like something . . ." said James, his voice trailing off. *I remember!*

"It seems like a whole lot more than something between the two of you," countered Adam.

"Adam, really, do you have to expose every bit of people's lives as if they were just video files to be sorted and cataloged?" responded Barbara to his general disregard for discretion.

Adam was silent for a moment, realizing that he had ventured into difficult territory in the friendly conversation.

"I'll field this one. I own this situation. Yes, Maya and I crossed the line, and I regret it. I also don't regret what we did. You have a mission to run here, I get that. I also get that you're worried about how we're going to perform tomorrow, that somehow this relationship will scuttle your hopes and dreams, and snatch it from your hands at the last minute." James stopped suddenly, worried that his raised voice would carry inside to the card table.

"Angry, are we?" asked Frank, doing his best impression of the *Star Wars* character.

"Yes, Yoda, a little angry, because we're just human beings and we make big mistakes sometimes. I'm on this team now, and nothing is going to deter me from our goals. Okay, you don't want me upstairs running around with the video. You have plans for me in the General Assembly. I get that too. I'm a team player."

"Again, James, we need to have the guys with combat experience go into harm's way. You've never handled a gun in your life. We'll rely on Maya, Frank, and Charlie to get the video to the projection booth. From there it's all a mechanical operation. Those three will defend the room while our accomplice does his job running the video. At the end of the flick, you are scheduled downstairs with me."

"Yes, I know, Adam. I know."

"Hey, that video came out really well, Adam," said Frank, trying to change the subject. "I strolled on over to that annex building to see how they were doing with the moviemaking, and it was fascinating to watch. The guys were very professional, even though I know the subject matter was getting to them. I'm glad we had a showing of it after dinner tonight. I think it was a nice editing job too."

"I'll pass along your compliments, Frank. This is only the beginning. The future is up to the three of you," said Adam.

"What, you're not seeing this through?" asked James.

"Oh, I'm seeing it through alright. It's just that I'm in my early sixties—"

"Middle sixties," corrected Barbara.

Adam stared intently at his associate, but the low light canceled out his intended body language. "And . . . I'm not getting any younger. I just think it's time for the younger crowd with new ideas to whip this world into shape—better than an old coot," he said, still glaring in the dark at Barbara.

"Looks like we have intruders, or June and Jacob are back," said Frank. Recognizable faces illuminated by motion activated spotlights brought a sigh of relief. Frank called to them through the screened windows. "How did you find your way back? It's really dark out there."

"Jacob has very sensitive eyes. He could see the trail very well," said June, unclasping Jacob's arm now that she could see her way up the steps. A certain unease came through in June's voice. She grasped the wooden handrail, more to mask the twitching in her hand than to assist her traverse of the stairway.

"Jacob has very sensitive eyes," whispered Frank in a singsong fashion, laying on the sarcasm.

Adam leaned into Frank and whispered. "You know, Jacob probably heard that. He has sensitive ears too." Frank remained respectfully silent.

Everyone's attention was drawn to an event happening in the field in front of them. With a slight hum, the alien ship materialized in the field, illuminated by the two spotlights. The portal opened and dropped to the grassy field. One inhabitant disembarked and walked towards the lodge. It was Bastian, the doctor. With purposeful strides, he crossed the field and climbed the few steps to the porch.

"Good evening, everyone. Jacob and I are leaving now. I must make one more check on my patient before we go."

"Thank you both," said Adam. "You obviously know you have provided invaluable service to this project—invaluable."

"It is our duty at this time," added Jacob.

"Excuse me," said Bastian, and he moved toward the door to the living room. As he came through the door, Maya looked up and smiled. She got up, and they both walked to a downstairs room and closed the door.

"She will be alright, James," said Jacob.

"What?" asked James, startled that he was discovered staring at Maya.

"I am sorry for reading you. With Bastian, it is different. I cannot read his mind."

"And humans are not that way," said Frank, stating the obvious to make a point. "You can read our minds like an open book—probably not a good thing. We will still want to limit our interactions in the future."

The bright light of the spotlights still bathing the field in daylight reflected Jacob's smile. "You are a surprisingly wise man, Frank Connors. He would be good," said Jacob directly to June. If it were not for the almost complete encroachment of darkness, everyone would have seen her blush.

It begins—all of it is true, thought June. She closed her eyes, and tears streamed down her face as a warm shudder shook her small frame.

"Is there anything that you need—some fresh fruit leftover from dinner? I know you're partial to our Bartlett pears. Why don't you have Nancy get you some?"

"Thank you for your kindness, Adam. We will be fine."

"I know you're fine," he said, getting out of the chaise and walking to the door to the living room. "But with these pears you will be finer." Adam was not going to take no for an answer. He brought Jacob with him and got Nancy off of the couch to search the refrigerator for the pears.

"Are you sure they will not help us tomorrow?" asked James.

"They can't," answered Barbara. "For two reasons: one, they truly want this operation, as we do, to be on our own; and two, Charlie says that the 'black hats' are using direct help. Two ships will be beaming down teams on two upper level verandas tomorrow. The last thing our friends want is an altercation between two space-faring species over New York City. We would prefer that the city still be there at the end of the day."

"Yeah, that would be a good thing. We don't want another 9/11 city-wide," said Frank.

"This is so amazing! You might be jaded by such a scene but for me . . . well, I don't think I'll ever forget this night. An alien from another planet is accepting a few pieces of fruit from an earthling. And in a few moments, the alien will depart in his spaceship, right in front of our eyes. No, I won't forget this!" said James.

"Nor will I, James, nor will I," said Barbara. The three earthlings watched the scene in the kitchen as Adam and Nancy selected the best pears from the basket in the refrigerator. Bastian and Maya came out of the bedroom at the bottom of the stairs and walked to the card table in the center of the room. Jacob and Adam joined them. James could not quite hear what they were saying, but that was fine for him. He knew they were saying goodbye. Everyone had smiles on their faces as they were apparently discussing the stack of chips sitting in front of Steve compared to the others. With handshakes completed, Jacob, Bastian, and Adam walked towards the door.

"I want to personally thank you, James," said Bastian, arriving first on the porch.

"I'm sure you are welcome, sir, but I'm not sure what service that I've performed to warrant your thanks."

"You have pleased Maya very much. It has helped in her recovery. We see that humans are learning that with a positive attitude and approach to their bodies, they can regenerate cell growth at an increased rate. She has healed faster than we would predict for a human. This is very good."

"I'm pleased that she is well, Bastian. I credit you and your skills as the paramount reason she has recovered. If I helped in some way, then I am very happy about that. I am very fond of Maya. She has done so much for us."

"I understand that you will be with Maya, Frank Connors."

"That's the plan," answered Frank.

"Please keep her safe . . . for me."

Frank looked at Bastian in the diffuse light of the spotlights. *Why 'for me'?* he wondered. Out of the immediate emotional rush of imagery to his brain, he discerned one salient idea that surprised him: *I love her!* Frank fidgeted in his chair for a second at the unabashed honesty of this new realization. "I won't let you down, Bastian. I will protect her."

"Thank you."

"We will leave now. We will see you again." With those few words, the two aliens turned, walked down the stairs, and started across the field. Jacob turned slightly and waved his arm, and the spotlights dimmed and went out. Adam went first, and the others followed out to the field in front of the lodge. The portal closed on the spaceship, and a slight hum could be heard. In a moment, the craft lifted off of the field and hovered momentarily at about one hundred feet. With a slight wobble, it lifted quickly straight up and disappeared into the dark night sky.

Adam turned back to the lodge. Looking up, he could see the card players who had remained inside, their faces pressed close to the window to catch the last glimpse of the interstellar travelers. It was over; nothing more could be seen, and again they were on their own, alone. Adam led his outdoor contingent back into the lodge; no one wanted to sit out on the cold porch any longer. The card game quickly concluded with Maya surprising Steve by taking the last hand.

"We all have a big day tomorrow," said Adam, stating the obvious. "I encourage you all to get a good night's sleep." There were no dissenters. Roommates paired up and progressed to their rooms. Maya lingered at the card table, collecting the cards and stuffing her winnings into her pants pocket. James held back, getting a glass of water from the kitchen sink.

"I'm going to miss them," said James, returning to the card table.

He sat down on one of the open chairs.

"Yes," agreed Maya.

"Do you think this will work?"

"I think we have a shot."

"It seems like a long time ago," he said, looking intently at her face.

Maya slowly set the stack of cards down on the table. "This is very hard for me. You may think that because I'm a young woman I find events like the other night to be no big thing. That's not true. In some ways, it was the biggest thing of my life. I know you don't look at it lightly."

James studied this new face. He knew it was Maya under the prosthetic changes to her nose, cheeks, and chin, but it was still hard. He'd had an intimate encounter with this beautiful woman, and now it was over. It was as if the new face not only replaced the woman he loved but had removed the experience altogether. "I don't know what to do. I have feelings for you that can't be turned off like a faucet. All I want to do is be with you. It's like you told me the other night, that there's only you and me and a snoring Frank."

Maya laughed at his joke, mostly for the opportunity to snatch a moment of emotional release from the difficult discussion. "There will be no time again. It is unclear what will happen if we succeed. You will be thrust into a new world of international dealings and corralling the secret government back into a group of government employees with regular oversight, just like everyone else in the government.

"I don't know if there's a place for me in this new world. I need the amnesty just as much as the 'black hats' do. We all need it, James."

"I don't give a damn about the President, the UN, or anybody's amnesty—except maybe yours. I don't care about any of that," he said. James stared at his knees. Maya leaned over, touched the side of his face, and kissed him on the lips. James returned the kiss. They embraced each other, their lips pressed tightly.

Maya slowly pulled away. “The tear ducts don’t work as they should. I can’t get a good cry going,” she said, pressing her lower eyelid for some moisture that was not there. “This is where you need to be a statesman and go for the greater good. This is where I give you and Frank one final push to make this mission a success. Let’s talk about this after. I will make time, but now we must get some sleep. We need to be at our optimum tomorrow.” Maya kissed him again on the lips and left the table for her bedroom.

James stood very still, concentrating on this woman who was walking away from him. He followed her shoulders, her waist, her hips as she climbed the stairs to her room. She whispered to him from the top of the stairs. “Go to bed!” Then she slowly opened the door to the bedroom and shut it behind her.

Chapter 11

Thursday, September 14 – Morning

The film was gone, but no one was worried. It was given a pre-dawn ride to a media outlet in lower Manhattan that supplied films and videos to the UN and other government agencies. Including the artifact in a regular shipment to the United Nations was Adam's plan.

Departure day brought a fleet of SUVs to the lodge to pick up the teams. All parties were involved. All were headed eventually to the United Nations. Maya and Carol left together before dawn. They needed to get Maya into Carol's home unseen. The white SUV parked in front of the house next to Carol's, close enough for Maya to get a visual fix on the front door.

"There's a clear open space just beyond that door. I don't leave anything in the hallway, Maya," said Carol as she watched her double prepare to jump.

"I need to get into a lotus position here, otherwise I'll bonk my head against one of your walls," said Maya. She tucked her legs under her on the seat. "I want one more check of the equipment."

Carol put on a pair of sunglasses and looked straight ahead at the back of the driver's head. She adjusted the glasses and fiddled with her earbud. "Okay, I see that you were looking at the headrest in front of you and now you're looking out the window . . . damn it, you're looking at the couch in my living room from my foyer! I wish you'd warn me when you're going to do that."

"I couldn't get a good sound check without a little separation. How are you reading me?"

"Like you were sitting next to me. These sunglasses linked to your implants are amazing," said Carol.

"That's what you get with quality workmanship. Okay, I'm taking a quick shower, and I don't care how much the driver will pay you—he can't wear the glasses."

"That's absolutely not a problem." The SUV driver swung his arm across his chest and mouthed the word "darn."

Rudy and Nancy departed next. They were to be the observers at a distance. Knowledge of the arrival of Charlie's teams was the key to the success of the plan. Nancy took up a position selling flowers within full view of the north veranda. Rudy set up a hot dog stand with a view of the south veranda. They would get very little notice of the arrival, but Charlie said the beam down would create an energy surge.

Barbara and June were next to depart. They set up a vehicular command post in the vicinity to monitor all electronic feeds.

No one knew exactly where Steve was going. He said it was a secret. There was no trace of him in the morning. Somehow it didn't bother Adam, and if it didn't bother Adam, no one else worried about it.

It was 6:00 AM, and last to leave in two SUVs were Adam in one car and Frank and James in the other. Only Adam knew how many copies of the presentation version of the film were made. All Frank knew was that he had one. He had two goals: get the presentation to the projection booth and protect Maya. He suspected that Maya shared one of his goals. The other he figured was to protect him. *Damn woman is making my life difficult*, he thought.

From a mobile command post in the area, Kathleen spoke into a microphone. "Any sign of Broadhurst?" Kathleen's voice crackled over into JoAnne's earbud.

"No sign of him or Connors," responded JoAnne.

"How are the delegates reacting to the security screening?"

"Not too well. They see it as an infringement of their rights as elected officials and all. Fortunately, as soon as we say we're looking for terrorists, they back off and submit to the screen. *Our* 'terrorists' won't make it through here."

"Are your teams in position, Charlie?" queried Kathleen.

"Almost. I think the pilot says we're over Albany now. We're on our way in. Any sign of our 'terrorists'?"

"Apparently not yet. We're watching all the doors and service entrances. Let me know when you're in position."

"Copy that."

"Good morning, Carol. How are you this fine day?" greeted Max. The watch captain looked intently as Carol (Maya) reported for duty.

"No, I'm not ready for the smiling, ebullient Max this morning. I got a cold last night," said Maya.

Good, Maya, said Carol over the com.

"You sound awful. That's what you get for taking a day off. You cavort with all kind of germs that you're not exposed to. Where did you go?"

"I hung out with space aliens last night and picked it up from them."

"I hear you. Last night Heidi Klum and a friend came over and invited me for a threesome. I said I couldn't because I was tired."

"Uh huh, and that was because you had to cover for me yesterday, right? It just wore you out. Too bad," jabbed Maya.

"That cold must have sharpened your wit, girl."

Ease up a bit, Maya. He acts gruff, but he's a cream puff and bruises easily. Ask him to put you upstairs on room detail, advised Carol.

"Hey, can you cut me a break here, Max? I'm not ready for all those delegates today. Can you put me upstairs on room detail?"

"You know you do have sick leave," he said, leaning forward and resting his elbows on the watch station counter. "My best guard wants a cake walk on a General Assembly day?" he said.

"Yeah, I'll take my sick leave if I can't handle room checks. It would be great if you could swing it, Max."

"Oh, alright. Hey, Johnathan," he yelled at a guard across the room. "Change of plans. You're heading up delegate duty on Floor Two." Johnathan grumbled a bit for his buddies but offered no more resistance.

"Thanks, Max. I'll owe you one."

"Give me a ride on your spaceship as payback?" he asked.

Maya laughed at the thought. "Sure, next time they come down, we'll hitch a ride. Invite Heidi and her friend."

"Go on, get outa here," he said directly to Maya. Then in a booming voice, "It's shift change, ladies and gentlemen. You all have your assignments. Have a nice day." The guards vacated the shift room and headed to their posts.

The blue sedan obtained access to the street in front of the UN and pulled up to the curb. Harold, standing on the sidewalk, came up to the passenger door and opened it for Don. "Is everything all right here, Harold?"

"Well, yeah, I guess," Don's assistant special agent stammered as they walked slowly to the delegate entrance.

"You guess? What the hell does that mean?"

"Well, there's a heightened security protocol here. There are some agents. They said they're FBI. They're checking everybody—something about a terrorist threat. I didn't hear anything about it."

"Who authorized this?"

"I don't know. We can't flash our credentials from Langley to get anywhere with these guys. We have no jurisdiction, and we're likely to get in a lot of hot water if they know the CIA is hanging around."

"It's that woman, Kathy something."

"Whoever she is, she's got quite an organization. I took a walk around all of the entrances, and these guys are everywhere."

"Don Petrulio and Harold Pinder," said a man of medium build in a dark blue suit wearing dark sunglasses. Another man stood next to Harold—dressed the same.

"Who wants to know?" responded Don, his voice quavering a bit.

"Will you come with us, please?"

"Why should I?"

"Because you want answers," was his response. "Please, sir, at this point we are not prepared to take no for an answer." The man patted his chest.

"You're prepared to shoot an agent of the US government on this sidewalk . . . in front of the UN?"

"We are prepared to take only 'yes' for an answer," he said.

"Let's tag along with these fellows, Harold. If they were going to shoot us, they would have already done so. Let's see if they have the answers we want."

"This way, please," said the man in the blue suit, pointing in the direction of the delegates' entrance. The two men dressed in business suits were waived on by the contingent at the screening station, which surprised Don. Inside they circumnavigated a group of delegates assembled in the hall. They segued past reporters conducting interviews with one dignitary or another. The blue suited men led them to a service elevator that took them to the twenty-second floor. After a long trip down a hall to the right then the left, they arrived at a small windowless conference room.

"Please have a seat, gentlemen. Someone will be with you shortly," said one of the men before leaving and closing the door behind him.

"You know, Harold, it seems to me that we are being sequestered here so we keep quiet while they carry out their operation," said Don, walking around the oblong table.

"You could be right, but let's give them the benefit of the doubt for a little while." Harold walked to the door and looked out a small window into the hallway. He looked left and saw nothing. Looking right, he could see the shoulder of one of the men who brought them there. "I don't know, but I think we're being guarded."

Don walked to the door to see for himself. "Damn! How could we be so easily hoodwinked? Try the handle on that door—slowly."

Harold pressed down on the burnished brass handle, expecting it to give easily. It did not. "We're locked in here!"

"I'm going to get an agent on the line about this." Don repeatedly pressed his earbud with no success. "I believe this bird has been captured, plucked, and trussed up for Thanksgiving a little early, Harold. We've been had! The only way we're going to save face here is if we can get the hell out of this room." Don and Harold sat down at the conference table to devise their escape.

Above the Assembly hall, a slight hum began to localize at the end of a wide portion of hallway. A half a second later, a few sparks glistened in front of a doorway, and Frank, sitting tailor fashion, appeared on the polished floor. He sat motionless for a second or two, looking left and then right. Getting his bearings, he stood up and touched his earbud.

"Maya, do you read me?"

"Yeah, and I see you too."

"I don't see you," he said, looking both ways.

"On my floor schematic, I see you. I'm a short walk away. Stay there. I'm coming to you."

"Any movement yet?" called Kathleen over the microphone in her command post.

"No Broadhurst yet, but we passed through that Adam Baines fellow a few moments ago," said the voice over the speaker.

"What! You let him through?" cried Kathleen.

"He didn't have Broadhurst or Connors or the film with him. He's a Senior Officer at the UN and—"

"I don't care if the President walked in with him. You should have stopped him!" yelled Kathleen. She pushed buttons on the console. "Everybody, it's going down now. Charlie, drop your men now!"

"We're in position, but we're having stability problems."

"I don't care. Get those men down there *now*!"

"Copy that."

Out of the corner of his eye, Rudy saw the briefest image of a saucer-shaped craft hover over the veranda. A bright beam deposited four men in commando gear on the surface of the veranda. In a flash the ship and the bright beam of light were gone.

"What was that?" yelled a passerby who was waiting in line for a hot dog.

"I think that was a plane behind the UN. It's gone now," said Rudy, discounting the reality for the benefit of the customers in line. He knew it was not a plane, but encouraging alarm among citizens was not part of the plan. "Excuse me, I have to take this call," said Rudy, pulling a cell phone out of his pocket. "Four bad guys, south veranda, confirmed," he whispered.

"Copy that, south," said Barbara.

"Ditto on north, ditto on the commandos," said Nancy.

"Copy that, north," said Barbara.

"Steve, if you're listening, we could use your help about now. Maya, you have less than a minute before eight pretty boys start crawling all over your back."

"God help us if you materialize inside a wall somewhere," whispered Adam, pacing around inside a conference room. "Any time now, my friend," he said out loud.

A soft hum appeared to emanate from the center of the table, then iridescent sparks projected outward. James Broadhurst popped into existence in a crouched position on the table. "I can't sit tailor fashion for very long like Frank. My legs don't bend that way."

"All that matters is that you're in one piece. These jumpers have never failed, but there's always a first time," said Adam.

"*Now* you tell me," groaned James.

"If you didn't want risk, you shouldn't have got out of bed this morning," said Adam, helping him down from the conference room table.

"Yeah, yeah, where do we go to pick up the movie?"

"Right this way," Adam said, walking towards the door of the conference room. "Wait a minute. You need a badge like mine." He pulled an identity badge out of his pocket and clipped it to the breast pocket of James's suit jacket. "Nice looking suit there, James," he said, adjusting the badge.

"Yes, it is. I'm used to old frumpy sport coats with elbow patches. I'm going to have to get me some more of these if I get to hobnob with the President."

"Whoa there, partner, one suit at a time. Let's go."

"Where's the projection room?" asked Frank as they slowly crept down a long hallway.

"It's not too far," said Maya. "James is right, you're continually untucked," she added, glancing down at his rumpled shirt more than half out of his pants.

Frank rolled his eyes. "I can fix that." He yanked his shirt out of his pants and pulled it down taut, grasping at the tails. "Now, why didn't we just jump into the projection room?" Maya smiled at his solution.

"We had to find a wide, open space for you, because you're not as skilled yet with these jumpers. Besides, the projection room is too small and too much interference with electronics. Anyway, it's more fun this way."

"Your idea of fun is highly overrated, sweet cheeks." Frank stood up and hugged the alcove of an office door along the hallway as he watched Maya peer around the corner.

Maya stopped and stared forward. Frank knew she was reading the schematics in her head, and he remained silent. "We have eight men approaching us from behind. Charlie's team is moving into position."

"Charlie . . . he's with us . . . isn't he?"

"He is, although I don't know if he's had time to turn any of his men," whispered Maya. The worry in her voice spiked an adrenalin rush. "They're about on us." Maya pulled out her gun and turned to face the approaching men. An automatic with silencer had replaced her small handgun. Two commandos came into view. Maya squeezed off one shot. The round hit one of the commandos in the shoulder, forcing the two men to quickly pull back.

"I'll take three men and work around to the other end of the hall," whispered Charlie. "You three, you're with me."

"Who put you in charge?" railed JoAnne, stuffing a white cloth under the wounded man's shoulder.

"Kathleen did. She said it's my operation at the UN. The fact that this has become the *only* operation hasn't changed anything," asserted

Charlie. The commandos crouching with their backs to the wall looked back and forth between the two leaders, waiting for a signal for the next move.

"Take care of him, and keep her busy from this end." Charlie poked his head around the corner. Maya was cautiously walking sideways with her gun held up in the direction of the commandos. She was also slowly pushing Frank down the hall in the opposite direction. Unseen by his other men, Charlie flashed four fingers to Maya and then leaped across the end of the hall to the other side. Charlie's men followed him in quick succession, ducking one more round from Maya that flew over their heads and lodged in the masonry wall above them.

Maya grabbed Frank's shoulder and shoved him into a recessed doorway, then collapsed against him as a barrage of silencer bullets sprayed down the hall.

"I'm going to have to keep firing at them. They don't get it; they're supposed to hide."

"Somehow, I don't think they read your playbook, Maya," whispered Frank, wincing at being slammed into a solid core door.

A phone on Maya's belt started ringing. "I think your boss is calling you," wheezed Frank. Maya fired off one more shot down the hall.

"What is it, Max?" said Maya, answering the phone.

"What the hell's going on up there? Someone said there's small arms fire on your floor. I'm ready to sound a general evacuation alarm. I wanted to hear from you. Are you under fire?"

"No! Do not do that, Max. I'm chasing some school kids with firecrackers."

"We have no school tours today; it's a General Assembly session, Carol."

"Everything is under control, Max. There isn't anything to worry about. Have I ever lied to you when the chips are down?"

Mention that one incident with the Laotians last year, barked Carol over the com.

"Didn't the Laotian thing go pretty well last year? Hey, I gotta run and catch these sniveling bastards. I'll call you when I corral them, okay?"

"Okay, copy that," said Max, reluctantly agreeing with her. She quickly holstered her phone.

"Now run down the hall and get around that corner. Go!" whispered Maya. Frank started running as quietly as he could. He reached the end of the hall and dodged one bullet from a commando who stuck his arm and shoulder out. Maya fired off a shot that lodged in the commando's shoulder and knocked him to the floor screaming in pain. While the others pulled him out of the line of fire, Maya made a break for it and slipped around the corner.

"What the hell!" said JoAnne. "How did she hit exactly the same spot on both of you? They weren't kill shots but I think she could have easily wasted any one of us. Does that bitch have telescopic eyes or what? Get Charlie on the com. We need an extraction for you two before you bleed to death."

As Maya rolled around the corner into Frank's shoulder, she looked down the short hallway ahead. "We have one long hallway to the left. Our destination is straight ahead to that only door on the left. Do you see it?"

"Yes, I see it," said Frank, gasping for breath.

"Charlie is going to be coming down this long hallway on the left. Your objective is that room. The guy is waiting for you."

"What are you going to do?"

"I'm sure that Charlie hasn't turned all of his men yet. You have to get to that room at all costs. You got it?"

"Yeah, I got it. When do we go?"

"No time like the present," said Maya, waving her gun in the direction of the projection room.

Frank and Maya cautiously approached the next corner with Maya still taking time to look behind her. Maya peeked around the corner and saw Charlie and his men rapidly approaching. "Run!" whispered Maya in a hoarse voice.

Frank complied. What happened next moved in slow motion in Frank's mind, even though he was running as fast as he could. He crossed the hallway, alerting Charlie's team who gave chase with Charlie and another man holding back. Frank turned his head from the hallway to look straight ahead again. Five commandos in desert camo materialized in front of him. He instinctively dropped to a sliding position, hoping to escape the oncoming bullets from this new team. He almost slid under their legs on the polished floor. Looking up, he saw it was Steve leading this new team.

The door to the projection room opened as if on cue, and a bearded man in his thirties grabbed Frank by the shoulder, dragged him into the projection booth, and closed the door. Maya stopped running as soon as she realized she had friendly agents in front of her. A second later, realizing she was in the middle of the impending firefight, she threw her body back against the wall. The two early arrivals from Charlie's team turned the corner and were astonished to meet opposition commandos with guns pointed at their noses.

At the same time JoAnne, on her own, flew into the center of the hall, took aim, and fired one round into Maya's right arm. Maya spun around from the blast and tumbled to the ground. Steve's men held their ground, waiting for the signal from Steve. Steve saw only one adversary—the woman firing from down the hall. He fired one shot and brought her down to the floor.

"Guns down *now*!" yelled Steve.

"Put them down!" echoed Charlie. "It's over. They have the day!" Charlie's men slowly laid their guns on the floor and instinctively put their hands on their heads.

"Is this how you take charge?" wailed JoAnne from the floor as she struggled to retrieve her gun from behind her. Charlie quickly ran to her and kicked the gun out of her reach in time. "It's over, JoAnne."

In the middle of an address by the Nigerian ambassador, the lights in the Assembly hall dimmed. The ambassador nervously looked around the great hall and at his fellow delegates. Murmurs from the Assembly grew until the view screens in the hall came to life. A title screen displayed in four languages, and a second with more information in the same four languages. Men and women in the translation booths, disoriented at first, jumped into their task and interpreted the words for their delegates.

The video opened with spaceships approaching a field in the desert. Shrieks of horror and bafflement rolled around the room. The world was seeing for the first time, proof that we are not alone.

"The delivery is here, James! Stop that man before he gets into the elevator."

James ran across the hallway and stuck his arm into the closing doors. The elevator doors jerked opened. "Hi. I'm James Broadhurst. That blue one is for me."

The startled deliveryman looked first at James and then at the stack of film reels on the cart. "This one?" he asked nervously. James nodded affirmatively, fishing for his wallet in his back pocket.

Adam arrived at the elevator and stuck his foot in the door to hold it open. "Show him your ID badge, James." James did, and the deliveryman looked at the blue film case. He read the label: "'For James Broadhurst, Floor 2, deliver in person.' Well, I'll be damned. I've never done this before. I pushed the button for the fourth floor expecting to get off the elevator there. I push this button every week, and it always takes me to the right floor. This time it takes me to Floor 2," said the delivery person, flashing a perplexed look.

"Strange things happen," said Adam. The deliveryman handed the film case to James.

"Thank you so much, sir," said James.

"By the way, projection room two is very busy right now. You might want to go to the commissary on the ground floor. They've got soldiers with guns upstairs. Not a fun place right now."

"Okay," said the deliveryman, clearly bewildered by such a claim. The elevator doors closed.

"Let's go. We need to get through final security to get you in there." Adam and James started back towards the main entrance to the Assembly hall. From out of a group of reporters walked Kathleen. Adam and James did not see her until they had turned toward the entrance to the Assembly hall. Kathleen grabbed Adam's shoulder and stuck a gun in his side.

"I'll take that," she said to James.

"You're too late, Kathleen. The delegates are watching the video right now. It's all over," whispered Adam.

"Not so fast, you bastard. Without this original film that's just another CGI fantasy flick conjured up by Industrial Light and Magic. We'll have it discredited in a day. Hand it over."

"We're going to do this real slow, lady," said Johnathan, coming up from behind her and poking his gun in her ribs. "We don't want to shut this place down for your little gun play. We're going to do this quietly, aren't we?"

"These are the terrorists, guard. Take them into custody. I'll explain it all to you."

"Mr. Adam Baines—a terrorist? That's a good one, lady. Besides you're the one with the gun. The other guy looks familiar, but he's obviously with Mr. Baines who I trust. I don't trust you, so hand it over nice and slow."

Kathleen relented and did as Johnathan requested. Another guard arrived, put cuffs on Kathleen, and led her away. "I will need a statement from both of you before you leave the building," said Johnathan.

"Of course, we will be most happy to clear this up for you. But right now, we are due in the Assembly hall."

"Later then," said Johnathan, waving goodbye and catching up with his fellow guard and prisoner.

"Take the film out of the case, James." James complied and left the empty case on the floor next to a wall. They proceeded to the main entrance where Adam presented an envelope to the guard. He opened it, handed it back to him, and opened the door. Inside the door, a second guard looked at the letter and pointed in the direction of the main podium.

The lights were still down for the last minute of the video. James knew that a short comment by him came at the end, but it was still a little disconcerting to see himself up on the screen as the last image everyone saw before the lights came up.

James and Adam walked side by side down the wide aisle. A few delegates looked up as they passed, but most were quickly conversing with their staff. The sound of hundreds and hundreds of voices added to the immensity of what James was about to do. No speaking venue in the past was like this. *Not a good time to pass out*, he thought as they reached the base of the podium. The Secretary waved them forward, and Adam and James climbed the steps as the crowd continued to buzz.

Before Adam seated himself in an open chair behind the podium, he shook hands with James. "They all want to hear from you, James."

"That's what I'm afraid of," he said, his voice quavering a bit.

"You'll do fine. Just imagine the smallest UFO conference you've ever attended."

James followed the Secretary to the podium and stood to the right of him as the official face of the UN thumped the gavel on the podium until the din of voices subsided.

"Delegates and honored guests, ladies and gentlemen, we apologize for the interruption, but this presentation could not be accurately planned. I would like to present to you James Broadhurst. He will fill you in on what just happened here today. Mr. Broadhurst," said the Secretary, standing back and giving up the podium. The crowd gave up a respectful applause.

"Mr. Secretary, I have in my hands the original film from which the short video you've just seen is only a small part. This film is the property of the American government, the American people, and now the world. Will you accept this artifact as a temporary loan from our country?"

The Secretary stood up and held out his hands, took the film, and bowed. This time the applause was a bit more energetic. James turned around facing the Assembly and waited for the applause to stop.

"What you witnessed just now was a chronicle of a moment in our past. There was no trickery in the production of this short video. Everything you saw except the introduction and the short epilog was a film of real events in history." A murmur of conversation disturbed the quiet of the hall. "What does this mean to us? It means many things, but at the outset it means humanity has been visited by species from another world. This is documented here in front of our eyes. The second thing we can perceive from this video is that this truth, that alien life forms, highly intelligent life forms that have visited us, have been hidden from us by our governments. As we speak, we are placing copies of the complete video into the hands of all the major news services. I imagine that special programming will ensue today and tomorrow on this historic artifact."

"He's doing a good job, isn't he?" said Frank, leaning back in a small chair in the projection room.

The bearded man nodded in approval. "Now we see what happens next. Will he persuade the shadow government into giving it all up? Will the public run screaming into the streets?"

"What do you really think?"

"I think that most people will still go to work tomorrow even after seeing the full video. People still have to pay their bills, feed their kids, and take Suzie to soccer practice and all that. It will all still go on like normal."

"But with a little twist. You can go to the internet and look at the surface of Mars from our meager efforts at getting around this solar system. Now you can turn on your television and watch someone that was never born on this planet, someone who may look a little like us but is more intelligent and knows how to go to Mars and get out there and take a stroll. It's a different perspective. Soon you'll be able to go there too, take that stroll on Mars. I think it's very exciting. I never thought I'd see this day, but I'm sure glad that I'm here right now," said Frank.

"I'm glad that you made it. I never thought you guys would succeed. The odds were definitely against you."

"I've got to go. I need to see how my friends did outside. We're going to see you again, aren't we?"

"If I get to keep my job, you will."

"That's not going to be a problem. For what you did, they're going to want your story. You and I, we made this happen. We're heroes."

"Call me tomorrow, and let's get together for a beer."

"You bet," said Frank, shaking his hand vigorously. Frank opened the door and stepped out into the hallway. He looked around and found no one. Something on the polished floor drew his attention. A sticky circle of blood glistened there. "Maya!" he shrieked.

Frank started running. He slid into a hallway, startling one commando dressed in desert fatigues.

"Oh, it's you," said the soldier, relaxing his drawn weapon. "Congratulations, Mr. Connors."

"What happened? Where's Maya?"

"She was shot. She got hit pretty badly, but she's supposed to recover."

"Did they take her to a hospital?" he asked breathlessly.

"I'm sure of it, Mr. Connors."

"Where's the elevator?"

"It's right behind you, sir."

Frank pushed the button and waited. "I'm sorry I'm so distracted. I can't believe I didn't check on Maya."

"You were busy, sir." The elevator bell dinged, and Frank turned to the opening doors.

"Congratulations again, sir," said the soldier. All Frank could do was nod his head.

The elevator doors opened to throngs of people moving in what looked like every direction. "What's going on?" asked Frank to the first person he saw.

"Because of the film, they cancelled the afternoon session. First time that's ever happened," said a young man with a British accent.

Frank pushed his way through the crowd to a clear spot in the large hallway. "Damn!" he said to himself. He had forgotten he had a communication link to Barbara. He tapped his earbud and started talking. "This is Frank. Can anyone hear me—anyone?"

"This is June. Where are you, Frank?"

"I'm in the middle of the entrance hall on the second floor. Where is everybody?"

"We're outside on the sidewalk. Come out to me now, Frank."

Frank made his way through the crowd to the exterior doors. The sidewalk was awash with reporters and delegates. Reporters were everywhere, hounding anyone who saw the video. What did they think? What would change in their country because of this revelation? For the moment, Frank walked through the crowd inconspicuously. Soon that would no longer be the case, he thought. The strained muscles of worry started to melt into a smile. "We did it!" he whispered. His team stood at the end of the long walkway out of the immediate crush of delegates and reporters. Barbara, June, Rudy, Nancy, and Steve clapped their hands as he approached. The smiling faces greeting him broadened his own smile. He was literally laughing in jubilation as he grasped their hands and hugged each one.

"Damn if we didn't pull this off!" shouted Rudy. "This is incredible!"

"It *is* incredible!" shouted Frank. "We turned decades of history around on its head."

"*You* did that, Frank," said Barbara. "Without you risking your life for this cause, none of us would be standing here in celebration."

"I couldn't have done it without this guy," said Frank, patting Steve on the back. "You arrived just in time."

"My mother always told me to never be late. I always do what my mother tells me to do," he said with a wry grin and laughter from the others.

"We *all* did this," said Frank looking around at the others in the team. "How is Maya?"

"They took her to the hospital with the others. In addition, three of their commandos were injured, nothing life threatening. Frank, Maya's injuries were more extensive. The shooter fully intended to do her in. Her shoulder will need extensive reconnection of tendons and arteries."

"Are we going to the hospital?" he asked expectantly.

"Yes, the fleet's here," said June, pointing to three SUVs lined up at the cordoned off area. "Your shirt, Frank."

"Hey, it's a fashion statement. The world is not only going to ask whose shirts I wear but how I wear them."

As the others groaned, June took Frank's arm and kissed him on the cheek. He turned to her and kissed her on the lips.

"Let's go," said Frank, giddy with unrestrained elation.

Chapter 12

Thursday, September 14 – Afternoon, Evening

"How's it going with that access panel, Harold?"

"I almost got it," he said, standing on a chair in the middle of the conference table.

With the noise that Harold was making in the ceiling, neither Don nor Harold heard the door open. "What are you guys doing in here?" asked Johnathan.

"We were escorted in here by some government agents," said Don.

"And that was an invitation to rip out the ceiling tiles? Come on, get down from there."

"Listen, sir, we need to know who's in charge here," demanded Don.

"Oh, I think that can be arranged. Come with me." Don and Harold followed Johnathan out of the conference room. Another guard joined them, and they proceeded into an elevator and down to the guard room on the ground floor. "This way, gentlemen," ordered Johnathan, leading the two CIA agents past empty rooms that looked like holding cells. Johnathan kept walking, but Don and Harold stopped to peer through the small window of an occupied cell. Inside was Kathleen sitting on a cot looking down at her feet.

"Can you open this one?" asked Don.

"Do you know this woman?" said Johnathan, taking the keys out of his pocket.

"Yes and no. Can I just have a word with her?"

"Okay, but make it brief. You're due down the hall with our watch captain." He opened the door, and Don stuck his head into the secure room.

"We meet again, Kathy," said Don with a sly smile.

"Go away, asshole," said Kathleen.

"Such a foul mouth for a woman dressed so well. They haven't got around to fitting you with your very own orange jumper? It must be a busy day."

"Busy day, huh? Didn't you just spend the last two hours locked up in a conference room while terrorists pulled off the crime of the century? You missed everything. Good luck explaining this to your candy ass friends at Langley. They'll laugh their asses off at your incompetence, and then they'll fire you. What a complete joke you two are."

"At least I'm not behind bars, Kathleen. We're walking out of here."

"So how do you know this woman? Are you working with her?" asked Johnathan.

"We've met once. That's about it. I don't particularly like her, and

I suspect the feeling is mutual. Whatever hole you decide to put her in is probably not deep enough."

"Alright, come with me. The watch captain wants to know how you got in here without proper ID and how you got locked in that room. As for you, lady, we have metro police coming to pick you up." Johnathan ushered Don out and locked the room.

Kathleen got up to watch Don and Harold disappear into a room at the end of the hall. She lay back on the cot and stared at the grey concrete ceiling. "Has it started to change already?" she asked herself. "At any other time, I would have been out of here, and any record would be expunged—no trace. It would be all cleared up." Then, "Where the hell is everybody?" The exasperated shout ricocheted off the smooth grey walls, but no one answered.

Bastian stepped quietly into the waiting room unnoticed by the team. "She is going to be alright." The pitch of his voice was so reassuring and comforting that it failed to startle a soul. Each member of the team looked up and smiled at the tall blue-eyed blond. He was wearing a doctor's lab coat that made him look almost normal. "She will be here for five days, more for the other doctors to observe and run tests than for her recuperation. Nonetheless, it is wise to give her body time to completely heal. The doctors gave her a sedative that will keep her asleep until mid-morning tomorrow.

"Maya was briefly awake after surgery, which is a good sign. She would like you all to go out and celebrate. With this money." He pulled out a wad of bills from his coat and handed it to Barbara. "You will buy drinks on her. Maya is so very proud of all of you."

"We are humbled by your service to Maya," said Barbara. "I believe we are going to be thanking you over and over again, Bastian."

"It is my pleasure to help. Maya is a wonderful woman. I have begun the sharing. Some of my instruments are with the doctors. We will be back when Maya leaves the hospital. At that time, I will participate in two surgeries to coach the doctors in how to use these new tools. Does this meet with your approval, Barbara?"

"Yes of course, Bastian. We want to get started in this cooperation. It will be the small-scale direct assistance that will go a long way towards convincing the people of this planet that what we started here is good for them."

"As you wish. I must leave now. Enjoy your evening, my friends." As soon as he finished his sentence, he instantly dematerialized.

"No, I don't think I'll soon get used to that, even when I do it," said Frank. The disclosure team laughed with Frank. Jumpers and communication devices embedded in the brain were tools that some would soon be using with increasing regularity.

"You know what I'm surprised at—no one attempted to arrest us." The quizzical looks Frank received signaled that he had ventured into unexplainable territory.

"Dear Frank, here's the explanation if you must. Maya did a convincing job when she spoke to Max. He could have called in reinforcements and evacuated the building. Maya saved it again. Second, as soon as you made it into the room, we sent Carol in as herself. She reported to Max and cleared it all up."

"What could she have possibly told Max that would have 'cleared it all up'?"

"The truth, she told him the truth," said Barbara. "Can we walk and talk? This is a nice room, but they don't serve margaritas here." They filed out of the room and progressed to the elevator.

"She told him everything?"

"Everything," answered Barbara, pressing the elevator button. "Max personally went up to where the action took place and assisted with a speedy exit of all of the commandos from both sides. He scheduled a special cleanup crew. The projectionist won't even lose his job over this."

The team members found their spots in the elevator and watched the door close. Frank and Steve entered last and stood at the door. "That's the other part of it, Frank. It's like when a big news story hits the airwaves and right on top of that a bigger story breaks—the biggest! The commandos were spirited out of there via a special elevator to the garage and loaded into quietly called ambulances and vans."

The elevator doors opened. Frank and Steve scanned the parking level as the doors opened and nodded for the women to disembark into the underground garage.

"I don't know, Frank. People get wrapped up in things like this and they don't notice anything else," said Rudy, unlocking the door to the SUV. "Speaking of noticing things, we have the keys to one SUV. I sent the three drivers home in the other vehicles. We're on our own now, with no security watching us."

"Hey, wait a minute. Steve and I can babysit you if that's what you need, Rudy," said Frank, getting a little indignant.

"I didn't mean it that way. Let me ask you, Frank, where are you sleeping tonight?"

"Well . . . I don't know."

"All of us are from DC except you and James—"

Barbara interrupted Rudy's divisive tangent. "We have hotel rooms for all of us for two nights and then we are back in DC, as you say, Rudy. James and Frank, you need to sign some paperwork if you're going to be government employees like the rest of us."

"I didn't think you were really part of the government. I thought you were part of that shadow government that James is always going on about."

"You are correct, Frank. You sign up with us first, and then we all divulge ourselves to the real government and resign with them—directly, on the books this time. No off the books black ops stuff anymore—at least not for the UFO connection. The legislation for complete amnesty has been sent to the President's desk. He's going to sign it but he doesn't want to upstage the actual disclosure."

"You know, I'm getting cold out here," said June.

"Let's go for a brew . . . in a warm restaurant," said Steve, opening the door for June.

The sun had long since set across New York City. With a light rain, the street glistened with a soft sheen of scattered reflected light from multihued sources along the broad avenue. Rudy turned left and sped up to the next street light.

"Where are we going?" asked Barbara.

"While you were socializing on the porch last night, I was doing some entertainment research. I was in the city on a job about six months ago, and I stumbled across this place. Well, I really didn't stumble; I was driving this guy around, and he met a contact at this restaurant—a nice Italian place. I'm driving, so it's our first stop."

"Okay," said Barbara, drawing out the word for effect.

"Is he still with us, Rudy?" asked Steve.

"Yep," answered Rudy.

"Is who still with us?" asked June.

"The guy from the hospital parking garage," said Rudy. "He's still with us."

"How do you know?" demanded Barbara.

"Listen, you don't pay me to knit sweaters. I've been doing this for more than awhile. He's following us. That's why we're going to some obscure little restaurant so we can force his hand. My guess? He's a reporter who spotted us on the sidewalk at the UN."

They were silent for a while as Rudy took one turn after another overtly to arrive at the destination and surreptitiously to force the lone follower to continue to demonstrate his intentions.

"One more turn and we'll be there," said Rudy.

"We'll take care of *him*," said Steve.

"I don't want him hurt," said Barbara. "We're done with that."

"We'll have a nice chat," said Frank.

"The rest of you go into the restaurant and get us a table," said Barbara. Rudy pulled into the last space on the short block fronting the restaurant.

"Good evening," said Steve, stepping immediately in the path of their pursuer.

"Uh, good evening to you," he stammered. "I'm going into this restaurant."

"Not until you tell us why you were following us," ordered Frank.

"I wasn't—"

"We saw you in the parking garage looking us over, and I saw it was you who just passed us in front of this restaurant. So, try again," said Steve.

He stood there quietly, not sure of what to do. His eyes nervously darted from Frank to Steve and then to Barbara, who was standing behind the two men. "I'm Jason Cox, a reporter for the *Times*. I saw that little applause for you in front of the UN," he said, looking directly at Frank. "Earlier I watched two ambulances with no lights or sirens quietly leave the garage lot. The story broke that a James Broadhurst released a film about alien visitation to earth. I take it he's a friend of yours," said Jason, trying to put them on the defensive.

"Jason Cox," announced Barbara, hovering over his name. "We attended a correspondent's dinner in Washington last year. I believe Adam Baines introduced us."

"Maybe," he said, nervously shaking his hand at his side.

"I'm familiar with your work. You seem well balanced in your reporting as far as I can tell."

"Thank you. There's a story here. Don't you want to tell the world how this came about and where you're taking the public with this?"

"Frank and Steve, go in and order. Jason and I are going to get a table in the bar for a bit," said Barbara, patting Steve on the back.

"Are you sure about this?" said Steve.

"Yeah, I'm sure. Go ahead." Frank and Steve left Jason and Barbara outside for a moment. "Would you like to talk?"

"Yes, on the record?"

"On the record, do you have a tape recorder?"

"Yes, Barbara, I do."

"Well, let's get out of this damp weather. Have you had dinner yet?"

"No, I haven't, too busy tailing you guys," said Jason, holding the door for Barbara.

"I'm feeling magnanimous tonight. Dinner's on me." They stepped into the warm restaurant and went straight to the bar to find a quiet table in the corner.

"Did you hear some man showed a video about aliens at the UN today? It's all over the news," said the waitress. Her big smile and breathless delivery verified her exuberance and support for the release of the film.

"Yeah, we definitely heard about it," said Barbara, adding a measure of enthusiasm. "Pretty cool, huh?"

"Yes, very, very cool," answered the waitress with a big smile. She turned and walked back to the bar.

"How about it, Jason, what are the early reactions?"

"Fairly positive at the moment; there are some naysayers who state that the video is a fake. Most of the networks are going to show the original film in its entirety with no commercial interruptions. Then we'll see how the naysayers get out from under that."

"You seem pretty supportive of what we've done. Is that from a personal interest?"

"Anything to shake things up a bit is fine with me. A slow news day is just that. I'm more content when there's something breaking and I just happen to be on the crest of it all . . . as I seem to be here."

"I have an idea that I would like to float. See if this has an appeal to you."

"Okay," said Jason with a little caution in his voice.

"How about I give you the exclusive to this story? Those guys at the table over there have been working on this for months now. Frank and James did a cross country journey with that film. They almost got caught a couple of times with every alphabet agency on their tail. It's a big story that I think could be a continuing series in your paper."

"Okay, I'm now sitting six inches off my seat here. I suspected some of this, but I'm afraid there's a catch, isn't there?" The waitress served up two beers and left again.

"I always like the first sip of a beer, don't you?"

"Don't tease me, Barbara. Give it up."

"Jason, this story of how these people got to this point is the biggest story of the millennium. The problem is that we're a part of a secret government organization with a specific mission now. We will be slowly bringing out more and more information and best of all . . . new technology. If you think the technological boom has been explosive up to now, just wait. We will be working with elected officials and scientists and the military to no longer keep this stuff hidden."

"All good stuff, but I'm still waiting for the proverbial other shoe to drop."

"I need a press secretary. That's the bottom line here. You would have unfettered access to anything and everything we do. We need a way to disclose all of this in reasonable chunks that the public can consume. You have a pretty good handle on the public pulse. Why not work on the biggest ongoing story you'll ever write?"

Jason pulled back, rubbing the smooth arms of his chair, and looked at Barbara's brown eyes. "We've just met five minutes ago, and you're offering me a job?"

"Listen, Jason, I can't tell you how I know this right now, but I can sense or read the honesty in you. There isn't anything hidden with you. You're excited by this adventure and you want to pounce on it, but your natural suspicion of humans has told you that there's always a catch. I'm being perfectly honest with you, and you sense that too. If you'd like, we can start with the exclusive story and then proceed from there."

"I'd like that, miss 'seer and knower of all things.'"

"There is a story in how I know what you're thinking and feeling, Jason."

"I'll bet," he said.

Someone at the bar turned up the sound on the television. On the screen were four men and two women. Each was an anchor of network news for their major network. The CNN newscaster spoke first: "As many of you have heard throughout the afternoon today we have a historic film that has just been, let's use the word 'liberated' for now, from a secret government agency. An excerpt of that film was presented at the United Nations today. All of us felt it was important to be here to present this full and unedited version."

Another anchor took up the introduction script: "The US government has not denied nor has it confirmed the authenticity of this film. We received a DVD copy of the film in the mail. Today, the apparent original was delivered by James Broadhurst, a UFO researcher, to the Secretary General of the UN. Our analysts from each of the major networks believe that this is an exact copy of the original."

A third anchor proceeded with her part of the script: "We will be showing this at 9:00 PM on the east coast. Of course, it is 6:00 PM on the west coast. Please use caution with your young children in viewing this film. The subject matter is alien visitation to our planet in the middle of the last century. Then President Eisenhower had a meeting with one emissary from another world. The video is not frightening in and of itself, but the themes and concepts that it addresses may be disturbing to young viewers."

The introduction on the TV continued, but the owner turned down the sound and shouted out to his patrons. "Is everybody in?"

A majority of the patrons raised their hands. "Anyone not interested, just look at your wonderful food and drinks instead." More nervous laughter, and the movie began.

The twenty-some restaurant and bar patrons shrieked and put their hands to their mouths at the site of three silvery spaceships landing at dusk in the California desert.

"Get their reaction to this, Jason!" said Barbara as the crowd stood up and walked up to the television to get a better look. The grainy fifties era images that looked washed out on the digital television did not deter the patrons. They huddled closer and watched as if they were examining each flicker on the screen. When the white leader spooled through, the anchors came back to discuss what they had just seen.

"Do you want to listen to the talking heads, Jason?" asked Barbara, taking another sip of her beer.

"No, those overpaid pretty boys and girls generally don't do much for me. So tell me, how long have you worked for the secret government?" Barbara explained it all over plates of spaghetti and chicken parmesan. There was no need to hide anything anymore. Jason filled his notebook with enough notes for multiple front page stories.

The cold rain continued outside, but in this little Italian restaurant the shared stories, ideas, fears, and hopes for the future warmed the hearts like a blazing fireplace.

Tomorrow would arrive with all its uncertainty. But that was tomorrow. Tonight was all celebration.

Chapter 13

Friday, September 15

Frank had spent the night with June, which surprised no one. At breakfast, he valiantly tried to deny that anything was going on between them, but after repeated physical jabs to his ribs from June and verbal jabs from everyone else, he relented. Adam and James joined them for breakfast and filled them in on the high-level meetings. The team was leaving for Washington that afternoon, but not before James scheduled an hour out of his morning to see Maya.

Something about what Maya had said to him in that small hotel room near Pittsburgh allowed him to accept the situation. He was pleased that she was alive and would fully recover. He reiterated to Adam that not one more person should die for this cause. On that Adam and James were in total agreement.

Jason was invited to join the breakfast, and he readily accepted, bringing a cameraman to take still pictures of the team members. His initial story was an instant success. It was picked up by everybody, making him the "go to" journalist on all things about the back story to the release of the film.

"Room 442, Mr. Broadhurst," said the duty nurse.

"Thank you," he said, turning quickly to find the room. He walked down the corridor and turned the corner to see a guard standing at a closed door in the middle of the hall.

"You're guarding this room?" asked James, approaching the guard.

"Yes, sir," replied the guard, standing stiffer as James approached. "Can I ask your name, please?"

"I already went through a metal detector downstairs. Why does Maya have a guard?"

"Your name, please," repeated the guard. "Please stand over near to the wall."

"James Broadhurst," he said as he stepped backwards toward the wall.

"*The* James Broadhurst?" asked the guard. "Please let me check this device. One moment please." He clicked some keys on a large handheld device, and James's photo and information flickered on the screen.

"I'm sorry for the delay, sir. You can go right in. She's awake."

"Thank you, but back to my original question, why are you here?"

"Ever since the . . . well, ever since you did what you and the others did, this hospital has received threats on Ms. Jablonski's life. Adam arranged for a complete security detail here at her room and throughout the hospital. It's to protect her."

"Thank you," said James, nodding to the guard. The guard opened the door, and James entered the large hospital room.

James's serious face faded into a broad smile as he looked at Maya. The bed somehow seemed oversized cradling this one-woman commando who now looked so small for the large goal she had achieved. Maya had a bandage on her head, and her arm was in a cast. James wanted to cry at the site of this beautiful woman violated so severely to make his presentation such a smooth and successful event.

"Hi there, Mr. Big," said Maya, squeezing out a smile from her bandaged face. "I've been watching you on television. How did you learn how to manage all those interviews so well?"

"I got all my confidence from you," he said, kissing her on an open spot on her forehead.

"Hey! As you can see, my lips aren't bandaged." He offered a nervous smile and came back to kiss her on the lips. She lifted her uninjured arm to hold his head as she kissed him. "We did it, James! You, me, Frank—it all came together. Adam is very proud of us."

"I'm very proud of you. I knew you wouldn't act in a safe manner on this. What were you thinking?"

"I had a job to do, James, and I did it. The bonus is I get to live to tell about it." James and Maya looked at each other, both recognizing that she was right. She had had a mission to accomplish, and it was accomplished as required. Everything else was indeed a bonus.

"Adam didn't tell me about your condition until late last night. If I had known—"

"I know, you would have rushed over here and missed important meetings that you attended. So, tell me, where did you go? What were their names?" asked Maya, getting as excited as a rock star groupie.

"Well, I went to dinner with the UN Secretary General, the US

Secretary of State, and two or three members of the Security Council."

"That's great! What's on the agenda for you today?"

"Enough about me, Maya. Tell me about you."

"Hey, I'm the sick one here. You're supposed to do as I want. Don't you want me to get better?" Her faux lament, brimming with condescension, destabilized the direction of the conversation, upsetting James in the process.

"What is it with you? When you're in bed you have your way with me."

"I do my best work in bed," she said with a little laugh that started her coughing. "I've got to stop laughing. It's going to kill me," she said, forcing the words as if out of a thin tube. James held her hand and waited for her to recover.

"I'm leaving today for Washington. Susan is coming into town. Maya, I'm going to tell her about us."

"Well, I guess that's something I can't laugh about. I'm glad you're doing this. James, I want you to ask her if she will take you back. You still love her, don't you?"

"Yes," he said, looking down at the floor. "Us, is there no 'us' in the future?"

Maya looked into his eyes and squeezed his hand hard. "What we had was beautiful. It took everything I had in me not to come to your bed that night at the lodge. I wanted you to hold me and make love to me again."

"Oh my!" he exclaimed, setting her hand down and walking to the other side of the room. He touched one of the flowers in a big bouquet sitting on the windowsill. "I laid awake thinking about just that—you coming to me in my bed, just like Pittsburgh."

"The damn mission took precedence as usual. It's best this way.

If we had made love one more time, we wouldn't have been effective yesterday, and you might have a different story for your wife."

"I'm not so sure that a different story would have been so bad," he said, looking out the window in a blank stare.

"Yes, it would, James. You have a task to accomplish now that few men ever get in their lifetime. You need a strong woman to support you through this."

"You're a strong woman," he said, turning to look straight into her eyes from across the room.

"I was fully briefed on Susan and your marriage. This is the way it has to be. She has to take you back, and you must get down on both knees and beg her to forgive you. If you want me to talk to her—"

"You! That's all I need—the two women I love to plot out my life for me!"

"I love you too, James."

"Then why don't you want to be with me?"

"Because, my mission has ended and yours has just begun. People in this country and for that matter, around the world, like nice, stable coupling. You and your wife, as leaders in this endeavor, will look and act the part of moral upstanding icons for the rest of the world. The inhabitants of this planet will trust you, and they really need to trust you, James. This is not going to be a piece of cake cobbling all these secret agencies together and convincing them to lay down their guns and open their warehouses for the elected officials of the world. 'The Amnesty Option' which you so eloquently described in your talks and in your books laid the groundwork. We chose you because a significant portion of both the black hats and the white hats trusted your plan. If they find out you had sex with your little commando friend, the trust level goes way down and we'll be back to secrecy all over again."

"Are they recording this through your eyes still?"

"No, Adam assured me that Bastian turned it off. They didn't remove the implants though—too dangerous with a head injury and all."

"How many times, were you hit? Adam said it was one bullet."

"The bullet was one of those nasty ones that shatters into lots of shrapnel. It hit my shoulder, shattered my clavicle, and flew off pieces into my head."

"Are you in a lot of pain?"

"It's not only when I laugh but . . . yeah, I got pains in my shoulder. The bullet JoAnne shot me with is illegal in most countries. They're designed to do what it did. She said she was aiming for my head. I'm damn glad she's a bad shot."

"How do you know who shot you?"

"I paid her a visit. She's just down the hall. The other commandos are here too—the ones I picked off in the fight."

"How can you talk to this woman? She was trying to kill you!"

"James, it was just a mission with us. She had a goal: to stop me at all costs. I had a goal: to get Frank into that projection room and keep him safe until the video was done. Each of us was fully focused on our goal. JoAnne's problem is that she got emotional at the last minute. She saw her men taken out of commission by my low impact rounds, and when she had me in her sights, she lost control. JoAnne saw the mission failing from her perspective, and she lost it."

"I suppose I should go down there and thank her then," he fired back.

"Stay away from the sarcasm, James. You're not good at it, and except for some comedians, it doesn't wear well. People want straight answers, and that's what you are going to give them."

"What else is there to say?"

"Don't end it like this, James. I love you and you love me. I want you to hold on to that forever. I will. It will sustain me."

"So, I go back to my wife, if she'll have me, and I go on to save the world. What do you do now?"

"I have another plan."

"Are you going to let me in on it?"

"Not yet. Bastian is going to be back here in a few days. When I'm released from the hospital, I'll have a meeting with Adam in DC. I hope to see you again. We will be able to hug, but I cannot kiss you then."

"Why is that?"

"Because a lot of other people will be there, and we have to keep up appearances. Susan will probably frown on me giving you a big kiss."

"Susan will be there?"

"I'm hoping she will. It depends on how successful you are in patching things up. Adam is organizing a news conference across from his office on Maryland Avenue. This news conference that was postponed, actually for generations, will be on the steps of the Supreme Court in keeping with your 'Amnesty Option.' Nothing is going to postpone it again, and I get to be there with you."

"You are always one step ahead of me, aren't you?"

"No, I just know about this one news conference. What's on your agenda today?"

"The President has invited me to dinner."

"That's fabulous, James. I've never met him, but he's a good guy, and he's really ready for this. Just be yourself around him."

"I'm having dinner with him, the Vice President, the secretaries of State and Defense, the CIA director, and the chairman of the Joint Chiefs."

"Oh. Well, I'm sure you'll do fine. I do know one last thing—your flight time," she said, looking at the clock on the windowsill. "Give me one last kiss, and I'll release you when I'm done. Again, I'm the sick one here, and you must do all you can to see that I get better. And I demand a long kiss." James smiled at her persuasive logic and leaned over to kiss her. She held his head for a long time as he pressed her mouth to his one last time. "Go forth and do well by your fellow man."

He squeezed her hand once more and left the room carrying a weight of sadness mixed with the warmth of Maya's kiss. His confused heart left him directionless, not about his new role on the world stage but about who should stand at his side. His wife was an immensely practical woman, but this affair would be untenable to her. James was about to lose both of them, for different reasons, for sure, but each culminated in an abandonment of all parties to the affair, declaring a singular living arrangement for the three for the foreseeable future. "What have I done!" screamed James, riding a deserted elevator to the first floor of the hospital.

James went to the dinner with the President with information for the Joint Chiefs. Adam had compiled a list of all known military attachés, enlisted men, and officers, from generals to corporals, and any consultants that he knew worked for the secret government. The plan was for the regular military to meet with each man or woman on the list and lay out their options. With immunity assured, the President felt that they could get all or most of them to cooperate with the new plans for disclosure.

The next couple of days were filled with meeting after meeting for James, Adam, Barbara, and Frank. James asked Adam about the news conference at the end of the week. Adam confirmed that it was scheduled and said they would work out the details later. That was enough for James. He trusted his new coworker on this project and was happy to learn new details about how the secret government worked. Some of what he had thought was true was mere rubbish. What he discovered was much more extensive than he had imagined.

Susan had left the next day after he told her what he had done, and she promised to be back with an answer in a couple of days. She let him kiss her goodbye when she left the hotel by cab. All that he knew was that she was going to her family estate in Albany, New York.

"Susan!" exclaimed Maya. Susan Broadhurst walked purposefully into Maya's hospital room. The tall, statuesque businesswoman dressed in a wool tweed suit was beautifully coifed. Her high heels clicked on the polished concrete floor. *The pictures didn't do her justice*, thought Maya. Susan's high forehead, aristocratic jaw and cheeks were wearing a frightfully mean look, bolstering a manifestation of complete superiority. Maya cowered slightly. "I wasn't expecting you."

"I bet you weren't," said Susan with unchecked anger in her voice.

"How did you get in here?" asked Maya, sitting up higher on the bed as she eyed this adversary warily.

"Easily. One of my companies owns this hospital. I sit on the board. Is that enough 'how'?"

"That works for me," said Maya. Her head bandage had been removed, revealing stitches and noticeable bruises on her forehead.

"You're not what I expected."

"What were you expecting?"

"What are you? Eastern Europe somewhere," asked Susan as

she paced in front of the bed.

"I was born in Pittsburgh, Pennsylvania."

"No, those features, the wide mouth, broad face with those brown eyes set just a little wide. What are you, Polish?"

"My ancestors came from Poland. I am an American, just like you."

"Are you second or third generation?"

"What the hell difference does it make? I still slept with your husband," said Maya, losing control. Susan stepped closer to the bed.

"I don't know whether to scratch out your eyes or hug you."

"Do I get a choice in this? If I do, I pick the latter," said Maya, pulling back in defense of Susan's advances. Susan walked away and paced at the end of the bed. "We didn't plan for any of this to happen."

"Can't you come up with something better than that? 'We didn't plan for this to happen'? That's a load of crap. Does that line work for all your Polish friends? I'll bet not. Not even with them would it carry any water."

"I know you're upset."

"Damn right I'm upset. What are you? Are you even thirty?"

"I turned thirty six months ago."

"Congratulations, I turned forty-three between the San Antonio conference and the St. Louis conference. Did you have eyes on my husband even then?"

"We knew him and you then, but I did not meet him until the St. Louis conference."

"Does he know?"

"Does he know what?" asked Maya nervously.

"Does he know that he's the father of your baby?"

Maya's eyes widened, and she stared at Susan in disbelief.

"How did you—"

"Oh, come on. I demanded to see your chart—the *whole chart*—or this hospital would have been left without a nickel for next year's funding. I can be very persuasive when I want something."

"No, he doesn't know. No one knows except my doctor."

"When are you going to tell him? You know he doesn't want you. He wants me back."

"Yes, I know. He said as much."

"When are you going to tell him?"

"In two days I will tell him, just after the news conference."

"Maybe I should just tell him. Maybe he'll change his mind and marry you if he knows that he's going to be a daddy."

"Please don't. You'll ruin everything."

"Ruin everything? Listen, sister, you've done a pretty good job yourself of ruining everything. You screw my husband, and you're going to have his baby, and you don't have the guts to tell him?"

"I have made a mess of things."

Susan was quiet for a moment staring out the window at the busy New York street below. "You knew of him and me, so you said. You must have known we couldn't have children. Is this some game? You want to throw this fertility thing in my face? Damn it, woman! You could have just slept with him. Why in hell didn't you use protection? Was it your intention to have a baby and slap me on the side of the head with your prowess as a procreator with my husband?"

"Having a baby with your husband was definitely not part of my mission. I made no effort to interrupt a pregnancy. It was a personal hope and a prayer. I am going away. I will not be coming back. Neither you nor James will ever see me again."

"Nice speech, but you're not walking away by yourself. You're walking away with his baby. Why?"

"You said you weren't sure whether you wanted to scratch my eyes out or hug me. The eye scratching, I understand. The hugging I don't get."

Susan walked back to the bed and spoke directly to Maya. "My husband has had this dream for as long as I have known him. I always fell for the dreamers when I brought boys home to Mom and Dad. They disapproved of all of them. I never change on some things. Your lover is a dreamer who through you is now living his dream. You made it happen for him. He told me what you talked about on the trip across the country, how you encouraged him to keep going, how you gave him the confidence to talk to Presidents. He's a changed man.

"I run corporations for a living. Up to now he dabbled in conspiracy theories. Who knew that some of those theories were true? You did, and Adam did, and you brought him to this place where he can stand on his own. I no longer have to support him. In a way, his choice of me over you is just incredible. You gave him his life, while all I could do was give him a home and enough money to play in his sandbox. And now just for good measure you're going to give him a child. He wants me over you. I don't know if he will want me when he can have this new life and the child too."

"Susan, you are an integral part of his new life. He is stronger than he's ever been before, but he needs you to stay strong in the coming months and years. This is not going to be an easy ride for any of you. With you at his side, you will accomplish great things for the people of this country and this planet. You have a role to play in this effort. Be content that he wants you over me."

"But what of the baby?"

"I want you to tell him you will take him back. I love your husband. I love him so much that I know that with you he will have a full and rewarding life. I did not plan on telling you this, but I will break the plan to reveal what I'm doing. Do you know about my doctor, Bastian?"

"Yes, I've been given a full report from the hospital staff of your treatment by this alien. He has jump-started new techniques in the operating theater that are, I guess, 'out of this world.'"

"I have fallen in love with my doctor, and he has fallen in love with me."

"Oh crap!"

"That isn't the reaction I expected, but I'll go on. Interspecies mating is not possible. I wanted a child, and he wants one too. I have been altered in such a way with various implants that I am a danger to the average man and woman on the street. These changes are irreversible. The only solution is for me to leave with the man I love and forsake the man I love on this planet. I think it's the hardest choice any person has ever made. I plan to tell James after the news conference and depart soon thereafter. I want you there to support him. I know him well enough now to know that he's not going to take this well, especially when our child, something he's always wanted, is thrown into the mix."

"Where will you go?"

"We will go to Bastian's home planet. It's very dry there. Not at all like here. He will resign his commission in the Expeditionary Force. He has enough credits saved to allow his future wife to live comfortably for the rest of our lives. He will continue to live for two hundred years after I die, but our child being born on his planet will enjoy the long life that he enjoys. He is not sure he can watch me die, but I love him so much we will work it out."

"Oh, Maya," Susan leaned over and clutched Maya's arm.

"This is so much better than having my eyes scratched out."

"I will take him back. Will I see you at the news conference?"

"Absolutely, I'm looking forward to it. I will tell him about the baby, and I will leave soon thereafter. Be there for him, Susan. He will need you."

"I will." Susan smiled faintly and left the hospital room.

Chapter 14

Monday, September 25 – Morning

"Kathleen Johnson," said the policeman as he unlocked the holding cell. "It's your lucky day. You're being released."

"What about the charges?"

"Do you really want to stay here in our lovely accommodations or go with your friend here?" said the policeman, looking toward the exit. Kathleen cautiously stepped out of the cell and looked at the gated exit. Standing behind the barred door was Charlie. Kathleen hesitated a moment and then proceeded to walk toward the entrance. "You can collect your clothes and your things at the guard's station. There's a restroom just beyond the station where you can change from your pretty orange outfit into your street clothes."

Kathleen looked at Charlie for a brief moment, said nothing, and walked past him to pick up her things. She immediately entered the restroom, coming out in a few moments.

"I suppose you have some kind of vehicle, or do I have to walk back to the office?"

"I have a vehicle."

"Let's not dawdle around here. Lead the way." They went through the precinct offices and out into a small parking lot behind the station.

"It's the dark green station wagon over there," said Charlie.

"Where's the company SUV?"

"Reassigned," answered Charlie as they walked through the crowded lot.

"What the hell does that mean?"

"Exactly what I said, our old offices have been shuttered."

Kathleen stopped in the middle of an aisle and stared at Charlie. A police cruiser pulled up behind them and tooted on the horn for them to move. Gently grabbing Kathleen's arm, he led her out of the way. "Where's my briefcase?"

"It's in the backseat. Why don't you get in? The wind is whipping up, and I left my overcoat in the car." Kathleen stared at her former subordinate looking for clues as to what was happening. "Please, Kathleen," he said, unlocking the passenger door for her.

He closed the door and got in the driver's seat. "You, Maya, the wounded commandos, JoAnne, me, and about a half dozen other people were listed in the first wave of pardons from the President last night. I couldn't get you out until this morning."

"Pardons for what!" exclaimed Kathleen.

"Well, for starters, you pulling a gun on someone at the entrance of the main hall of the UN and for all the other nefarious things we did in support of our causes."

"Did Broadhurst get away with it?"

"In a word, yes, and I did my best to help him."

"Why, you bastard!" screamed Kathleen. She swung her arms wildly at Charlie, hitting him in the face multiple times. The door of Charlie's car was flung open, and two arms yanked her away from Charlie and threw her body onto the hood of the police cruiser.

"What the hell are you doing, lady? That really looked like assault. What's your problem?"

"Officer, arrest that man. He's a traitor!"

Charlie quickly regained his position and showed ID to the officer. "I don't want to press charges, officer. She just left this police station, pardoned by the President this morning."

"Well, for what she just did, she's going back in."

"Please, sir, let her go. I'm trying to explain that things are different now since Mr. Broadhurst made his speech at the UN. She's a little out of it. I'll take care of her."

"I'm not insane here. Broadhurst—that's the guy you should arrest," yelled Kathleen still spread-eagled and pressed firmly on the hood of the car.

Charlie gave a knowing look at the officer, and he released his grip on Kathleen's shoulder. "Listen, lady, Broadhurst is a national hero for doing what he did. Yeah, he is guilty; he stole government property to do it, but the President pardoned him—just a formality for him. You, I don't know. Seems like you need to earn that pardon," said the officer.

"I'm taking her to the airport, sir. She won't be a bother to the city anymore."

"Is that true? I don't want you attacking this man on the way to the airport."

"Yes," said Kathleen, staring at the ground.

"I didn't quite hear that."

"Yes, officer, I'm done attacking good ole Charlie here."

"You sure you don't want to press charges, sir?"

"I'm positive. Thank you for letting her go."

"Go on, get out of here," said the officer. He turned away and walked toward the police station. Kathleen and Charlie drove for miles through the city streets and on the freeway to the airport without talking again. Each time he looked at her, she was staring out the passenger window at the factories and low-rise apartments along their way.

"You have a private jet waiting to take you to Washington. A driver will then take you to a meeting with Adam Baines."

"Then, I get to meet the instigator of this whole mess." Charlie chose not to respond. "So how long have you been working with Adam?"

"If I tell you the truth, are you going to start hitting me again?"

"No, no. I promised an officer of the law that I wouldn't beat up on poor Charlie even though he deserves it."

"I probably do deserve the thrashing—but not for the reasons that you think. Adam assigned me to work in your unit. I've been working with him ever since."

"You sound very proud of that. Don't you know you are a traitor to your country for all the assistance you've been giving them?"

"Frankly, Kathleen, I and most Americans don't see it that way. They've been doing polls constantly in the last few days, and over seventy percent of the people think this is a good thing. Over eighty percent would want to shake hands with an alien."

"You're talking about polls! Polls! This isn't a popularity contest here, Charlie. We have to protect the American people here. They don't know what the hell they want. You watch. The first alien that starts ordering an American around and you'll see a change in your bloody polls!"

"We are proceeding slowly for just those reasons, Kathleen. We're not rushing into anything."

"Nothing except closing down the New York office and reassigning my SUV," replied Kathleen. "What happened to our organization?"

"First of all, it wasn't your SUV. Second, we are disbanding our offices around the country. Agents are being offered positions with real agencies that have direct command and control that is public. We recognize that we have a lot of good people with useful skills. One by one they are being offered these positions, and we're verifying their allegiances to this country." Charlie pulled up to a gated entrance and passed an ID card through a reader; the gate opened.

"At least you're still using our east entrance access."

"The staff here is all on board with the new agenda, Kathleen. If you're thinking of mounting a coup here at the airport, forget it. All of the hardcore, recalcitrant characters like you are gone, reassigned to less sensitive positions or released with big severance bonuses." Charlie drove up to a small jet plane waiting on the tarmac.

"So why don't you give me a golden parachute and get on with your little game with your alien friends?"

"Adam wants to talk to you personally. I don't see the point in it, but I agreed to get you on the plane, nonetheless. You will have that option. But this is where you get out, Kathleen. If you change your mind, then I guess I'll see you again. If not, have a nice life in the private sector."

"You're not going with me?"

"No, I still have some more things to do to dismantle the company. There's a news conference in Washington today that I will attend. I'll catch the return flight to DC. Please walk to the plane. That burly guy with the sunglasses over there is ordered to throw you into a seat and strap you down if you show signs of unwillingness. If you get on the plane nicely, I believe they have a nice bottle or two of your favorite Chardonnay kept at just the right temperature." Charlie reached into the backseat, retrieved her briefcase, and handed it to her. "Have a nice day, Kathleen." Kathleen looked at Charlie with a blank expression on her face, grabbed the handle of the briefcase, and left the vehicle. He watched as she purposely walked to the plane and climbed the steps, disappearing inside.

The plane with all on board, did not land in Washington, DC. It was officially listed as "missing" by the FAA.

Chapter 15

Tuesday, October 3 – Morning

As with most things in Washington, schedules are hard to keep. The news conference was scheduled and rescheduled twice. Barbara was adamant that the third of October was not going to be as forgotten as the last three attempts at scheduling the news conference were. "This one will not slide into Halloween!" she exclaimed from her new desk in Adam's old office space that she now shared with James.

"This is the secret inner sanctum. It looks like a pretty plush office for 'an undisclosed location,'" said Maya, walking around Adam's office.

"It's homey," said Adam as he took his seat behind the desk. Barbara rolled her eyes. "Come sit down, Maya. You must be tired from your plane flight."

"Actually, I got here earlier today. I wanted to take one last look at all the monuments and famous buildings. I didn't walk all those steps to the top of the Washington Monument. I did that as a girl of fourteen, but this time I just walked around it."

"I'm sorry. I could have arranged a meeting with the President and a special tour of the White House," said Adam.

"That's okay. He called me when I was in the hospital. We had a nice chat."

"Good show. He sometimes forgets to do those nice things. I think he's getting better at it. I know that you covered Anthony in your debrief. I just wanted to personally thank you for doing that. By letting him yammer on like he does sometimes about his favorite subject—"

"Himself?" asked Maya rhetorically.

"Yes, he was wavering. You cajoled him off the fence to our side. Everything in Wright Patterson is intact, and the extensive private sector with artifacts that he controlled is secure. Nobody shredded anything." Maya displayed two thumbs up.

"Did you have time to collect your personal things?" asked Barbara.

"I'm really not a collector of stuff. I have a picture of my parents in my wallet. A few other things I stuck in here," she said, patting her purse. "Besides, that last upgrade provides me an enhanced memory. All that I saw since the beginning, even before the system crash in Pittsburgh, can be called up at will and replayed on the screen in my head. It's pretty cool."

"I would have no idea about that," sighed Barbara.

"You could have had the extended implants, Barbara," warned Adam.

"Yeah, but then I'd have to leave. I don't think my husband would understand."

"No, I don't think he would," agreed Adam. "I'm not sure we did the right thing by you, Maya."

"Stop, Adam, it's working out okay. There are enough people, humans, already there and with this contingent, we'll have a real community."

"That original protocol, signed by the last President, says anyone who receives Level Three implants must go off-world when the mission is complete."

"And the mission is complete, isn't it?" asked Maya, correlating the simple cause and effect.

"I mean how dangerous are you, my dear? Here you are, you provided immeasurable help to getting the mission accomplished, and now we banish you to some far-off distant world," said Adam.

"Far-off is distant," corrected Barbara.

"Everyone is an English critic," he said with a scowl on his face. "What would a hero like you do on the dark side with your skills?"

"I would get bored around here. The missions they could assign me won't be exciting enough for me. I could easily become a master thief. All I'd need is an accomplice," said Maya, staring at Barbara.

Barbara picked up on the game. "I could feed you intel on your com, and with your photographic memory you could easily circumvent security measures. Yeah, let's do it! What I want to know is, is it 'Barbara and Maya' or is it 'Maya and Barbara'?"

"Here I am pouring my heart out to you, and you ladies want to play."

"Oh, don't be such a ninny," said Barbara.

"What are you taking, Adam?" asked Maya, returning to the serious side after laughing heartily at Adam.

"I don't have much either. Some mementoes and a picture of my wife are all I'm taking. I got permission to take one mechanical artifact that we've never been able to figure out. It was discovered in Lebanon back in the thirties. I showed it to Bastian, and he'd never seen anything like it. He said if I could bring it with me, his science guys would work with me on it when we get there. Nice little challenge, huh?"

"Bastian says after the baby is born, I can work with the Expeditionary Force in planning recon of some new worlds. Now that's exciting! He said my implants will have even better acuity on their home world. I'll be able to synthesize pictures, text, and data to work out some protocols and plans to make their missions more organized. Yeah, they could do this without me, but they really want me to participate. New world, new husband, new baby, and a new career—I can learn to like my banishment, Adam."

"Good! I want you to be happy."

"Does James know about the baby?" asked Barbara.

"Not yet," answered Maya with downcast eyes.

"What were you waiting for?" said Adam.

"I don't know. It never seemed the right time to tell him. I'll tell him after the news conference."

"You do know what's happening after the news conference?" warned Adam.

"I was hoping that you or Barbara could take the microphone and deal with the deluge of news questions while I pull him aside and explain it to him."

"In the middle of the pandemonium, you're going to pull the man of the hour aside and say, 'Oh, by the way you're the father of my baby, and oh, I'm leaving forever. Bye!' No, Maya, this is what you're going to do. I'm giving you one last order, soldier. I'm meeting with James and Frank in about an hour. He's got about an hour between meetings, and you are now on his agenda. I want his head cleared up by the time of the news conference. Do I make myself clear?"

"Yes, sir," responded Maya, her voice halting in her throat.

"Let's go for a walk. I saw a deli up the street when I came in this morning. I don't really want a lunch, but I want something."

"Well, we have an hour. How far of a walk is it?"

"It's not as far as the Cathedral of Learning was from our SUV. Do you remember that?"

"Yes, I'm glad it's not that far. Let's do it."

James and Maya exited through the heavy glass doors of the white granite building and descended the short flight of marble steps to the curved driveway and onto the street. Newsmen were already doing sound checks for the afternoon event on the Supreme Court steps across the street. The reporters looked at them briefly, wondering if they were someone special. Before they could decide, James and Maya were already gone, bundled up, walking arm in arm down the concrete sidewalk. Another sunny day greeted them, but each day's march toward winter was a descending step to colder temperatures. The street trees were rapidly discarding their coats of leaves that eventually swirled into little triangular mounds in every nook and cranny.

The warm smell of baked goods greeted them as they entered the deli. "What would you like, Maya?" asked James as he made his way to the counter.

"Apple juice and wheat roll for me, please."

"No coffee?"

Maya jerked her hand side to side, gesturing no. "No coffee for me, James. I'll grab an open table back there."

James smiled and focused on the barista waiting to take his order.

This wasn't the perfect place, thought Maya, *but it'll do.* She mulled it over in her head and retried each possible script. She had been ordered by her superior officer to do this. Maya laughed. At this point, that line of authority had little sway over her actions. She agreed with Adam and Barbara out of courtesy to them as friends. She was done taking orders, at least for a little while. The demands of motherhood would soon be upon her, and her allegiance to her child would hold sway.

"Juice and wheat roll for you, and coffee and I'm not sure what for me," he said, sitting down at the table.

"What is that anyway?"

"They call it a jumble."

"The jumble is going to rumble in your tummy. How can you eat that?" said Maya.

"I get away with this when my nutritionist is not on duty."

"I'm glad she took you back, James. It's going to work out wonderfully for you."

"Everybody has my life plan all sewn up. I'm not quite sure if they're sewing me a straitjacket or an Armani suit."

"Oh, you would look good in Armani! There's a store just down the street. I'll buy one for you," she said, portraying a sense of excitement that was not very convincing.

"Hold on there, partner, what gives?"

"I want to buy you something nice. Can't I buy you something nice?" Maya's exasperation was dissolving her trumped up excitement. She was becoming completely destabilized. Tears poured down her cheeks. She fumbled to retrieve the napkin from under her wheat roll, and it careened into the jumble and stuck to the glazed confection.

"Okay, what is it?" he asked, grasping her free hand. "You know you can talk to me about absolutely anything, Maya."

His comforting words had the exact opposite effect. She started sobbing. James scooted his chair around the small table so that he could put his arm around her.

She had to come to grips with her troubles and find a way to tell him everything before she left. After using both napkins to dry her eyes, she spoke haltingly to James. "This is so hard, because you are the last person I want to hurt or burden with anything. I'll give it to you in pieces, James. You've gone back with your wife, and you are happy, aren't you?"

"Yes, Maya, you are a wise person for such a young age. Susan and I talked for hours about us, about you, and about what we have ahead of us. I love my wife but—"

She pressed her fingers to his lips. "Don't say it, James. It will just make this harder. I'll say it for us. What we had was very beautiful. It was wrong, but I would do it again. I haven't been completely honest with you. In fact, I've downright lied to you."

"What are you saying?"

"Bastian and I are lovers," she said, staring through her tears.

James stared back at Maya. His eyes questioned, but with a sense of knowing and understanding. "You're not the first person who's fallen for their doctor, Maya."

"It's really more than that, much more. Ever since I had these implants, we developed a bond with each other. All I wanted to do was spend time with Bastian, and I have. I could tell you many beautiful stories of our time together."

"I don't think I would find them pleasurable. It's too soon. The time may never be right."

Maya kissed him on the cheek. "I made love to you because I

felt such a bond with you as well, James. No matter what you say to me today, that bond can never be destroyed in my heart. Bastian knows how I feel about you."

"You talked about us?"

"We tell each other everything."

"But apparently, you haven't told me something that is very important. Am I going to be upset at you?"

"Yes, James, you are going to be very upset, but you need to recover to perform at this news conference. Every day is vital, and your face during these monstrous changes must be fearless and unequivocal. Do you understand?"

"Yes, but I'm getting a little apprehensive here. Are you going away, going away with Bastian today on the ship?" Maya started to sob again, signaling to James that he was right. "You're a part of the contingent that is leaving today. Damn it! I'm so absorbed in what I'm doing that I didn't have a clue about your situation. All the Level Three implant humans must go off-world. I didn't look at the names on the list when someone handed it to me." He pleaded vainly, hoping she would deny it.

"I'm not coming back, James."

James retracted his arm from Maya's shoulder and rubbed his face. "I've been so stupid here."

"No, you haven't. You've done exactly what you were supposed to do. You made it easy for me—up to now."

"There's more to this unveiling?"

"Yes," said Maya in a low voice. "Bastian and I can never have children; the biology doesn't work. I didn't know I would get close to you like this but—"

"Am I supposed to guess this one too?"

Maya grasped his arm. "I'm pregnant, pregnant with your child."

The revelation crashed onto the table, heaved up, and splattered his consciousness. He was going to be a father. He would never see his son. His lover was having his baby. His wife could not have his baby. Did she know about this? The thoughts coursed across his mind, and his face telegraphed the shock and confusion to the mother of his child, gazing helplessly into his eyes.

James had to do something. He picked up his coffee and attempted to bring the paper cup to his lips, but he could not find the orifice where it normally went. He unconsciously set the container back down on the table. He stared at the cup wondering what just happened.

Maya held her hand to her mouth as the slow motion mental disconnect transpired in the human she loved most. "Say something, James."

He still stared at his cup, trying to decide to reattempt his previously unsuccessful muscle movements. "Who else knows about this?"

Maya looked at him with frightened eyes. "Everybody," she sighed.

"And I'm the last to know this because all of you wanted to protect me, because an upset James Broadhurst upsets the apple cart of your schemes. You and Adam and Barbara—you're all in on this conspiracy against me!" He thumped the table, raising eyebrows around the deli. James knew this was not the time and place for his anger.

"Listen, James, this baby is between you and me."

"It is, huh? So as soon as you knew, you came to me to tell me of the impending blessed event. Thank you so much for sharing your joy."

"I felt I needed to protect you."

"Correction, little lady, you were protecting yourself and the mission. Nowhere in your mind was there a thought about me. Really, be honest for once." Maya stared at the table. He was right in a way. She should have told him much earlier. "For a woman who has a lot of stand-up qualities, courage in the face of death, you failed miserably at handling a decent relationship. I feel like chucking this whole project into the dust bin. Adam and Barbara can handle it all from here."

"Barbara is staying, but Adam is on the list. He hasn't told you?"

"Oh, this is rich! I've got the two most capable people in the world today, but they can't manage to tell me anything important. What is it with all of you? Is secrecy so ingrained in your brains you can't be honest with the man you want to lead you out of this cesspool of compartmentalization? So, do I have at least one human on my side? Tell me my wife doesn't know you're pregnant? Tell me," he said in a hoarse whisper.

"I cannot tell you that. She came to me in the hospital, and I confided in her. She knows."

The last nail was struck. The box was now closed. The destruction was complete. The weight of the secrecy was lifted from her shoulders at the expense of the man she loved sitting across the table from her. As he stared at her, anger and fear gripped him. The only thing that kept him from total rage was something Jacob had said to him: "The passion of anger when engaged destroys indiscriminately." Something snapped inside him, and he detached himself from the physical environment. He had only a viewpoint above his body. He looked down on the sad people at the table. *How painful it is to live in a body. How painful are these emotions of the flesh.*

Do you see that the anger consumes you both? Maya is afraid of you. These impressions came from somewhere else.

They sounded like the cadence of speech he heard from Jacob, but there was no face or body to confirm the source. *It's true, Jacob. This is a pretty pathetic situation, isn't it?* he thought, attaching the name to the impression.

You can end this cycle of painful anger, James. We need you to bring yourself to a new place above these destructive emotions. Can you do this, my friend?

It is not easy to do this under these circumstances.

You can do this. You alone must choose. You have the power and freedom, and I believe you now have the wisdom to see it through.

James momentarily suspended all contacts. He existed as only a viewpoint, untethered and unrestricted in any way. The words took form as if in front of him as an object in and of itself. The content and meaning of those syllables strung together took shape. They reverberated in his mind.

Yes, Jacob, yes I can. Immediately he was pulled back into his body. Maya was staring at him. She projected fear and uncertainty, the same emotions that had strangled him just moments ago. James blinked his eyes once, twice and looked at her troubled face.

"Can you eat on the run?" he asked with a look of wonderment overriding his former negative emotions.

"What?" asked Maya, startled at his change in tone.

"Well, if you're going to buy me that suit, we better get going. Does the offer still stand?"

"Well, yes . . . yes . . . of course," she answered in bewilderment.

"Good, grab your wheat roll and juice and we'll be off."

"You looked like you were in another world. Are you okay?" she asked, still confused about what had happened to him.

"Yes, I was and now I am. I'm sorry I raised my voice to you. You don't need to feel bad about anything you've done, Maya." Maya picked up her roll and juice.

"Don't you want your jumble?"

He stared down at the mound of doughy confection dripping with sugar glaze. "It doesn't look very appealing to me now. Shall we?" he said, getting out of his chair and offering his arm once again to Maya. She tentatively took his arm, stared into his eyes for a moment, and smiled.

"Something happened to you, didn't it?"

"Yes, Maya. I now have clarity. I know this now. I *thought* I knew where I was going. Now I *know*." They walked briskly towards the front entrance.

"About the suit, James," said Maya as James held the door for her.

"Maya, I can pay for it myself, don't worry. I just wanted you to help me pick it out. I can't wear this ratty old thing in front of all those reporters."

"No, I said I would buy you a suit. Dollars don't mean anything where I'm going. What I wanted to say is, this place will do alterations while you wait. Their claim to fame is a suit in about an hour, and we have a little less than that. If all they have to alter is the pants, then we have it made."

"I don't intend to use my name to get extra special treatment, but extra dollars may do the trick."

"Are you alright about the baby?"

"I will be. It will take some time. I know this now. I know this!" he said with a level of excitement that startled Maya. "I will be alright about everything, Maya. Tell him about me if you can. Tell him or her that I love them from afar. Tell your child that the three of us will be together again. There are wonderful things ahead for three souls that intersected in this world so briefly. Of that I'm convinced."

Maya had difficulty walking. Unconsciously, James held her tighter, steadying her as they made it along the sidewalk. The wind whipped around her head, tossing her hair in rolls of auburn brown. Her mission *was* a success.

Chapter 16

Tuesday, October 3 – Afternoon

"Are you ready for this, your first news conference?" said Adam, sitting in one of the guest chairs in his old office space, now reconfigured for Barbara, James, June and an analyst. As federal employees with direct congressional oversight, the two thousand square foot office could no longer be justified for one man. James stroked his chin and framed a pensive look on his face for effect.

"It seems I don't have a choice. You know you could have told me earlier that you were leaving on the next spaceship out of here. I could have handled it earlier." The surety of these facts slowly dissipated as he finished each word in the sentence.

"One of the things we learned from our friends, James, is how much the human being can take. From our earliest work with you, we kept filling your tank with just enough new information and knowledge that you could reasonably carry and not lose it entirely. Maya, Barbara, and I have been trained in this art. Barbara will continue to pour the good stuff into you. I know you want to take on much more. You want to know everything right now. You are different now, but please resist that greed for immediate knowledge."

"Different? In what way am I different?"

"Jacob spoke to you. You need to develop that out of the body skill. It will serve you well in managing this new knowledge that you will unleash in measured amounts to the world."

James leaned back on his chair and stared intently at his mentor. "It seems that I have a lot to learn here. Exactly what does Barbara know how to do?"

"Do you mean out of the normal human capabilities?"

"That's what I'm asking."

"Barbara has been augmented in very subtle portions of the brain—areas that are suited to reading minds so to speak. Her intuitive skills and organizational abilities and the ability to project six, ten, maybe twenty steps ahead are now legend in our organization. We taught her to play chess. Six months later, we put her up against Big Blue, the computer chess program, and she beat it over and over. There's more, but I will let her tell you those. Now, lean back in that chair."

"This chair?" asked James, looking around for something special about the chair.

"Yes. Tilt it back and close your eyes for a moment. Try to recall how you felt when you were with Maya a little while ago . . . above your head. Just let it come slowly to you in a relaxed way. Don't force it."

Adam waited while James attempted to recreate the experience that he'd had earlier in the day. He moved closer to James and whispered. "This chair is an enhanced apparatus. Don't open your eyes. Just relax. It's all perfectly safe. No harm will come to you here. I'm going to be quiet for a few moments while you lightly concentrate on the screen behind your eyes. Just think softly about being outside your body. The chair will do the rest."

Adam stepped lightly and carefully repositioned himself in the guest chair facing the desk. He studied the face of his student and wondered how successful he was. In a few moments James's face took on a soft, almost imperceptible glow. Adam knew he was out and experiencing another dimension. He sat down as quietly as he could. The seconds turned to minutes until twenty minutes had transpired and James opened his eyes.

"How was that?" whispered Adam.

"I went somewhere. I'm not sure where it was. It was very beautiful. Was I talking out loud?"

"No, James, you spoke not a word."

"I was with Jacob. We had a conversation, but I can barely remember any of it. I do remember we sat by a soft waterfall that was quiet enough to not interfere with our conversation but loud enough so I noticed it. Jacob seemed to be making adjustments as we spoke—just little things."

"To what was he making adjustments?" asked Adam, already knowing the answer.

"Oh my! He was making adjustments to me—to me, Adam!"

"That's what I'm talking about. How do you feel right now?"

"Very relaxed but focused," said James, blinking his eyes.

"Remember this, James. You should sit in this chair no more than twenty minutes at a time and only once a day. More than that is tantamount to gluttony. It is designed to help you. In time, you will remember all that transpires with Jacob. He is not a god, James, no more than you or I are. He is an advanced being that has some skills to teach you. It will help you in your work."

"Can Susan use this chair too?"

"Yes, James, Susan can use it too. We want her to participate in all that you do. You will find that you will grow together in love and understanding with this apparatus. If you are diligent in your use of it, you both may graduate out of the chair and do all of this on your own. There are other teachers out there. With the right discernment, you can select one to be your spiritual guide. By the way, do you remember the guy who gave you the film in San Antonio?"

"Yeah!" said James with the excitement of a child.

"He was one of our first field tests with a jumper. As soon as his feet hit the water, he was transported to the parking lot where our man picked him up. He immediately retired to a farm in Pennsylvania. Thought you would like to know that he made it," said Adam wistfully.

"Thanks, I needed a happy ending on that one."

"Barbara will work with you for one year. After that she is free to go. You are going to be the leader. You will be with this program, hopefully for a long time. Our friends want you to try it for at least that one year. The use of the chair is a package deal. Do you see?"

"Yes, I see how it fits together." James looked at his watch. "We only have a few minutes before the new conference. I still have thousands of questions for you, but I'm surprisingly unconcerned about the answers right now."

"Good, Barbara knows everything I know. She will be happy to answer your questions. Unfortunately, you have one big loose end. Have you been briefed on who Kathleen is?"

"Yes."

"She was on her way to Washington on an agency-chartered jet. She never arrived."

"What does this mean for us?"

"It means you and Barbara have a whopper of a loose end. We don't know the extent of her connections. She's going to stay off the grid for as long as she can. James, she's nothing but trouble. She will thwart your every effort. If she can cobble together an entourage of like-minded souls, she will decrease the effectiveness of this whole mission."

"What do I need to do?" asked James.

"You have to find her and stop her in her tracks. Barbara will give you the latest intelligence on where her plane went off the grid. I have confidence in you, James. Right now, we have a public to meet."

The sun was a whitish orb behind high cirrus clouds that gave the afternoon a matte finish. The four o'clock news conference had brought out all of the major networks and print media. The reporters were flayed out on the pavement at the lowest level of the Supreme Court steps just above the sidewalk. The podium was affixed in the middle of the steps overlooking the pool of news media below.

"Why are we here?" demanded JoAnne, standing in a tight group of spectators across the street. Maryland Avenue NE was barricaded as was 1st Street NE near the capitol. Kathleen and JoAnne chose the anonymity of the lawn on the capitol grounds to observe the press conference. The two women wearing hooded jackets looked like everyone else in the crowd trying to keep warm.

"Because we get to observe history in the making, and we get to see all of this without any CNN or Fox News filters. This cadre of characters is why we are standing out here in the cold. They are the ones we are up against, and we need to know their screwups, their stumbles, and their perceived successes. There's something in here. Something that is the key to taking this stuff back to ground," said Kathleen.

"Why did they cordon off 1st Street NE?" asked JoAnne, looking south towards the intersection of East Capitol Street.

"Beats me," answered Kathleen. "See, you noticed something that just might be important that we wouldn't see on the news."

"I'm not following what they're saying. What's happening now?" asked JoAnne.

"Drop your hooded jacket then. Jason Cox did introductions and asshole Baines is flapping his lips now," said Kathleen, scanning the crowd for unfriendly agents.

"This secret government organization was in itself a crime," said Adam, his voice booming across 1st Street NE with the loudspeakers placed everywhere that there were crowds of onlookers. "The organization in recent years divided along the lines of disclosure or no disclosure. The organization started on the 'no' side of the fence. More than half of those in these secret organizations, and there are multiples of them, were on the disclosure side of the equation at the time of this final operation.

"All this is important because we want those with information to come forward. We have almost everything now, but we need to give the remaining operatives freedom to come forward. Please believe me. The blanket amnesty is about to be approved by both houses of Congress, and the President assures me he will sign it. It will be retroactive to January 1, 1940. We will take your questions now."

"Are you going to 'come forward,' JoAnne?" asked Kathleen with a nullifying smirk to clearly position herself.

"No way," answered JoAnne flatly.

"Wait, wait, here we get the admission. The little bitch is going to speak," said Kathleen.

"I insist," said Maya, stepping around Jason to get to the microphones. "I am directly responsible for that man's death." The crowd of reporters and public moaned. "I truly regret what happened to him. He was an operative employed by this secret government just as I am. James, Frank, and I had just picked up the film and were going back to our car when this man stopped us at gunpoint. We had no intention of giving him the film, and we fought back. In the ensuing fight between him and me, he was killed. To his family I offer my deepest regrets. If it is any consolation, he fought admirably well. My mission was to get that film out to the public, and I achieved that mission. May his death be the last in this sordid affair."

"Are you buying any of that crap?" said Kathleen. JoAnne shook her head no.

Adam moved forward to the podium. "Remember, the first pardon was for the people standing in front of you. Next question, please."

"John Donovan, *New York Times.* Do you expect the American public to accept this—this woman clearly stated that she killed this man. That really sounds like murder to me. Is there no recourse for the family of this man?"

"As James pointed out earlier, the secret government was more homogeneous in its purpose and secrecy. Secrecy at all costs. Liberation of artifacts did not easily occur. The would-be liberators then were dealt a harsh justice. Much mayhem was inflicted on those outside the secret government who tried to expose the alien presence.

"Recently, the 'war' against disclosure took on the appearance of a civil war within this secret government. Anyone who has studied civil wars will understand how inhumane they can be."

Kathleen doffed the hood of her jacket to hear more clearly.

"I too am disheartened that one of the events that brought us all to stand before you today was the termination of the life of a colleague, a family man who—" Adam paused in midsentence, stared blankly at the crowd, and turned away from the microphone.

Kathleen stood motionless for a moment as Jason returned to the podium. "He did care. I don't believe it. The loss of life mattered to him," whispered Kathleen.

"Yeah, you're right, they may delete that cherry on the six o'clock news. There is a spark of humanity in him. I wonder how many more cared?" asked JoAnne.

"Don't start going soft on me, JoAnne. One momentary dip into cheap sentimentality is not going to rescue these criminals in my heart," said Kathleen. "What do we have here?"

"We have cordoned off a portion of 1st Street NE behind you, and we have temporarily obtained clearance for the restricted airspace around the city. Ladies and gentlemen, we are expecting the arrival of a spaceship behind you." The crowd began talking immediately to one another.

"Max Crawford, CNN. What are you trying to pull here, Mr. Baines? You don't expect us to buy this kind of grandstanding with no substance."

"I'm not pulling anything, Max. This is no joke. Please be calm during the landing. The ship will wobble slightly as it lands. It will be completely silent and safe for all of you."

The crowd of reporters, not knowing if it was a hoax, was reluctant to turn around and look at the sky for clues.

"Please tell us this is a joke, Adam," said another newsman with a frightened look on his face.

"Grandstanding—they're going to land a ship on 1st Street NE, simply grandstanding!" said Kathleen.

Adam stepped to the microphone. "Please be calm everyone.

Maya, Barbara, and you too, James, we need to calm them down or else we don't get a landing. Circle now," he said, and the four people quickly formed a circle. "Concentrate on a calm day in the country, a soft breeze on a sunny day. Spread that feeling outward in a big circle," he whispered. "Cover everyone." The team held hands and closed their eyes. "Soft breeze, warm sunny day in the country," Adam whispered. Slowly the crowd of reporters stopped yelling at the presenters. The team was succeeding.

Jason began a slow play-by-play of the event for the cameramen. "This is truly an historic day for humanity. Over the Capitol building we can see a soft silver light. It's descending slowly and coming down the street. As it slides through the trees, it is taking full shape now. It's so large it's going to fill up the entire street and cover the sidewalks." The silver ship wobbled at the end of its descent, then rested on pods that silently extended from the bottom surface of the craft. The team broke their huddle and opened their eyes.

"That went well. The arrival didn't scare them away," said James, off-mike stating the obvious.

"James, would you like to do the formal greeting?" whispered Barbara.

"Something's happening!" shouted a reporter.

"A door is opening!" said another. James chuckled to himself as he descended the white marble steps. *Oh! "A door is opening!" Shades of the fifties sci-fi flicks. I'm sure it's not Michael Rennie or even Gort*, thought James.

James reached the street and stood at the gangplank descending from the wall of the ship. A big smile was on his face. "It doesn't get any better than this," he said aloud.

"Did anybody get that? What did he say?" said a reporter standing in the back.

"I think he said 'it doesn't get any better than this.'"

"There's a man walking out of the ship," said another reporter. The men and women watched the event unfold in silence. Jacob extended his hand to James, and the humanoid and man shook hands, smiling like old friends.

"The calming blanket that you extended over the reporters was quite effective, James. Adam, Maya, and Barbara held themselves back. They wanted to see what you could do, James, and you mastered the technique."

"I did?"

"Your connection to the spiritual, undying parts of you is very strong, James. This is very good for the successful completion of your work. Rely upon it. Use it confidently in all that you do."

"Shall we introduce you to the rest of the world?" said James. Jacob nodded in agreement and climbed the steps with James.

"Ladies and gentlemen, we will take a few questions after we handle one last task. Adam," said Jason, stepping away from the microphones.

Adam spoke to the reporters for the last time. "The people assembling in front of the spaceship are special humans. They volunteered for physical enhancements to perform supra-human tasks on this project. Now that the first phase of this project is over, the President has wisely ordered that these people who have served their planet in this fashion must leave it.

"When they volunteered, they understood that this day would arrive. They are going off-planet with their heads held high and proud of their efforts to bring this story out to you and change history. This is their legacy. We leave you in good hands," said Adam, looking over his shoulder to the team. "On behalf of all of them, we thank you and . . . goodbye. Oh, and Mr. Broadhurst will walk out with me to wish them farewell. Join Maya and me for one last time, James?"

"No, no, no! They get to fly away unscathed! No accountability?" cried Kathleen. Individuals in the crowd around them started turning heads at Kathleen's outburst.

"Maybe we should vacate the premises," whispered JoAnne, pulling on Kathleen's arm. JoAnne nudged her boss in the direction of a low wall on Maryland Avenue just across the street from the news conference.

The crowd of reporters gave way for the two men to walk down the steps of the Supreme Court building, through the crowd on the corner, and to the front of the queue for departure to another world. James shook the hands of the ten men and women assembled to leave. Charlie was positioned third from last.

Kathleen and JoAnne were no longer sitting on the wall. Kathleen was pushing through the crowd, dragging JoAnne, who was kicking and silently screaming for her enraged boss to stop. They managed to reach the front of the crowd to observe James Broadhurst say goodbye to the last three.

"I hardly got to know you, Charlie," said James, giving him a hug.

"Likewise, James," said Charlie, clasping his hands. "Take this project we started and make it your own. Give them the truth."

"I will," said James, shaking his hand. Charlie followed the others.

"Here, James," said Adam, stuffing an envelope into his hand. James gazed at the brown envelope in his hand and looked up at Adam for explanation. "It's the quit claim deed to my Chesapeake Bay beach house. I don't have any relatives that I want to leave it with, and you and

Susan will need some time away. Enjoy it, James. I obviously have no more need for it."

"You humble me again, sir."

"Follow your plan, James. It's a good one. But be flexible when the need arises. I put Jonesy's cell phone number in the envelope. Call him sometime if you like. He and Mary are good people to test new ideas. They've been around for more than a while, and they have this kind of knowing whether or not something will work with the public. They'll tell you straight."

"I will." Adam hugged his replacement and walked toward the spaceship. Jason initiated the question-and-answer session with Jacob. The reporters turned and faced the podium again. Only a line of spectators unwilling to give up their front row position observed James and Maya saying their goodbyes.

Maya pulled him close and whispered in his ear. "Be careful what you say, dear. They are recording everything."

"Right up to the end, you're concerned about the mission," lamented James as they stepped closer to the ramp of the ship. Maya offered a little smile. "That smile, I can't be sad with that smile. I still cannot fathom you leaving us, leaving . . . at all."

"This isn't easy for any of us. Some of those people are giving up families to meet the President's edict."

"This is not going to happen again if I can help it." Maya continued to gaze into his eyes to record the cut of his jaw, the smooth skin of his forehead, and those twinkling blue eyes. "Does Bastian have a nice home?"

"That's an odd question."

"I can't ask all the things I want to ask."

"And we don't have time either, James. Bastian is sending me messages that we must go. There are citizens pressing the police at the end of the block to get closer. We need to protect them."

"Alright," he said, leaning over to kiss her on the cheek.

"You'll have to explain that to the public," whispered Maya. "Goodbye, James."

Maya stepped quickly towards the spaceship. Bastian waited at the opening to the ship with an outstretched hand.

James called to her, "Goodbye, Maya." An impression flooded his brain, something cool and hot at the same time. Not so much as word or phrase but a feeling of contentment. James looked up at Bastian. The received message formed into words in his head. *I will love her as long as she lives, my friend. We will love your child with our hearts conjoined. This is my pledge to you. Have a happy life and do good deeds. The planet awaits your direction.* With no cameras to capture the last few moments, Maya's whole body shuddered, and she broke into uncontrolled tears. She reached vainly for James—her arms trembling. James burst into tears and yelled, "Don't go!" The door slowly closed with Bastian encircling her waist. Maya doubled over, and the door closed.

James dropped to his knees sobbing. A policeman scooped him up and positioned his body against a lamppost in front of the US Supreme Court.

The intimate encounter brought tears to the spectators' eyes. Some were openly sobbing along with James. Kathleen, just minutes ago, was ready to break the line and lunge at Maya passing just a few feet in front of her. She too absorbed the intense emotion of the ending of a singular and remarkable relationship. One that would endure in memories for all who witnessed the departure.

Two pairs of ancient eyes took in the departure. No one saw them shed tears for two particular souls. "I'm glad we came to this news conference."

"Yes, dear," sobbed Mary. "James has so much to go through in the next ten years. It hardly seems doable for just one man."

"But we'll finally be there, side by side, working with him," whispered Jonesy.

"To fix our mistake," said Mary. Seth's eyes absorbed the emotion, the utter hopelessness in her heart. There was still a spark of knowing, confident that together they would rectify the mistake.

"They're here too," said Jonesy. "I feel them close to us. They will make a difference in the outcome."

"To be sure, Seth, to be sure."

"Someone special," said a policeman to James as a declarative statement.

"Yes," he said, still sobbing.

"We are all going to make some sacrifices in our lives. The love of a wonderful woman is almost too much to surrender," said the policeman. Frank approached and slowly leaned against the lamppost on the other side of James.

"Hey, Jimbo. We need you at the podium." Frank couldn't help himself. He scanned the teary-eyed spectators not really looking for a threat, but he thought he found one. Frank's and Kathleen's eyes met. He slowly rose to his feet, not taking his eyes off of his quarry. "It's Kathleen and JoAnne in the crowd," he whispered to James.

James slowly turned his head. "And they're off!" said James.

Frank grabbed the policeman's arm. "Wanted felons!" yelled Frank. "I got this, James. You stay," said Frank, running with the policeman.

James turned away from the chase scene and stepped backwards until his back was at the cordoned off area and the row of spellbound observers at the bottom of the Supreme Court steps. He stared at the gunmetal surface of the interstellar craft as it slowly lifted from the street. It wobbled slightly as it silently lifted straight up. He watched as the edges of the craft brushed against the almost bare limbs of the trees along the street, dislodging the remaining leaves in a cascade of brown to the black pavement. Once above the trees, the craft lifted quickly to the height of the concrete pillars of the Supreme Court building and disappeared in an unworldly acceleration straight up and then off toward the setting sun, out of sight.

"Unbelievable!" said someone in the crowd standing behind him at the barricade.

"Unbelievable . . . until now," responded James, still looking at the empty sky. He slowly made his way back to the reporters on the steps. Two sets of ancient eyes turned and disappeared. Jacob alone caught the departure and smiled.

"We taught you how to be men and women, and in return you took us as gods," said Jacob. "Some of us enjoyed that exalted position and took advantage of it. In time, you tired of our indiscretions, and you grew stronger, but you adopted our bad traits as well as our good ones. While we have been away, you have secretly met other races from other worlds. Being the superior race, they took advantage of you. This is the way of all interactions of peoples, even among those of your world."

As Jacob finished his speech, Frank appeared toward the back. He shook his head no. James mouthed the words "it's okay."

James stepped to the microphones as Jacob bowed and stepped back. "To those who say you cannot handle these changes, I say they underestimate humanity's ability to adapt. Jacob and I are not just looking at throwing some new motor into your car that never needs fuel. That's a physical solution that keeps the same old societal structures in place. We are looking at a transformation in how you and I look at the world. Maya, the last woman to board that interstellar craft, is looking forward to joining the Expeditionary Force. They go to planets that are ready for just such an intervention. On other planets, she will be working behind the scenes to uplift the beings and help them to understand their true spiritual nature. What a wonderful job description! We are not only getting the benefits of Jacob's benevolent assistance, but we are asked to participate as citizens of this galaxy. Yes, I know, some of us are not quite citizens of our own country, let alone citizens of this planet.

"We will all grow at our own speed. We will hold open the opportunities of the millenium to move beyond service to just ourselves and on to service to all throughout the galaxy." James lifted his right hand and held it straight out above the podium—thumb up. "I hold out my hand to welcome you aboard on the greatest adventure of any lifetime. Will you take it?"

Acknowledgements

The meeting with the alien in Chapter 1 was closely tied with the work of Michael E. Salla, PhD, specifically Research Study #8 titled “Eisenhower’s 1954 Meeting With Extraterrestrials: The Fiftieth Anniversary of First Contact?” The research study itself has forty endnotes, resources that Dr. Salla identified that were used in support of his study.

The thorough, well documented, and well written study made a significant impression on me when I read it over ten years ago. It inspired me to use it as a powerful springboard for this first novel in the *Alien Disclosure Trilogy*. Thank you, sir.

My thanks to my early readers for giving me wise criticism and guarded optimism for publishing this book.

JoAnne who asked me upon reading the unedited first version, “When’s the movie coming out?”

Norm who rated the unedited first version “outstanding,”

Alyssa, my daughter, for performing the first technical edit,

Charlotte for support and confidence that I had something others would read,

And Jennifer, my editor, who with her skills and heartfelt support brought this book with significantly fewer flaws and the right word at the right time, to you.

Printed in Great Britain
by Amazon

21350794R00169